Observations
and
Reflections

Observations
and
Reflections

John Bennett

First published in 2005 by Stamford House

© Copyright 2005
John Bennett

The right of John Bennett to be identified as the author of this work has been asserted by him in accordance with the Copyright, Designs and Patents Act 1988.

All Rights Reserved

ISBN: 1-904985-28-9

Printed and bound in Great Britain

OBSERVATIONS AND REFLECTIONS

Introduction

I was born in Bracondale in Norwich in 1933 and moved to Thorpe Hamlet in 1938. This is a book of my reflections and observations as I trod the mine-strewn passage of life. It's about how I viewed life, how we were and how ephemeral is life's hour. From the 1930's up to the beginning of the 21st century my generation has been privileged to witness more changes than in the former history of mankind. As time goes on the progression of change is hardly noticeable, but in science and technology we hurtle through time with little idea of from whence we came and even less of to where we are bound. It is not until we look back that we realise just how rapid those changes were and how swift and fleeting was our moment.

*

'The clock ticks on.
It neither stops nor pauses.
It witnesses each of life's transitory moments and sees all,
but changes not in its consistency.
It is relentless in its pursuit of the future'.

* * *

Contents

Chapter One

In 1933 many events occurred, some happy, some sad, some traumatic, but the two main events were Hitler's rise to the top of Germany's political ladder, and a boy child born to the Bennett household in July of that year (but not necessarily in that order of importance).

Adolf Hitler became Germany's Chancellor and adopted the title Reich Führer (State Leader). Born in Austria he fought in the Great War and his meteoric rise to corporal demonstrates that the powers that governed the German military were far wiser than Hitler's latter day supporters. Hitler believed in ridding the world of anyone who did not measure up to his perceived standards. He led his beloved Germany from total despair, confusion and chaos through blood, torment and tears to *total despair, confusion, and chaos.* After viewing his achievements he decided to make a fast exit and promptly departed.

The more important event was my birth. This event was of greater importance than Hitler's rise to power, the wheel, or even elastic garters. This event was so great it took me by shock, my sister by surprise, my mother two weeks to recover and my father two months to sober up. So at least the event was the most important to the Bennett household.

On the ninth of July 1933 came my introduction to a world under stress and although my birth did little to add to this stress neither did it do much to lessen it. At around 7 am I lay warm and comfortable, sublimely happy, cocooned in a soft and balmy environment little realising the trauma the next hour or so would bring.

At 7.15, or thereabouts, after a determined struggle to maintain my position against overwhelming odds and stiff opposition I was suddenly and violently thrust into a hostile and completely unnatural world full of giants. A counter attack was just about to be formulated when up stepped a ruddy-faced giant of a woman and snipped my bungee rope. My route back was irrevocably removed.

There I was, stunned into silence amid foreign sombre faced giants. Not wishing to upset the strange beings, I remained silent. Then swiftly and unceremoniously up stepped the ruddy-faced woman again and for no reason fetched me a mighty smack across my arse with such force it made me cry out in pain. The reaction of those gathered around convinced me that I was entering a world of troubled souls. They beamed and twittered away, copious amounts of alcohol were sunk and hands were vigorously shaken.

I was washed in warm water then I was dried and handed back again to the lady who had so unpredictably evicted me. However, she *was* benevolent as she allowed me my first feed. After which there were regular feeds, accompanied by after feed burps and ablutions etc. I was by now getting my bearings.

After a cursory inspection in the first few months, plus making sure my rations were not going to be removed as arbitrarily as my former dwelling, I began a period of more intense scrutiny. The place was a disaster. It had little to recommend it, and the ceiling certainly looked unsure of itself. It was bowed and seemed to have no more than what I would call a tenuous grasp on its duty, a duty which after all only required it to stay up. I tried to tell my grocery lady, but she took no notice, so I concluded that either her mental ability, or her hearing was impaired.

We did have visitors occasionally but conversation was very difficult, as they were completely incoherent. If they weren't flapping their lower lips and making bub-bub-bub sounds, they were gurgling and imitating ape-like noises. There was little room for doubt in their cases; their mental ability was definitely impaired. It could be that they were the products of cousins who had, to put it delicately, formed an over zealous bonding. Benevolent lady, who I had by now discovered been designated as my official mother, and I were struggling in the voice communication area, but at least I felt comfortable with her and felt she must only have been slightly mentally impaired, as she at least understood when I was hungry. Food and cleanliness were the two operations prioritised. I felt food was my priority, cleanliness was just an interruption to sleep and with no true benefit as far as one could tell.

There were two other worrying aspects of life around this time, one was a big gruff voiced giant the other was a little annoying thing. Big gruff voiced giant I later discovered was my father and little annoying thing was my sister. Everyone, that is to say, my mother and my father seemed absolutely obsessed with my looks in the bright shiny department. I'm sure I could have gone much longer with no ill effect without being immersed in water every few hours, at this rate my body would soon grow scales and fins. Later on, as I reached boyhood (much to the displeasure of some, I might add) it became obvious that all those ablutions were quite unnecessary, I was able to go for quite long periods without suffering too much harm. Avoiding water and soap of any kind it was discovered that the natural tendency of the resident dirt collected was to get just so deep and then stay pretty well constant, in fact, after the first layer took up house other invading grime would realise it had no future and would depart. The only blight was mothers who insisted that necks should be spotless. Behind the ears was also nominated a grime free area. After exiting the bathroom my mother would always make the point of asking, "Have you washed behind the ears?" and "Have you washed your neck?" The rest of my anatomy never came under the same detailed scrutiny. I never over-tormented my mind as to the reasons for these strange hygienic fixations on those particular areas, but have since wondered if mothers belonged to some mysterious sect. Given that my sister never had to be interrogated on her personal cleanliness it must have been just boys who were in peril from the ear-neck ogre.

Although my sister seemed quite sociable, she did tend toward the odd disobedience. I believe she felt the need for more input into the situation. There was a certain conflict of interest there, because my mother was thinking more on the lines of allowing her less input. So odd wayward acts of defiance such as the removal of covers from my cot (to ensure I didn't overheat) and the odd nip now and then (to make sure I was still alive), although well intentioned were not regarded with any degree of pleasure by my mother - or me. Later on I found out that if I bawled loudly enough my sister would rapidly vanish.

It is noticeable that not only small children, but also adults tend towards disobedience (even when they are going about their law-abiding business). Most orders seem to bring out the worst in people . . . As soon as we are able to read we tend toward the small unlawful acts, like notices: Wet Paint, Keep off the Grass, Do Not Touch, Break Only in the Event of Fire, Emergency Cords on Trains, 'Pull Only should Emergency Occur'. These directives have an outstanding chance of being disobeyed. The latter carries a two hundred pound penalty, in which case the unwillingness to part with money probably prevents the act of wrenching the chain more often than actually happens. Were it not for that I doubt if any train would ever move more than one hundred yards nearer its destination.

Wet Paint! Do not touch! Now there's a challenge, in life's journey we pass many thousands of lampposts. Hardly ever, if ever, do we notice them. Dreamingly bumping into one may highlight its existence, but under normal conditions, along with stones in the road and other mundane objects, lampposts must be at the end of a long chain of insignificant nonentities. Useful yes, but interesting no. Now hang a sign on a lamppost declaring 'DO NOT TOUCH: WET PAINT', and without exception this object will, with immediate effect, become impossible to ignore; elevating you to a fever pitch of excitement it will need your undivided attention. After glancing around just to ensure no one else is in the vicinity, you will reach out and touch it. Why? If it is dry it is likely the notice is now out of date.

Do you remove the notice? Of course not, having been entertained yourself why spoil the experience for others? If it is wet, paint is now daubed all over your fingers and impossible to remove. Armed with useless information, the fingers are now full of paint, so was it really worth the aggravation? Of course it wasn't, but it is a safe bet that the next time there's a wet paint notice the desire to prove it wrong will still be just as strong. So you risk having your sanity being brought into question just to prove that curiosity is alive and well. We're all guilty of such wanton stupidity, it's just another way of saying to authority '*UP YOURS*'.

Is it an innate sense of curiosity or a hankering to be just outside the law without the fear of being inside prison? When women are discussing their partner's many awful traits, the one which comes up most often is, of course, the old faithful, and it never fails to get the utmost sympathy, 'He never puts the toilet seat down'. We never complain that it isn't put up after the ladies use it. If it is such a big deal, I would suggest sticking a notice on it 'PLEASE LEAVE SEAT UP', this would guarantee an immediate end to the problem. Never again would it remain erect, (c'mon! I mean the toilet seat).

These trivial, but pleasing, little deviations from normally upright citizens, carry no custodial sentences and only incur a few sleepless nights as you lie wondering about the stability of your mind. There were others which did evoke the displeasure of the law.

Take for example the disobedience against Prohibition in America between 1920 and 1933. Anyone with knowledge of how the human mind works would have seen almost at once that, had a study of 'WET PAINT', 'KEEP OFF THE GRASS' notices been observed, the act of prohibiting the legal vending of alcohol would increase its popularity *and* its illegal sale by the vat load. And that's just what happened. Man's natural bent toward that which is not allowed led to even more alcohol being sold than would have been the case had the sale of legal alcohol continued.

Now America had to enforce a law that was virtually impossible to enforce. It produced an ethos that stated very clearly 'We the people, because we are not allowed by law to drink, will do it anyway'. It criminalized citizens who were mainly law-abiding and gave the real criminals the opportunity of making vast fortunes. Now that it was illegal to imbibe alcohol it became more interesting to do so. As there was also no check on the contents, no clarification of the constituency of the contents, any kind of gutrot could be sold. Even today, with distilleries coming under strict control, it would be hard to imagine a less palatable substance, at least until the taste is acquired. In America during the period of prohibition I would assume any concoction would be sold as long as it produced the inability to walk, talk, or think, but made man into superman. In the wake of the act of prohibition sprung up the whisky joints and the illicit drinking places called speakeasies. What a misnomer this was. After absorbing a few glasses of this rotgut I would think it highly unlikely one could speak at all, and probably would be ill-advised to even try. The alternative names that spring to mind of less sense are stand-easies or walk-steadies. It was thought at the time that alchemists used some of the illegal distilled whisky to turn base metals into gold. Unfortunately, it only turned base metals into dust and men into gibbering idiots, so it hasn't changed as most of us can gibber idiotically and at length without any bogus stimulus. So it would seem that it is the forbidden which makes things sweet, exciting and tempting.

In my youth people would talk of the joys of wine, women and song being exciting and tempting, but for me, being completely toneless this left just the wine and the women. Unfortunately, after the wine I usually fell asleep, or as some would put it 'blissfully paralytic'. Toneless is not necessarily too much for a girl to handle, but it is easy to see alcoholic paralysis could be a bit off putting. In my case they'd hardly notice the difference anyway.

Debauchery and depravity were two other things mentioned as being quite the thing, but they never visited me, at least not to any great extent. If they did, then it must have been in extremely small amounts, or I'm sure I would have detected them. As you can see, I'm not an authority on all sins, so anyone hoping for licentiousness on a global scale may find this book a touch disappointing.

Another disobedience is swearing. Now, unlike my limited acquaintance with debauchery, of which there is little to reveal, I have encountered swearing and, I must confess with some reluctance, entered into the odd irreverent word. The use of the profane, irreverent, blasphemous, vulgar or just indiscreet seems to fit all occasions. Although these words are not illegal, in the main they are sociably unacceptable. This unacceptability is that which keeps them at the top of the most often-used words table. To reach this height of popularity a word must be capable of causing old ladies to go into fits of shock. It must also send parents into long diatribes on the torments of hell should you continue down the road of the blasphemer. The good old f-ck is one of the more endearing and enduring of the four letter words, there are some who would become almost bereft of any sort of speech without constant reference to the four-letter thesaurus. The fact that it will lead one down the road to perdition is entirely disregarded when the car refuses to start, or the cat's just tripped you up.

Maybe if these words were given respectability they would be much less used. As always it is this craving to disobey which makes use of these words compelling. My own introduction to words that must not be injudiciously used came upon me quite by accident. A certain four-letter word learned at a very tender age almost prevented me from reaching a more mature age (I use the word *mature* in its capacity of longevity rather than in any wisdom it may convey, as I wish no false impressions to be construed). This word only increased my vocabulary by a minimal margin, but it decreased my life expectancy by a spectacular amount.

A friend of mine (and I use the word 'friend' advisedly), some two years my senior, had latched onto one of the aforementioned four-letter words; not wishing to keep this word all to himself, he found a willing student in me. Prior to this, I 'swear' all the words I'd used seemed perfectly acceptable and had in no way ever been challenged. But at this point my vocabulary almost doubled, not just with my new word, but also with a few my father expressed with which I was quite unfamiliar and did not know existed. My new word beginning with c, ending with t, and rhyming with punt, nearly had me beginning with d, ending with d, and rhyming with bed.

After my friend and I had been totally absorbed in play *and* our lovely new word, we had actually arrived home late for tea. It still crosses my mind, did my friend suspect this *suspect* word? Next time we met he never mentioned any sort of crisis in his life so either he had avoided the pitfalls by not uttering the word or else he was too embarrassed to say.

Like all four-letter words this word just rolls off the tongue and is easily remembered, on top of which I was eager to show off my new word. It was the word that would transform my life. On entering my house the first thing my father said was, "And where have you been?" Thinly veiled was an undertone of "This had better be good." Now overtly standing out in my reply to his question was my new word which I was about to display in all its splendour and in all my innocence. "Out playing, you" then my new word. Unfortunately, it never reached the heights of "good" that was expected. In fact on a scale of decency it struggled in the lower regions of unacceptability. It did much better in the heights of enraged fury, in fact it animated my father beyond that which I would call reasonably acceptable.

From that very moment it became quite clear my lovely new word was going to have certain restrictions placed on it. From ashen white through to traffic light red via a myriad of shades my dad's face seemed to travel, black being the one it finally decided to settle on. This rapid transformation was impressive, to say the least, however it was not impressive enough to encourage me to stay around for the next change. It would have been interesting to stay and hear his explanation for such pique, but I suddenly realised that this word was far more potent than had previously been envisaged. My next move was rapid. My legs received the message from my brain that this was not the place to be at that precise moment. Goaded on by fear and panic, mixed with a good deal of surprise at such an alarming reaction I hurried off. To their eternal credit the legs responded by accelerating the body at sufficient speed to enable it to cross the threshold just before my dad's boot collided with the wall adjacent to where I had just passed.

Luckily the door was open and I managed to get safely out of range before any more missiles could be propelled in my direction. My hurried exit delayed my tea by a considerable amount of time and extended my life by some sixty years - up until now, and a substantial amount more if I can manage it. Only hunger, and the knowledge that utter rage would subside into an acceptable level of feeling that I would call petulance, on my father's part, plus a dash of courage, prevented starvation and all because my father allowed himself to get upset over some silly little word. I don't know! Parents! Who'd have them?

These forbidden words are often short on lettering but long on potential and this one was no exception. They have the ability to induce a gamut of emotions, emotions that sometimes we don't even know we possess (feelings I certainly never knew my father possessed). They can create laughter or rage just as easily as they can cause hate or embarrassment. In my case its debut caused haste as I had to hurtle through the door to avoid personal injury.

It's this versatility that makes them so interesting, but it is that same versatility that makes them words to be wary of. It should always be a considered judgement whether to go for the four-lettered blasphemy or take the more acceptable route. When hitting one's thumb with a hammer is it best to count to ten before delving into the four-letter phrase book? Of course not. Have a good swear, let it all out, it won't hurt any less, but it proves you are still alive in spite of the fact you wish you weren't. Who for instance would condemn a man who, after crushing his thumb with a hammer, uses a few expletives? Having just displayed an inability to control a hand tool, he could hardly be blamed for mismanagement in the vocabulary workshop.

It used to be boys who swore, girls very rarely did so, but now they seem to be rapidly catching up. Unfortunately, they can't quite manage to swear as effectively as their male counterparts, their voices are far too high. They never have that same menacing tone, in fact the female curse is about as scary as watching hedgehogs mating, and just as prickly to the senses.

Now, a man with a ruddy angered expression and a foghorn-like voice, who stands about six feet eleven inches with a dimensional chest to match it, and a body which even Arnold Schwarzenegger would envy, is the sort of bloke who gets my greatest respect, especially when he's issuing violent curses. Mind you, a man of this ilk gets my respect even when he's not issuing any curses at all. This is the kind of image which brings me to one of my favourite words.

I have discovered a word that can be as potent and just as entertaining as any profanity ever to grace the pages of a dictionary. The word is *awesome*. This word brings to mind great events of nature and can be used in company even when members of the armed forces are present, and it won't even offend them. The problem is that too much overuse of it could lose its *awesome* power.

For instance, one day I was watching television and the focus was on some men taking a leisurely stroll around some park or other in a foreign land, Scotland I believe it was. Breakfast had finished and I didn't wish to waste the rest of the day doing anything too energetic, so I decided that here was something more interesting than just sitting and vegetating. Usually I will sit and vegetate quite happily, but on this occasion I felt really energised and knew that given the chance I could move mountains. As there were no mountains in desperate need of moving I decided to settle down and view the activity on the box, and that turned out to be a game referred to as golf.

To appreciate this 'game' it must be understood that it is not going to make you laugh unless you play and then it will only make everyone else laugh. But it's not too sad-a-game (now me with bugger all to do but sit in front of telly watching this golf thing, that *is* pretty sad) and it will not get too exciting, therefore it's hardly likely to cause you to have a seizure. Another upside is that you can read a book between any eventualities that occur. Although with golf, as I was about to find out, nothing actually does occur, things just unfold in a gentle-like way. It's a bit like paddling, but without the danger of being stung by a jellyfish or eaten by a crab.

Whilst sitting there drifting between pathos, boredom and sleep, I was suddenly jolted out of my gathering apathy when the commentator aroused my curiosity with that wonderful word *awesome*. In the past I had always associated that word with the colossal demonstrations of power that Mother Nature enacts. The mighty seas of the world unbounded as they boil and roar in a caldron of uncontrolled rage and throw their anger at the shores of rebuffing rocks, rocks intent on preventing the ocean's advancement beyond their parameters. The dynamic lightning as it releases its destructive charges between lowering black clouds, with ear-splitting thunderous crashes booming down displaying the wrath of the gods, ever threatening to destroy even the universe, and causing me such fright that it puts my washing machine to extra work.

The German Luftwaffe, whose destructive explosives tumbled great man-made structures, and whose incendiaries illuminated the skies, left in their wake total ruin and decimated cities throughout our land. Once again over-stretching the family washing machine (which in the days of the Luftwaffe happened to be my dear old mum, her carbolic soap and the faithful old scrub-board). These things were indeed *awesome* (not my dear old mum and her washing paraphernalia, she was quite gentle on most occasions). Men walking around a park and occasionally assaulting a small ball stretches the use of the word *awesome* beyond the realms of the appropriate.

The commentator was salivating over a golfer, a man called Tiger. On show was a clean-cut young man, but it was not he who was being declared as *awesome*. It was the way that he abused the little white ball that was portrayed as being *awesome*. This ball was not much bigger than an old-fashioned gob-stopper and Tiger was beating it with a strange looking stick. It got so frightened (the ball not the stick) that it tried to escape down a hole. Tiger was having none of this and swiftly dragged it out again whereupon he meted out another goodly measure of abusive violence.

Sometimes the little ball would seek refuge in that which was termed a 'bunker'. In the days of conflict a bunker was a place in

11

which to seek sanctuary, unfortunately there was no such comfort for this poor little sod. Unceremoniously he was given another thwack and along with about two yards of sand (a builders measure for sand for the uninitiated) out he flew. Then displaying the intelligence usually reserved for the study of quantum physics, the little fellow flew into the thicket. This is the kind of defiance that really upsets these golfers and so began the sort of manic display of grass trampling, hedge hacking and bush bashing that gets vandalism a bad name.

Accompanied by officials, spectators, and just plain ruffians out for a spot of bother, they'd go hacking, hewing, chopping and cursing. This was okay to watch because it was the most lively anyone had been up to that point. But what I couldn't understand was why the golfer didn't use another ball, after all they must cost less than replacing half the forests in Scotland.

At the end of the game the winner was awarded a cup big enough to contain the entire product of the vineyards of Southern France and required a special delivery from one of Pickford's low loaders. Anyone intending to carry it could and probably would incur a hernia of such agonising dimensions that he would never play golf again.

But the most *awesome* event was the presentation of the winner's cheque, well not the presentation but the size of the cheque. It is read out in numerals which would suggest that the national debt was only a piddling little amount, and beside this it is. So great was the amount that it would have kept Imelda Marcos in shoes for at least a year.

However, it is almost certain that the payment, were it to be paid in coinage, would require a second low loader to carry it to the bank, should a bank be found that was big enough to accommodate such bulk.

Incidentally, if anyone intends to report these fellows to the Royal Society for the Protection of Golf Balls, it seems that it is only a game and I'm assured that the ball doesn't mind because it does it for a living.

My point is, it is the word *awesome* that suffers. In order to keep it high in the rankings of *awesome* words it needs to be applied much less to mundane sporting events and used only for nature's performances.

Chapter Two

Anyway! Back to my early years before I was waylaid by other thoughts. By the age of two I had learnt little and even my walking was retarded because of some bone trouble. So although I am now two I'm still confined to sitting and lying about, but with my retarded brain it doesn't much matter. My interests are such that now I stay awake after meals and no longer get thumped on the back after I have eaten. Mum's soft feed bags have been banned, this is a pity as although the food lacked variety it was comforting. Little hard pieces of ivory have started to sprout in my mouth and I believe this has caused the removal of my right to milk.

The previously mentioned bulge in the ceiling had become more pronounced and I had just been placed well away from it when a few moments after breakfast and giving no warning, tired of clinging to a ceiling of whose company it had grown weary, it crashed to the floor. The noise and dust was terrifying, it seemed that the whole house was disintegrating. Luckily there were no injuries, casualties or deaths; the mess was cleared up and the damage repaired. The repair was done by a man who had lost all interest in plastering so he actually put strips of board up. The ceiling now looked similar to the floor, but of course you couldn't walk on it, unless you were a spider or a fly, and it did little to enhance the beauty of the room, but it looked much more stable. Well actually, more like a stable door. No one was too concerned about giving it a coat of paint so it maintained its natural inverted splendour for the duration of its life's term.

And so it transpired, my family's first home was a humble abode or to be more accurate, a hovel. There was a large room downstairs, of a utilitarian nature, purposeful rather than decorative, and it was its desire to push home this point in every aspect of its being. In fact no one to the best of my knowledge ever accused it of having any decorative qualities. This living space was also the kitchen, bath area and laundering room. There was one bedroom that accommodated the four of us. The plaster had an unconvincing grip on the walls and the walls seemed to lack any ambition to remain focussed on staying vertical. All in all any aspiration the building held in the past had long since departed, and it was by now crumbling into sorrowful decline.

Our water supply was a communal tap standing in the yard. The toilet was also communal and was for the use and abuse of all (well, all who dared enter therein). And if Charlie at number ten had been on stout the night before then only the desperate, the unwary, or the suicidal would enter within (that's to say at least not within an hour of Charlie's exiting).

In the early part of the twentieth century the yard house complex was quite normal and had been so since the nineteenth century. Many families lived in these dwellings. They brought up their children and then *their* children raised families under those same conditions. People had very little in the way of material possessions, but were probably just as happy as we are today, although happy is a fairly fleeting concept which I must admit seldom burdens itself on me. But women in the early part of the twentieth century would think their present day sisters privileged indeed. Just consider the amount of laundering and the amount of work this entailed. Everything had to be washed by hand, the biological detergents used today were not available, the method was scrub board and carbolic soap; heavy sheets, blankets, grimy clothes, all had to be washed and rinsed in a tin bath after being boiled in a copper boiler. Quite a few of these houses had no individual water tap; the water had to be carried from the communal tap in the yard.

In a lot of cases the boiler was heated by a coal fire underneath it, later came the gas-fired boiler, but the work was still slavish. After the wash and rinse came the chore of putting the lot through a hand turned mangle (wringer). In those long gone days life was a constant struggle but the people managed because they had to. However, I would not wish to return to those times.

My mother seemed to manage pretty well, and people survived and in most cases flourished. Although it was a way of life for many, today's generation would find it quite intolerable. There was one fire and it allowed more heat to escape through the chimney than ever managed to get into the living room. There was however plenty of smoke exiting the grate and coming into our lungs. This would make you cough and once the cough got into a good rhythm you would quickly warm up. These places existed more for the profits of the landlords than for the comfort of the tenants.

In 1937 at the age of four my education began in earnest. My first school was Horns Lane Infants. The only thing I can recall was having some biscuits packed up for lunch. They were wrapped in clean greaseproof paper and tied with a piece of string, leaving a loop by which to carry them. My name was written on the packet, more to warn other hungry little sods not to touch than for me to recognise. Off we would all trip, one hand clutching those *vital victuals*, the other clasping my mother's hand, as if she would vanish should I let go. On arrival at school, tears running down my cheeks and my mother releasing my hand and disappearing down the road, here I was about to embark on life's great adventure and all I could think of was "How will she manage without me?"

At that time there was a cattle market in Norwich where every Saturday drovers would bring their animals to sell. Herds of cattle and flocks of sheep would be walked into Norwich from nearby farms to be sold in the open market place. It must have been hard work farming in those days before farm machinery. Long hours were spent toiling and tilling, sowing and reaping and all the work was done by hard sweat and slog. Horses were the main source of power so that even after long hours in the fields the animals still needed care and attention.

Occasionally as the drovers herded their livestock into the city a steer would detach itself from the herd and set off on its own journey of exploration followed by the farmer and an entourage of small boys waving sticks and bellowing stop, stop! This of course had exactly the opposite effect, the animal ran even faster, those following shouted louder and in the general confusion life and limb were placed in mortal danger. In the end the boys got over excited, the farmer got exhausted and the steer stopped of its own accord wondering what all the fuss was about. The steer got sold, the boys got a whack across the buttocks for their over enthusiasm and the farmer feigned disappointment, at the price he got for all his trouble. But farmers are always feigning disappointment that's what keeps them cheerful. Anyhow it was all good fun and a great diversion from the normal humdrum existence and everyday tedium. These markets continued until the 1950's although it hardly seems possible now that roads were used in such a way, droves of sheep and cattle, each and all depositing their dung in little packages as through the streets they trundled. I can't recall if anyone was ever delegated the job of clearing up the mess so it must have been kicked around until it finally disappeared. If anyone can throw some light on the subject, *please!* Not in my direction.

In those days there were very few motorised vehicles on the roads, the roads were merely that which we would consider narrow lanes in today's world. The horse and cart were the main carriers of goods for delivery and the horse's generous deposits were viewed with more reverence than were the cattle's as they were better for the growing of roses. Gardeners would follow a horse for as long as it took in order to collect a good dollop of horse sh-- um manure. Bucket in hand, patience a by-word, a prayer that nature would soon take its course a keen rose grower would pursue the animal until it could hold out no longer. Some, the more devious rose enthusiast it's been said, would feed the horse something to induce a more rapid conclusion to the hunt but only when the owner wasn't looking, a sour apple, or a few prunes. However, I do find this hard to swallow; as possibly did the horse. As there is no detailed account to prove the case, and to prevent the lawyers becoming involved, it will be, perhaps, as well if I just leave it to speculation.

Public transport was the mode of travel for most people. The bus was taking over from the old trams. The bus (or omnibus, meaning in all ways and to all places) was far more convenient. The trams required lines or rails on which to run, but the bus could go anywhere, that is anywhere the conditions allowed, and as roads were widened the bus became far more practicable. It required no rails or lines and could progress further and faster than railed transport.

The horse was also losing its viability, and was required less and less, it was becoming redundant. This was in some ways a good thing, but in other ways not so good. The horse was a part of life and certainly a major part for the rose grower, the demise of the horse dropped him right in it . . . or should I say out of it?

This was a way of life which would soon disappear, a way that meandered along, where people had time to observe. Even city dwellers conducted their businesses in a far more leisurely way, people had time to stop and reflect. Life was more tranquil, people were not rushing headlong in order to reach something or somewhere they would never reach anyway. One destination only brings into focus the next one which it seems must be reached before the last one has hardly been left.

The better side of progress is that, although most horse owners treated their animals with kindness, there was also much cruelty toward the beasts. 'Black Beauty', a novel by Anna Sewell published in 1877, is probably as factual as it is possible to get whilst writing fictionally on the subject. The advent of trams initially and the infernal, (or is it internal?) combustion engine must have relieved the horse of much suffering.

That was the way of life in those long-gone days. Life was not idyllic, but it was less frenetic, less frenzied, and it allowed the children to grow and mature into adulthood at a less alarming rate. However, in many ways it was a much more cruel age; abuse of a physical nature was not frowned upon but enthusiastically encouraged. School was, or could be, a fearful place. Teachers could be brutal and also very insensitive. But that's for later.

Chapter Three

In 1938 my family was offered a choice of a council house, in fact three choices. The first was at Lakenham, the second at Cadge Road and the third at Pilling Park Road. My parents opted for Pilling Park Road. The house was situated opposite a wood and the grounds of a mansion called Mousehold House. It stood at the end of a long wooded drive in its own grounds. The mansion and the estate were all part of the land that was called Mousehold Estate.

My family visited our new abode one Saturday in the middle of July. I remember it was a day of real heat, a genuine summer's day. As we walked along Wellesley Avenue, turning into Pilling Park Road we could see all the way down the valley which divided the woods into two sides. The aesthetic beauty of the place was poetry to the eye. This was the most desirable place on earth. The sun beaming through the heavily leaf-laden trees, but was full in grandeur as it reached out to bathe the grassy regions beyond the trees. There was a child way down the valley dressed in the garb of a North American Indian. With flowing wide trousers, a buckskin top and the crowning glory of a fully feathered Red Indian head-dress. This vision was as a promise of things to come. They never arrived, but even now my optimism is such as to believe they are en route, just delayed.

Pilling Park Road was just one that helped to make up Plumstead Estate. As the houses filled it became apparent that most of the new tenants were escapees from our former area of existence. Ber Street, King Street, Brooke Place, St Julian's Street, off here was St Julian's Alley, and off all these streets was a plethora of yards, Cogman's Yard, Lock and Key Yard, Fiddy's and Hewitt Yard, Scotts Yard, Jolly Butcher's Yard (Butchers were about as jolly as it got, at least they were employed), Russell's Yard, Fox and Hound Yard and Mason's Yard. Then there was Thorn Lane, Chapel Loke and Finkelgate. All these Yards, Alleys, Lokes etc., housed families where hope triumphed over despair by a margin of infinitesimal proportions, but triumphed nevertheless.

Hope gained a much wider margin of victory with the new housing estates. These were built by the local council or rather for the council. New homes that were far removed from and far superior to the Yard Houses. The first of these new estates was Mile Cross. Next came Lakenham, then North Earlham and Plumstead Estate. The latter two were built in the mid thirties and they were palatial by comparison to the yard houses in which people formerly lived.

They were much better in their construction and inside afforded much more comfort and convenience. The plaster carried out its formal duty of loyally sticking to the walls, while the ceilings spent their days unquestioningly gripping the joists, in fact they even seemed to cherish the work. This was a great relief as in our old house both the plaster and the ceilings took their work with a rather lackadaisical attitude inspiring confidence in no one. These new homes contained a living area more spacious than the Yard dwellings. This area was separate from the kitchen, and we had a toilet we only shared with our visitors, but with two provisos: the first was, were their feet clean; the second was, were they desperate. Such opulence, such luxury! We had three bedrooms and a coal cellar under the stairs. This coal cellar was to become very important later.

The living room was as large a room as in our former house and it was only required for living in. It had an open fire beside which stood an airing cupboard which also contained a hot water cylinder. There was a back boiler and the water was heated by the open fire. The water gravitated through two pipes, a flow and return. Although the system was very basic it was also fairly efficient. To maintain that efficiency the chimney had to be swept about twice a year. Chimney sweeps were quite numerous in those days and in spite of the nature of their work were usually quite cheerful chaps. They did give a lot of black looks, but that was only to be expected.

Even now it is hard to believe the number of coal merchants there were in and about Norwich. There were: E Barker, W & R Bell, W Berry, Bessey & Palmer, S Betts, Collier & Son Ltd, A Dufour, F Eglen, H Fulcher, Chas Gardiner, J H Girling, F Grint

& Son, Edward Groom, Geo Garrett, G Kerrison, Thomas Moy Ltd, Sadler & Sons Ltd, Arthur Spurgeon, H Edwards and many more. They were all hacking (or maybe sacking) a living from coal.

With the amounts of coal being burnt and the amount of smoke being produced, it was hardly surprising that the city became obliterated from view occasionally. It's a miracle we weren't all obliterated from earth permanently. No wonder all those chimney sweeps were in popular demand. I should think they had very little time to do their real job, which was attending weddings in order to bring good luck to the happy couple. It worked well because since the demise of the sweep there are far more divorces than when the sweep donated his services. Not everyone was demanding of his chimney sweeping services, there were those who, being knowledgeable but quite irresponsible would, with the aid of a few pints of paraffin (litres to the younger ones) set light to the soot in the chimney, the smoke would exit the chimney and engulf the entire neighbourhood obliterating everything from sight. The people would condemn the reckless reprobate for his lack of consideration. Women who had spent the entire day washing clothes would dash out to remove them from the line swearing liberally and threatening profusely. The fire engines would arrive, the kids would shriek with excitement, the pyromaniac's wife would quiver with fear, have a nervous breakdown, and piss off to her mother's. The mother, who was having a passionate affair with the milkman and didn't want the daughter to know would arrange the daughter's admittance into the local asylum and advise immediate divorce from such a degenerate. The neighbours would condemn the act as sheer irresponsibility, they'd all have a good coughing fit and go home.

The firemen finally got wise to this chimney cleaning fiasco and stuck a massively big hose down the chimney, poured in half the contents of the river Wensum, fucked up the lino and any adjacent chattels, then rolled up their hoses and left. The tenant was left to clear up the mess, and the community spectators went home safe in the knowledge that the villain would act less imprudently in the future. The culprit's wife would refuse to return to sanity and flatly refuse to leave the sanatorium until the house was returned to its former glory. The tenant had wrecked his marriage, destroyed his relationship with his neighbours, and upset the fire service, but saved himself 3/6d.

In the early part of the twentieth century open fires were the only option for heating the home. They were mainly wood or coal. Both of these fuels created much smoke and much heat. The good thing was that some of the smoke went up the chimney, the bad thing was that most of the heat followed it. Also, a coal fire was only able to heat one room and the chimney. This left an awful lot of house that never got very warm. Open fires were also hard work, much effort was required in order to re-light the fire each day. Kindling had to be chopped, coal fetched in, the ashes had to be cleared, the fire re-laid and re-lit and if you managed to light it at the first attempt it was considered a miracle. After you did finally succeed in getting it to stay alight it was ages before the room actually got to any sort of decent temperature, but then we weren't such an impatient society as is now and nothing was ever instant. Anyone leaving the room had to shut the door as soon as they were able, or everyone would be on their case with deafening shouts of "Shut that door," followed by death threats. No one would leave the room unless it was absolutely essential; bladders would have to be near to bursting in order to make a person vacate their position near the fire. Another problem was that as the fire got to its optimum temperature it would be like a foundry furnace roasting flesh and incinerating bone. As there was no thermostatic control on the hot water, the cylinder would be frantically gyrating about like Billy on speed attempting some ritual tribal dance whilst the water would be transformed into steam and have to be drawn off; this was a great waste. When the fire died down the room would once again return to arctic conditions, everyone would have to move almost onto the fire in order to prevent frostbite.

Most of the week's refuse was the ash that was left from the week's fires. There was not the rubbish of pre-wrapping that is the bulk of modern day living. The hazard of hot ashes must have been a nightmare for those intrepid men who had to collect them. The dustbins were made of metal so even red-hot ashes had no effect on them. If you didn't like the dustman you could put hot ashes in the bin just as he came along and set light to him. In those days the collector carried a large bin into which he would tip several household bins. The passages were long, down which he had to carry the refuse, so he could be quite a fair distance away before he spontaneously erupted into flame. I'm only kidding of course, most of the dustmen were friendly people who would not have relished being set on fire, and would have thought it most thoughtless were you to do so. In the days of my youth dust was the main type of refuse hence the name dustmen; the job has now changed and so has the collectors' title. I think they are now called waste technicians.

When mains gas reached most towns, people began to use it as a means of heating their water and their homes, but coal was still the main source of heating the rooms. Big houses installed central heating. This however, required a large boiler which was usually installed in the kitchen or a utility room. Because the heated water from the boiler had to flow to the radiators by means of gravitation, the pipes servicing the radiators had to be big, as did the radiators. Flow and return pipes needed to be of a substantial size; had these systems been put into small premises the families would have had to move into the garden shed to give them room. Then there was the problem of getting the rises and falls right, if they were not correct the system just would never work. In the early sixties someone came up with a great idea; make a small pump and the pipes could be less substantial, the rises and the falls would not be so critical and the pipes, because they were smaller, could travel (not that pipes actually move by themselves). So it would be more logical to say installed all over the place. Smaller houses could now enjoy the luxury of what was termed small-bore central heating.

The great heating revolution was now upon the country. Although coal was still the main source of heat it now became far more efficient. Smokeless fuel was now the thing: anthracite, coalite, nuts, single nuts, double nuts, you could now painlessly burn your nuts without smoking the country into invisibility. Parkray and Rayburn boilers were the main appliances and they were completely enclosed. They would only burn smokeless fuel but relied on the control of the air supply in order to make them burn efficiently. Once lit they could be kept alight day and night, the only problem was that if they were given too much air they would burn out quickly, too little air and they would die. These systems were a huge step forward both in home comfort and in the work that was needed to keep the home warm.

In the early nineteen fifties we had the smog phenomenon. This was caused by too many fires pouring out too much smoke. Visibility was restricted to about one yard. Even in familiar surroundings you would be totally lost, places became unrecognisable. Traffic came to a complete standstill and walking was also a nightmare. London acquired the nickname 'The Smoke' and so it has from then on been called.

This next piece is not only for people who didn't concentrate at school, but also for those who did, but missed this next piece of intelligence through truanting, or falling asleep. You are now given a second chance of redemption. Coal is a sedimentary rock formed from vegetation. Over millions of years this vegetation gradually decomposed in swamps. This happened during what was called the carbon coniferous period, and although I was not there to oversee it myself, it managed quite well. The vegetation was first turned into peat, (unlike myself where the process was reversed and I began to vegetate, in fact it's a wonder I wasn't called Pete) which was turned into coal, as heat and the compression of other rocks impacted on it. The coal then lay dormant and undisturbed, troubling no one for millions of years and would in all probability have remained in this blissful state for many millions more. Then along came these men with illuminated heads and picks, disturbing their tranquillity. I bet the poor old coal was really hacked off (no pun intended).

Coal is a carboniferous mineral of which anthracite is the hardest element and is made up of 90% carbon (during the war, because of its shortage, it was termed black diamond). The coal we burnt on our fires was made up from 80% carbon and is a bituminous mineral. Newcastle-upon-Tyne was the centre of the coal industry in the 18th Century, but coal has probably been worked in Britain since Roman Times (AD43-AD407). The County of Yorkshire too had a large coal mining industry. Derbyshire, Nottinghamshire, and other parts of the Midlands along with parts of Kent were also large coal mining areas, Wales too had a massive coal industry. The Midlands was a heavy industry area, and the West Midlands extending from the north of Birmingham up through to Wolverhampton was called The Black Country. It got the name because of the grime and dirt associated with its industrial nature. In the Midlands a multiple of iron and steel commodities were manufactured, everything from pins to traction engines. Great canals were built and railways were formed in order to transport all the materials needed to keep these enormous industries flourishing.

In the early years, coalmine managers would employ children to toil their lives away working in terrible conditions and at which would now be classed as breadline wages, or even below. In the 1920's 1.2 million people were employed in the coal industry, and this doesn't take into account all the subsidiaries, the transporters, the coal merchants and the likes. Almost all our power came from coal: there were the electricity generating stations, ships, trains, the great industrial factories, the home fires, gas generating works, in fact everything you could name needing power relied on coal. By the 1990's the coal industry had shrunk to a mere 27,000 as by now other methods were being used in order to fuel all the above.

During the 1939-45 World War Ernest Bevin was the Minister of Labour in the coalition government under Churchill. Ernie had the power to take conscripted men and put them into the mines rather than have them join the forces. These miners were called Bevin Boys. Bevin was a dockers' leader in the 20's and 30's and formed the Transport and General Workers' Union. He was a Labour politician who served in the Atlee government in 1945-51 and held the post of Foreign Secretary. It is possible to get him mixed up with Aneurin Bevan, who was the Minister of Health in the Attlee government and set up the National Health Service (NHS) in 1948. He too was a trade unionist, he was also an ex-miner. Bevan was a good orator, but then aren't all politicians? Aneurin was called Nye for short; he was Welsh and, and, and he was long-winded, I bet the House was glad there was something short about him if it was only his name.

Around the 30's, 40's and 50's Norwich was blessed with three railway stations: there was Thorpe Station, City Station and Victoria Station. Where Thorpe Station now stands was the original site of Norwich's first passenger station and it had two platforms. City Station was privately owned by the Midland & Great Northern (M & GN). In its day City Station was an ostentatious affair, a monument to an affluent railway company and served Norfolk and the Midlands. During the Blitz it was blown to pieces, that is to say its finery was torn from it and its splendid arched front was destroyed, but although it lost its beauty it still remained a passenger station until around 1958/59. A very good friend of mine (John Rogers) remembers it, as he once travelled up to Derbyshire by train, setting out from City Station. It was in 1948 when the railways were nationalised that rail services lost their individuality and became known as British Rail. This was under the Attlee Government. In the late 50's City Station lost its passenger carrying status and became a goods station, and this continued until the end of the 60's when it was shut down completely. In its heyday the City Station had four platforms, although the main passenger station was Thorpe. Only Thorpe Station remains today. When the City Station and Victoria Stations became goods stations, their intake was mostly coal and I remember these two stations being stacked high with it. Just outside Thorpe Station there was a turntable used to turn locomotives round at journey's end. We used to watch from Carrow Bridge as this was pushed round manually by two men using long handles attached to this device. In spite of the weight of the train, the turntable seemed quite easy to rotate. I only assume this because as boys we were not allowed to have a go ourselves, such was the mean-mindedness of the adults. Trains were always fascinating to watch. We used to look over Carrow Bridge and watch them leaving, bound for bewitching and enchanting places. In reality of course they were dirty, smelly, noisy little buggers which got you filthy and deposited small specks of soot into your eyes. I expect boys have always had an affinity with trains and that is probably because, for the most part they are dirty, smelly, noisy little buggers themselves. When I was a lad we used to put coins on the line to see the effect the train had on them. Quite astonishingly, it just flattened them. This game would end when we were spotted by one of the foot-up-ya-arses brigade garbed in railwaymen's attire. But railways, and all the paraphernalia that went with them, could keep small boys entertained for hours. Now there are the diesel train and the electrically propelled train, I don't suppose they're half as interesting.

Those colossi were magnificent, metal masterpieces of mechanical manufacture. They snorted and bellowed their way into the twentieth century from the nineteenth century bringing their *awesomeness* into our lives. Then still vehemently bellowing and protesting they snorted their way into obsolescence, but fortunately not into obscurity. There will forever be a place in our records, museums, and in our hearts for those fire eating, coal consuming, mighty steam monsters of yesteryear.

As they transported the human race to pleasure, to business and even to war, we will remember them. Their ghostly rhythmic 'diddle-de-de diddle-de-da' will echo through the passing of time. We, who rode them and were privileged to witness their occupation, we, who listened, enthralled by their rhythmic heartbeat but were suddenly surprised by the break in rhythm as the iron wheels crossed over points or crossings, were excited by their endurance and speed.

Each break in the rhythm was like a heart going out of sync, and the 'diddle-de-de diddle-de-da' would become 'sha-widdle-da-diddle-widdle-diddle-da-dum' (or noises to that effect). It was most distressing and may have required the medical services of a defibrillator to restore it to good health. But then it would soon be back to its well-orchestrated best.

There was always a great surge of expectancy as the mighty boilers discharged their duty by creating the steam to power the engines into a gigantic effort in order to heave the weighty load of coaches, passengers and freight into motion. Aboard would be people whose objectives were east to west, north to south, county to county, country to country, even continent to continent. All and each with a destiny to fulfil, riding those fire and smoke breathing iron giants of transportation. The thrill of the experience as they, slowly at first, and then accelerating to speeds hitherto not known hurtled through the countryside announcing their approach with bellowing roars and shrill whistles. Passing fields and hedges so rapidly that they almost became one massive canvas of painted beauty. Telegraph poles dashing by, their wires continually rising and dipping like sea waves. Streams, rivers, sheep, cattle, trees and hedges, miles of scenery all condensed into moments of time as these rail-restricted mammoths unerringly and hurriedly delivered their cargo safely to its destination. These were not the carbon monoxide lung destroying monsters detrimental to life of the road transport. These giants of power only gave out nitrogen, sulphur and carbon, evaporated water and non-harmful ash which went back into the soil. The exhausts were almost as exhilarating as were the shrill sounds of their whistles as they told of far off places about to be visited. There were no tricks with these honest workers as they travelled their allocated routes on rails as shiny as newly minted shillings. The exhaust products had no need to be encased and sealed in lead containers for thousands of years in the hope that they would not escape, as with nuclear fuels, neither had they the detrimental toxic effect on the environment of the carbon monoxide fuels such as diesel and petroleum. Also they could transport as much cargo with one engine that can be transported by a fleet of lorries and more people than four or five hundred cars, on top of which they didn't take up the huge mass of countryside road transport requires. The rail lines lay beside big industrial firms, so not only did they bring people but they also brought raw materials for our industries. It's only a pity that Herbert de Losinga (founder of Norwich Cathedral) didn't invent the locomotive. Just think what a boon that would have been to those that had to transport the masonry and other materials that were used to build Norwich's cathedral. In the 900th centenary year a postman delivered a slab of stone from Caen to commemorate the building of the Cathedral, I am reliably informed he is still in hospital with a hernia. With all the slabs of masonry that had to be delivered when it was originally built, I wonder how many postmen suffered the same fate then.

Chapter Four

Going back to our new house and the living room: on the other side of the fireplace were two built-in ovens but they were as much use as lead lined boots strapped to a drowning man's feet. They had no controlling device and either got too hot or not hot enough. As they were made of cast metal they would need a good seeing-to with black metal polish, and even then they struggled to enhance the beauty of the room. Ultimately, one by one they were removed and tiled surrounds were installed.

Then there was the family entertainment, a small wireless called a relay which would enrich each and every little life with a choice of two channels, the Home Service and the Light Programme. At a quarter to seven each night a serial called 'Dick Barton, Special Agent' was broadcast. This was heralded by a stirring tune called 'The Devil's Gallop'. Such was the power of this entertainment that it would clear the streets of children for the quarter of an hour it was on. It was on every weekday evening and captivated an audience that even the main television soaps of today would envy. Each night's ending had poor old Dick trying to extricate his two side-kicks (Snowy and Jock) from, usually, self-inflicted, life or death situations. The serial ran for a good few years and was replaced by 'The Daring Dexters' but they never had the same appeal. After that came 'The Archers', and that is still running (or at least jogging). There were many fine programmes on the radio: Tommy Handley, Valentine Dyall reading ghost stories in a programme called 'The Man in Black', 'Hancock's Half Hour', 'Monday Night at Eight' and many more greatly entertaining shows.

ITMA (acronym for It's That Man Again) was Tommy Handley's show. It was about the most listened-to programme on the wireless in the 1940's. This programme was a quick-moving, quick-fire piece of entertainment. It consisted of parodies, songs, puns and largely nonsense. Tommy was Liverpool born and kept Britain laughing through the 40's. He died an untimely death of a stroke in 1949 at the age of 53, and he was as much mourned as was Eric Morecambe at his death.

ITMA was not the most sophisticated show, in fact for sophistication it probably ranks alongside the Goons. Its main laughs were drawn from quick one-liners and catch-phrases. Where it really scored well was in its anti-German banter. To appreciate this it must be realised just how terrible the threat from the Germans was. There was this massive war machine menacing the world and trying to intimidate our country and yet here was this Liverpudlian taking the piss at the whole evil structure. It was the relief of knowing that, in spite of their overwhelming power that seemed almost unbeatable, they couldn't stop this man from making them look absolutely foolish.

The laughter of the audience was another factor. Laughter has that magical effect: even though the lines may not have been the greatest ever delivered the rub-off result, plus the realisation that the Germans weren't invincible, gave the people a feeling of things not being as bad as they first saw them. In retrospect I suppose people such as comedians and other entertainers were as vital to the war effort as were the factory workers, and the roles of entertainers should never be underestimated.

Then there was another programme called 'In Town Tonight'. At the beginning of the show the presenter would introduce it whilst talking over the recorded sound of traffic. He would pronounce in a grand, authoritarian voice "Once again we stop the mighty roar of London's traffic to bring you some of the interesting people who are . . ." the title he would then drag out almost in the regal fashion of today's big boxing bouts "Iiin Towwwn Toniiight." The recorded sound would then be turned off and a deathly silence would ensue. So realistic was this to a seven/eight year old I truly believed that London's traffic actually stopped. Those were the days before London's traffic had become so fouled up that it was at a grinding halt anyway. After the celebrities had been soundly grilled (sorry, interviewed) this voice would boom out "CARRY ON, LONDON!" I rather suspect that not too many drivers would dare disobey that grand voice so, with the help of the pre-recorded traffic noise, off they would go again jollying along their merry way. It's a fair bet that drivers of today would love to jolly along their merry way given the chance.

Later on a third programme was added, this was more an addition to enhance the mind than cheer the soul. There weren't too many frolicsome little joys for urchins of my age, so while my mother was being entertained by Delius, Strauss, Tchaikovsky and Sir Yehudi Menuhin (playing about with his Stradivarius), not wishing to become cultured too quickly I stayed well away.

I feel culture is something to be entered into gradually and with a certain amount of caution. Boys from my generation and from Plumstead Estate frowned on anyone with too much culture, so we tended to err on the unrefined, seedier side of nature. This is the very reason why there were so few male ballet dancers bred from this area. Another point was that boys were a bit apprehensive about wearing tights. However, I can remember a boy wearing his sister's shoes, but that was because he had no shoes of his own. Although now I feel, had he have worn his sister's tights it may well have enhanced the whole ensemble; of course, she may have only had stockings and I'm not too sure they would have enhanced anything and certainly not his street credibility. The fact that the shoes had high heels was a bit of a give-away as to the actual owner, but she did stipulate that they must be returned in good order and to disobey a sibling sister could spell a fate worse than death. Personally, I rather feel death would have been preferable, but that is only the view of one not too acquainted with the indignity of wearing ladies footwear, well only on the odd occasion anyway.

There were about eleven picture houses in Norwich, about three hundred and sixty-five public houses, one for each day of the year, and fifty-two churches. The picture houses were the Electric (later renamed the Norvic), the Regent (which became the ABC), the Theatre de Luxe, Cinema or fleapit (this became the Mayfair), the Haymarket, the Odeon, the Ritz, the Regal, the Carlton (this later became the Gaumont), the Capital and the Empire.

For the most part the visual effects of cinema and television detract from something that the wireless gave. I believe it loses out because there is not enough left to the imagination. It fills the sense of sight but leaves void the need to create our own images.

In later life when I was more 'adult' I tried to get round the pubs, unfortunately after the first eight I would lose my balance, sense of direction, be sick and had to be carried home.

Anyway, back to my new home. In the kitchen stood an electric copper for boiling the weekly laundry and this was beside a shallow clay and ceramic-coated sink. The copper was supplied by its own tap positioned directly over it. The sink had its own taps, one hot, one cold, for which I am sure it was suitably grateful. By today's standards it would seem austere, but for us it was splendid, almost bordering on opulence.

The coal cellar took on a very significant role during the days of the air raids. It was observed early on that, after the raid ended and sleepy little eyes had caused the Luftwaffe pilots to withdraw, the houses hit in many cases still had the stairway standing. People took this as a sign that the coal cellar positioned under the stairs was the place to be. As far as I was concerned the place to be was about a million miles away.

The bathroom consisted of a 5ft bath with round ends and the bog, or toilet as our new-found status required we called it. It had a flush cistern at high level, which was functional without being flamboyant. I did discover that if I stood on the seat I could reach my hand under the lid, press the float down and cause it to overflow. I know it is sad, but we never had computers so this gave me good wholesome amusement. It also gave me power, here was a piece of equipment which could shut itself off automatically but now it would never know if I was about to arrive and spoil its little party piece. The whole house was newly decorated and fine it looked, but the best thing was that the ceiling appeared capable of remaining in place for the foreseeable future.

The garden was long and spacious and looked quite able to grow enough vegetables to feed us. Unfortunately the earth was of poor quality. The main yield was stones. One barrow load removed and two more seemed to appear. I believe the bloody things got it together during the night and copulated. That many were there that the gestation period must have been hours rather than months. The earth itself was almost sand; this was possibly the reason Mousehold was never cultivated.

My father could never get anything to grow, but give him a piece of wood and he would make a beautiful fire, but he knew less about gardening than I know about nuclear physics, apart from how to spell it. I even had to fumble through the dictionary to discover that.

My sister and I soon made friends (not with each other obviously) and life improved by a bucket load in our new and exciting home. Most of the families came from the same background so we all had this in common. We all assumed that only adults grew up, so life would never alter. We could not see a life beyond our constant search for games and pleasure. These were people who stuck by you through all your troubles, mainly I suspect because they were the instigators of most of them.

In the first years of life on Plumstead Estate my friends were: Terry and John Whall, Kenny and Brian Soer, Brian Meadows, Kenny Westgate, Michael Catchpole, David Goulding, and Ronnie Mann. My sister Freda made a friend whose name was Margaret Wymer and their friendship lasted through child and adulthood until my sister's death.

Those were the kids of my childhood, they were the ones who beat out the fires that I accidentally lit in my pyrotechnic days. Together we played, chased, learned to swim, sledged, annoyed Ted and confused Parky (two characters I will introduce later). We feuded and hired boats from which we lost valuable parts. We picnicked, played football, cricket, rounders, releaso, made popguns, and catapults trimmed out of the woods, fought wars with Red Indians and threw stones at the morons from down

Wellesley Avenue (sorry, lads, just a joke). We collected scrap metal in an effort to shorten the war, also because it was fun and it upset the neighbourhood. We walked, biked and bussed many miles, not because we had anywhere in particular to go, as we always finished up at home, but we just enjoyed it.

At that time school holidays were one month in duration and for the first week things were fine. Mostly the sheer exhilaration of leaving school behind, although only for a month, would seem to be an eternal and heavenly experience. After that and with brains sufficiently rested, more adventurous pleasures needed to be sought.

Picnics were a great affair. Food would be packed (sandwiches and a few pieces of cake, a bottle of lemonade or limeade) and off we would go. The best place was just outside Norwich at a place called Postwick, pronounced 'Possic'. We would wander off down to catch the bus and after about a five-minute ride we would reach our destination. Tumbling from the bus and clutching in our mucky hands our tasteful sustenance, we would make our disorganised way towards the mysteries that awaited us in our quest for excitement and our thirst for knowledge. Our thirst for knowledge was but a fleeting attempt to justify our existence and it never reached the same heights as our quest for excitement. We would go swimming, bird nesting (not actually building the birds a home but just making sure they were comfortable), climbing and fishing, in fact all those things you could not do during school term.

Postwick lies on the east side of Norwich and about 3 miles out. It had a fairly regular bus service that took you to within about ½ mile from the marshes. It was just off the main Yarmouth Road and to get there a couple of stiles and the rail track had to be negotiated and arrived at from a little narrow lane. Once over the second stile the land opened up to a massive marsh that ran beside the river. The river lay some 60 or so yards across the marshland. There was a path about 300 yards long to the left of the marsh that led to some grassy hills. This was an ideal place to picnic; also small sandy bays had developed due to the constant ebb and flow of the tides. To the left of the path was a dyke (not a sexual orientation, just a ditch filled with water) and a tall hedge. This was the ideal terrain and habitat for all sorts of wild birds. There were swans and ducks, moorhens and all kind of waterfowl to be found nesting on the marshes. There was a large variety of other birds nesting in the hedgerows, but the best part about it was that there were very few people ever to visit it. It was always good fun to go there on the Easter or the Whit Holidays when the birds were nesting. Unfortunately, most of it has now gone and the land has been developed for housing. It was a wonderful experience in the days of our childhood and we spent many hours there.

On one occasion we took with us one of the less privileged of our companions. To save him any embarrassment I will call him Vic instead of using his full name, which was Victor. Kenny (Soer), who found most things amusing, was about to become not only a philanthropist but a not too amused philanthropist. Poor Vic had brought no drink with him on this particular occasion so Kenny, rather thoughtless in his thoughtfulness, gave to Vic his bottle of drink. This was all very laudable and would have been okay had he awaited the swallowing of the mouthful of bread that Vic had just offered his mouth and his mouth had ravenously received. Vic, with the impetuosity and enthusiasm of a man just returning from a 40-day drought in the Kalahari Desert, grabbed the bottle from Kenny's hand and drank deeply. The mouth actually took in more than the throat could cope with and it promptly returned the surplus to the bottle.

Kenny watched in horror as his pristine and clear contents of the bottle of drink now became clouded with the infiltration of the former contents of Vic's mouth which was not only drink but included a rather larger than could be foreseen portion of Vic's meal. Whereupon Kenny now extended his generosity beyond the normal course of duty. He did that which we all considered a magnanimous and charitable act: ignoring the fact that the bottle was now well fortified, he allowed Vic to keep the rest of the contents while he himself shared with someone else. I rather suspect Vic has never forgotten Kenny's generosity, neither I would think has Kenny forgotten his irresponsibility in not waiting until the contents of Vic's mouth had subsided to a reasonable level – a level that could have prevented the regurgitation that followed Vic's avaricious gulp.

It was Terry who reminded me of this day of charitable proceedings and although he recalls the event with some merriment I also detect an air of relief in his attitude. I do believe that he was about to embark on that same bountiful course until Kenny beat him to it. I think it was a race that Terry was quite relieved to have lost.

It is a fact, and I'm not sure why, but those boys I called my friends always wanted to hold the high moral ground. There was one time during a Whit holiday when it would have been best had we minded our own business. This also happened at Postwick. We were getting near to the end of another day filled with the delights of doing nothing in particular and very little in general when we noticed three older boys from our home area. They seemed to be nesting. Now earlier on in the day we too had been searching out the little feathered ones' nests. As soon as they had left the scene of one of the nests we had found earlier we went to investigate. We discovered that the eggs previously four in number were now but one solitary egg. Suddenly endowed with a feeling of sadness for a mother who had just lost three quarters of her family and filled with a sense of outrage and a desire to avenge the little one's loss, we pursued a course of action that might be called naïve at the very least and dangerous to a degree.

Those boys who had offended our sensibilities were by quite some distance older and bigger than we were. They had by now moved from our sight, quite oblivious to the fact that they had engaged our need to bring some retribution into their lives on behalf of the feathered population of Norwich and its domains.

We knew that they had cycled there and had rather unthinkingly left their means of transport home to the mercy of six revenge-seeking boys. On reaching their bikes we decided to let a little wind out of their tyres, thus letting the wind out of their sails. On reflection I think it all got a bit silly and before you could say "Whoops!" the tyres were very, instead of a bit, in fact, *absolutely*, flat. Someone then noticed that there was a pump attached to one of the bikes and so we removed the connection and replaced the pump minus the connection back on the bike. Then we strolled off to catch our bus.

Now buses in those days were more punctual than those of today, but in no way were they what might be termed as perfect. There we stood, and the longer we stood the more chance there was for the three nesting delinquents to discover that cycling home was no longer an option afforded to them. For the first quarter of an hour this was a mild irritation for us, but as the minutes ticked by it became increasingly likely that they would appear over the horizon. Then horror of horrors from out of the distance came three figures, disconsolate, dejected, but looking very annoyed. As they approached I realised just how big they were. Although I had seen them around it had never struck me as to just what fine specimens they were.

When they finally arrived at where we now stood trembling, a sudden thought invaded my mind. Amidst the images of my past life rushing through my head I realised that I hadn't kissed my mother goodbye that morning. Each of us was trying desperately to hide behind the other and hoping that a spokesman with some debating skills might perchance come to the fore. I loved these friends, but I knew that anything spoken by any of us was more likely to inflame the problem rather than quell it. So here we stood, not a dry pair of pants among us. They had obviously elected their shop steward because the biggest of the three then asked, "Did any of you lot see anyone fucking about with our bikes?" (Big boys were allowed the odd fuck here or there and this boy could use it almost as a weapon of intent.) Now for some strange reason a lie seems to be ejected from the mouth much quicker than the truth; and when your life is threatened it really gets a shift on, this is a fact, I know, and that was the moment I discovered it.

Suddenly and with little consideration, at least four mouths issued that fact that we had seen nothing. It all seemed a bit too hasty, too deliberate, but it did the trick. Although not that convincing, a denial in unison was what was called for. Then the whole effect could have been ruined when someone tried to embellish the lie by adding another lie. I believe it is termed 'to gild the lily'. From out of his mouth, hastily bypassing his brain, came the words that he 'saw someone earlier and they were acting in a funny way'. I felt at the time that *funny* was not how they viewed their plight. They now had a long walk home and some urgent bike repairs at the end of their journey.

It is not impossible to appreciate how the condemned man feels when standing on the gallows with his heart in his mouth and his balls drawn up to his stomach; when you are in the same delicate position yourself. You seem to be able to relate to other people's dire struggles in quite a sensitive way. The first answer didn't produce the salvo of interrogative requests for the truth that we'd expected. These boys had either picked the wrong brief, or they had resigned themselves to the fact that giving us physical pain would in no way diminish their mental pain. It would be hard to believe that they did not know who had pissed on their parade but they managed to come to terms with the fact that no plea of guilty was going to be lodged. As a parting shot and in a voice that I would describe as threatening but thinly veiled, their leader said, "When we find out who did it they'll get a foot up their arses." There were these three lads, hardly into manhood and yet already with the rhetoric of the adults. They were going to be a great addition to their new club of arse-kicking adults. I could even imagine a time when one of them would become president of that club.

I watched sadly as they turned and mooched off into the distance, unloved and without their revenge. I rejoiced in the fact that I would once again see my dear old mother, have apples and custard for tea, and knew at that very moment there was a God and He loved little birds and that He protected little boys that protected those little birds. What He didn't like was older boys who stole little birds' eggs. I don't think He's too concerned about chicken's eggs as He lets us eat them with impunity, well apart from the odd bowel binding occasionally, but I believe that to be only a token gesture to appease the god of chickens.

The bus finally arrived and we caught up and passed our three heroes as they wearily wound their way home. As we had to leave the bus a little later we thought it best not to call out of the bus window and wish them happy hiking. By now they seemed in a better frame of mind and they might have taken it the wrong way, so to upset them again would have seemed a touch churlish.

Egg collecting was always a source of entertainment to boys. There seems little logic as to why they should attract such interest; in fact I rather think that the birds would prefer a much less high profile for their babies. The smooth roundness could be the attraction, or maybe the hunt rather than the find is that which goads small boys on to ever more frenetic egg searching.

It is usually an interest confined to boys which appears to be the problem. Girls seem to pay more attention to gossiping and dolls than getting down to the serious business of intrepid egg finding expeditions. However, it is not the baffling dismissive attitude of the girls toward this undeniably pleasurable pastime, it is the lengths boys will go to in order to gather the results of our feathered friends' reproductive efforts.

During my school days I nearly witnessed the death of one of my best friends who, had it not been for his speed of thought combined with a certain speed of foot, would almost certainly have arrived at a premature end. Not only would his end have been about sixty years premature it would have probably been the bloodiest ever in the history of egg collecting.

It was at school and during one playtime that one of my friends named Roy happened to mention that he knew of a place in the darkest part of Norfolk where there was a certain field. He went on to explain that fortuitously this place was not far outside of Norwich. In this field were some trees of great girth and height. As luck would have it, or rather nature, these trees were built for the express purpose of housing the entire population of mating pairs of rooks within the radius of Norfolk and its satellites, or so Roy related. Roy, when pressed, could not put a figure on the exact number, but did nail it down slightly by saying that there were a lot. This estimation, although slightly loose, could have meant anything from one mating pair to upwards of one hundred mating pairs.

Roy was quite an intelligent boy, as boys go that is, and where he was about to go may not have suggested that he was less intelligent, but maybe less prudent than he ought to have been. As I stood in awe of this egg Utopia now being related I did notice that my friend Popeye was also standing in wonderment of Roy's story. Although Popeye was eavesdropping on a private conversation and had no need to join in, he must never the less have felt it was his duty to get this information authenticated.

As he listened I watched his face and it was quite evident that he had plumped for the larger of the two estimations. One hundred mating pairs, if each pair laid say only four eggs per pair, one hundred divided by two, multiplied by four, allowing for some miscalculation, that would be, now let me see, well anyway more eggs than it is possible to count when God only provided you with a ten finger abacus. Maybe there were only five mating pairs and they produced only two eggs per pair. Yes, that's what it'll be I expect and with the number of fingers He provided it was much easier to calculate.

Now whatever total Popeye had arrived at, and I'm not in any way questioning his mathematical ability, it was quite enough to rouse him into an excited mood. At this point Popeye challenged Roy's account by saying that if it were true then Roy should divulge the whereabouts of this egg phenomenon. Here it would have been more sensible for Roy to have said that he didn't actually know where it was and anyway he had loads of homework to do. Unfortunately, at this juncture I feel that pride plus indignation took precedence over sanity. "Right!" said Roy, in a voice that carried an air of irritation, "we'll go out tonight and I'll prove it to you." It is quite unclear why I ended up in the middle of this, but I agreed to accompany the two fearless egg enthusiasts. This seemed to me to be one of those occasions when the voice of reason was overcome by the whisper of curiosity. So there we three stood, optimist, idiot and innocent all with thoughts of an egg bonanza.

In the first place Roy had only come by this information through the shadiest of sources, and in the second place I always felt much more at ease just idling around than forcing myself to waste energy on a wild goose chase, or in this case a wild rook chase. Listening to the conversation, there was either a tremor of annoyance, or more likely a tremor of doubt, etched in Roy's voice when relating his account. Second hand accounts are always a bit shady, especially when being handed down by schoolboys. There was no logical reason to assume this story was any more valid than other flights of fancy passed from boy to boy. At the time I recall thinking that if all goes well and we find an abundance (I didn't know abundance at the time so probably thought 'lot')of eggs, great, if not then the night could become quite eventful.

The evening turned out to be quite tranquil. It was late spring and the sun was warm enough to make the ride out to the country pleasant. It was obvious that Roy had never been here and was trying to remember the directions he had been given some time in the past by someone he was probably by now wishing he'd not listened to. However, we three rode our cycles amidst an air of speculation and expectation, each with our own vision of the treasures which lay before us. Then by chance we came to a field, which I must admit looked strangely familiar to the place Roy had previously described in our conversation in the playground.

The field we were about to trespass in was as described. It was surrounded by an iron fence and there were five large oak trees growing, or truer to say standing there, by the look of them their growing days were long since passed. They were gnarled old buggers, they reminded me of the Quasimodos of the woodlands. The most worrying feature was that there was no sound. Had there been the plethora of bird life described in Roy's telling of the story one would have expected some noise. None of us wished to be deafened by a cacophony of squawking out of control, but I did feel the *odd* squawk would not have come amiss.

Undeterred by the silence, and assuming that the parents had possibly gone out for the night, we started to climb up the trees. It was a simple matter to climb them because they were all humps and lumps, but each step convinced us that the whole evening was going to be a shambles. For me, most of my life up until that period had been a shambles, so this was just a run-o'-the-mill experience, and I must say, so it has continued for the greater part thereafter.

However, by the third tree it was noticeable that there weren't as many eggs as Popeye had envisaged there would be, or in fact that Roy had prophesied. By now Popeye was getting quite upset by the low yield, not to mention the complete absence of birds or their associated families, namely the eggs. There was reluctance on the part of Roy to precede Popeye into the third tree, as by this time Popeye was becoming a little upset and with Popeye, a little upset could rapidly change into a large upset closely followed by anger and violence. Now anger and violence in the hands of Popeye was something to observe from behind metal bars, or from a long way off, and if you were the object of that anger it was best that you were too far away to witness it at all.

The third tree saw Popeye frantically climbing and searching for eggs whilst Roy was frantically searching for an opportune moment at which to leave this egg barren field whilst he himself remained in one piece. It has never been my wish to compete in open warfare but as a great observer of human traits I soon realised that Roy's life was quickly becoming forfeit to the vagaries of egg collecting.

Popeye was by now possessed of the knowledge that there was no egg bonanza to be had and was conveying his thoughts to all in earshot. All in earshot were Roy and myself, but Roy, realising that he was rapidly becoming the main contender for maiming or worse was by now taking steps to be quite quickly out of earshot and to preserve his life as best he could. The steps he was taking were long and quite urgently hurried.

We now had a duel and the two protagonists were anger versus panic. I liked Popeye in spite of certain homicidal tendencies he was apt to display at times, but I also liked Roy, and was relieved to see that Popeye's anger was no match for Roy's panic. The speed with which he shot off left me quite breathless, and had Popeye's speed been greater I felt at the time it would have left Roy lifeless. As Roy disappeared into the distance I swear there was smoke coming from his tyres.

I gathered my bike and drifted off behind them. I didn't see them again that night and as there was no sign of blood, for which I was very relieved, I guessed that Roy had made home base in safety. By the next morning at school my two friends didn't say much and soon the whole incident was forgotten.

It is highly unlikely that they ever went birds nesting again, well not together anyway. By now Roy had in all probability learned the lesson of staying silent on issues of which his only knowledge was scant and gained from dubious and speculative sources. He certainly would never again involve Popeye in his plans, at least not unless he had completely lost the will to live.

As for Popeye, the rage subsided and being taken over by a more calm state of mind he would probably only use the incident when psyching himself up for an encounter with one of the schoolmasters. Popeye always considered schoolmasters were fair game on which to vent his wrath. Most masters would put up a good fight, but with the egg incident by now feverishly eating at Popeye's brain and supplying much energy to his legs enabling him to wield his steel-clad-public-assisted-paid-for-boots with deadly effect, thinly covered shins would fare badly against such weaponry. All this because some obstinate rooks would not oblige and build homes where Popeye thought they should, or where Roy wished they had. For my part I'm still pondering my own stupidity at getting involved. Even to this day I'm not too sure what we could have done with the number of eggs we were hoping to find. Now in my later years I reflect on silly and daft events of my past, and there are quite a considerable amount, I do believe egg collecting must rank with the most inane and pointless, unless you had friends like Popeye and Roy and then it could be quite exciting.

Chapter Five

Norwich was much smaller in the 30's and 40's; at least the urban spread was small compared to today. All roads leading from Norwich soon passed from residential and built-up areas into wooded regions, grasslands or cultivated fields. Many more people used bicycles for both getting to and from work and for leisure activities. It was deemed quite normal for families or an accumulation of friends to get together and cycle from Norwich to Yarmouth or Hemsby or any other resort.

One inventor who in all probability has given me more strife than any other was a man called Kirkpatrick Macmillan, a Scottish blacksmith who either wouldn't or couldn't splash out a few quid on a train fare and decided to invent a bike. This blacksmith attached pedals to rods that turned a back wheel and this was the beginning of life for the instrument of torture I was forced to endure during my younger years.

Now it is an unbelievable fact that there are people who regard this cycling thing as a sport. There are some who regard it as a pleasure. It is my belief, and I must stress that it is only a personal opinion (although I do speak from experience of having been delivered of aching legs, a sore bum and near dehumanisation by this gismo), that anyone who remotely enjoys this ultimate in unforced, self-inflicted agony should be detained for psychiatric reports. Before anybody (cyclists in particular) rummages through the list of solicitors, just remember it is only *my opinion.* It must also be said, however, that the rack, the stocks and the ducking stool were marginally worse, but of course I was never able to test that theory (some would think that a dereliction of justice). But I still feel my limits of endurance were tested way beyond my comfort *endurance,* and all because a Scotsman wouldn't dip into his pocket and buy a rail ticket. (The Scots are talked of as being mean, but this idiocy was taking it too far). At this point I would like to say that in my travels I've met many Scots and Scotsmen are not mean, frugal maybe, mean never.

45

The roads were less dangerous in the 40's and 50's than they are today. There were fewer motorised vehicles on the roads. The juggernaut was not around, boy racers had not been born, so mostly those people actually driving were older men, in possession of some sense, men whose main object was to get a job done but seemed to have more time in which to do it. In today's society the main consideration of young men is spreading their genes all over the place, and they rely on the car in order to allow it to be done more quickly, and over a much wider area than in the days when only bicycles or shank's pony were available.

Gene spreading has always been high on young men's agendas, but now with cars as status symbols and with ever-increasing speed, the young male can be in and away before his quarry can catch her breath, never mind his name. Even if the Don Juan is caught he can give a false name, not like during the war years.

During the war years it became necessary to remember not only who you were, but *exactly* who you were. So the government issued a proclamation that all the peoples of the land should carry some sort of identification and the identity card was introduced. In 1952 came the end of this edict, the authorities now respected the notion that most people knew who they were. And, as no one else gave a pig's whit who you were, it would no longer be required that you were forced to carry one. After the abolishment of these cards there were people wandering around for ages wondering who the hell they were. Even today, in this enlightened age, we hear of people declining commitments because they are still trying to find out who they are. Only the other day I was watching a television programme in which a young lad said he was trying to find himself. Apparently some young girl had managed to get herself pregnant, and this lad had in some way assisted her, but as he put it: "I've only just come out of Borstal, I'm trying to find myself and need to find out who I am before I can commit."

I just hoped that he found himself before her father found him. This must surely make a good case for bringing back identity cards (or maybe it would be more beneficial to her if he remained lost). If someone has even, just temporarily, forgotten who they were, another kind person could read the card and put them right.

It would also assist the law in tackling crime. I know there is the theory that the reintroduction of identity cards would dilute the rights of ordinary people, but people with nothing to hide would have no need to fear. It could also help to save life, especially if it carried some important information on health problems etc.

During the war years because of more pressing matters crime took a back seat in the papers, but it was still being committed. There were murders going on but it was seldom if ever made an issue of. When a culprit was caught swift justice was meted out. From the crime to the gallows was a very rushed affair. As for burglary, people had very little to steal, so it would have been a futile exercise anyway. There were plenty of fights and when people got liquored up they would punch each other, gouge each other's eyes out, kick seven bells out of each other and try to rip each other's heads off. The men were nearly as bad.

In the late 40's to the late 60's cars were too expensive for the majority of young people to own, so youths had to rely on pedal power to transport them to their assignations. Afterwards, these Romeos were in no condition to make fast exits, so they could be pinned down more easily.

Cycles could be hired from certain shops around the city. The cost was not prohibitive and for about three pennies (equal to one and a half pence in our new decimal coinage) you could secure an hour's pleasure, or torture, much depending on the individual's point of view. One shilling would allow half a day's torture (five pence in decimal coinage) or one shilling and ninepence (9d) (nine pence in decimal coinage) would allow a whole day's punishment. Of course I am not talking sophisticated pedal ware, these machines were battle worn old steeds that had seen better days long since. They had been punched up and patched up so many times it was difficult to see where the original parts ended and the repairs began. Once hired, it would be a miracle if the hirer did not have to return for some sort of repair, or even exchange one bike which was beyond human help and demanding of its last rites, for another bike heading in the same direction and onwards to the same infamous demise.

Those iron warhorses would have lasted much longer had they been less imprudently hired out. It was mostly young schoolchildren who hired them. I am sure those poor old bikes, which had become nothing but objects of abuse rather than the efficient refined pieces of equipment produced by their maker some years previously, gave out squeals of protest tempered with sighs of resignation whenever a schoolboy clutching his accumulated fortune in his hand came into sight.

My affair with pedal power began when I was presented with a three-wheeled demon we will call Trike. He was named Trike because he was a tricycle, so for a bit of originality I named him thus, no his name wasn't thus, his name was Trike (do try to keep up). My friend Terry Whall accompanied me in the following disaster. Terry and I were indeed well matched, roughly the same age, same amount of brains, and both enthusiastic riders of Trike.

For the following account I feel it would be unworthy to blame Terry, or in fact for him to blame me. Maybe it was entirely Trike's fault, yes! Now I look back on it, the onus was definitely on Trike. Terry and I were just normal intelligent (although I'm slightly inclined toward the over use of the word normal, I believe in this case it is not incongruous with the facts) six year olds, whose mission in life was enjoyment and staying out of trouble. However, our secret agenda was helping our parents, and anyone else needing our particular expertise. Now I've heard said of 'people being touched by greatness', at the time and place I grew up people would often mention the fact that children were 'touched', regretfully. I don't think they meant by greatness.

On this particular day, with no one needing our help, (or if they were they were keeping mighty quiet about it) we decided to occupy ourselves in a few downhill rides on Trike. I believe, in hindsight, that we should have taken turns each. Instead, we doubled up and it is my humble opinion that Trike took umbrage. We had one or two rides before tragedy struck. The format was that each took turns at steering whilst the other rode shotgun standing on the frame of Trike and holding on to the other's shoulders. All was progressing well, or so it seemed, when all of a sudden Trike became possessed of the devil. It was Terry's turn to ride shotgun so I was steering. Now in spite of the psychiatrist's report I swear we were doing nothing other than that which we had done up until that moment. All at once it seemed that Trike lost the plot completely. From the normal of that which we were entitled *and* had the right to expect, Trike, with a very limited intelligence, decided to take charge. *Deciding* that the path was a better option than the road, he duly attempted to jump onto it in one leap, ignoring the fact that the kerb was about four inches high. Trike, having quite obviously had no previous experience in kerb climbing, failed miserably in his first attempt. It was at this point that Trike's forward motion ceased, rather abruptly, but unfortunately our forward motion did not. Not being aware of the coming events, it saw no reason at that exact moment to change its plans. The suddenness of deceleration caused Terry to exit Trike via the aerial route, passing over me at quite a phenomenal rate of knots. Not wishing to be outshone, I then left Trike by the more direct route *via* the handlebars. We both visited the unforgiving pavement at an interval of milliseconds, but in quite ungainly circumstances. Most people would consider that two six year olds with limited mental capacity and riding on Trike, whose cerebral acumen was to say the least sub standard, were verging on (no pun intended) the irresponsible, but then everyone is entitled to an opinion.

With tearstained eyes and wounded knees we limped off to whatever medical aid was available at the time. We both carry scars of that little piece of misjudgement even now. We have remained good friends throughout the years, but I still shudder when I think of that piece of reckless stupidity (Trike trying to mount the path I mean). As for Trike I never knew what became of him, what destiny had in store for him, only that he was left neglected and dejected, to fend for himself. Whether Trike was acting out the human trait of disobedience, through lack of good sense, or just malevolence, I don't know. Whatever the case, it was quite a wilful act.

We were never restricted to one or two pursuits. There was a diversity of games and pastimes, at which we could illustrate an ineptitude that beggared belief. They were categorised as: A dull, B dangerous, and C deadly. Boating was one such diversion, but as no one actually died it can only be classed as B. This was one of our favourite pastimes which upset no one - apart from other river users, bank-side dwellers, the river police and making the wild fowl a little wilder.

We would hire our boats from Clarke's Boatyard in Thorpe; coincidentally, to get to this yard you had to pass the local asylum. I think Mr Clarke must have wondered at times if we were escapees from there. On the other hand, he probably thought he should be a detainee for letting out his boats to twelve and thirteen year olds.

He may have even thought we were adults with stunted growth, or even Pigmies with great knowledge of the Amazon, so a stream like the Yare would present few problems. It would have been unlikely he would have succumbed to such indiscretion; had he had prior knowledge as to the folly he was to endorse he would have at the very least doubled his insurance policy. It is just possible that he was temporarily mentally bereft of plain common sense, and he may even have been in need of the establishment down the lane.

Under his watchful eye we would all pile into the boat. He might have been reassured of our competence when we actually managed to board without anyone falling into the water, but this confidence would soon be dispelled when, after pushing the boat off, the first dozen strokes of the oars hardly touched the water. He must have thought 'things can only get better,' but he was wrong of course, things never do get better in any radical way, as times past will recall, especially when 'single brain celled boys' are involved. The poor man's face would go ashen and be veiled in alarm. I don't think he expected a Cambridge eight, although he could have been fooled by the fact that there were eight of us. This would have been the only clue that we had any knowledge at all of boats and the next few actions would certainly not have over-burdened him with confidence. By now he would not be looking for capability, the best he could hope for was sanity. A forlorn hope; many a fore runner had this objective in mind, but none found any sign of it approaching, and much less of its arrival. Mr Clarke had by now lost interest in life and was turning his back on us. He looked quite small as he disappeared into the distance and it was suggested that it was because he was further away from us, but I could swear he was kneeling, hands clasped together.

Before his regrets had time to alter the course of history, we would be drifting with the tide. The 'oarsmen' should have been struggling with their technique, or at least making an attempt at some sort of technique. Instead, they were still struggling to get back on their seats. Then one of them, just to demonstrate that incompetence was not quite dead, actually lost an oar. We then had to paddle furiously with our hands in order to catch and retrieve the wayward oar, I say wayward because the harder we paddled our hands the faster the oar went. It was almost as though it had some premonition of an approaching disaster and wished to distance itself from it.

After recovering the oar we set off in search of crocodiles, someone had said they lazed around these parts. Later it transpired that it was only in *these parts* if you included Africa as these parts. The only things we found, apart from fish (and we never saw many of those), were frogs and that was about as dangerous as it got. The greatest dangers were right there in the boat. By now the two rowers had reached a certain proficiency, I am not saying that their technique would impress the rigid pedant, neither would it be entered into the textbooks, but they were managing to do a few strokes without catching a crab. On top of which, they were now inspiring a bit of confidence into the rest of us. The rest of us, ignoring the fact that competence was only a relative thing, now wished to put our own skills to the test, it was 'move over time'. Anyone who has tried to play musical

51

chairs in an overcrowded rowing boat will realise just what a delicate operation it is: The first miracle was not turning the boat over, the second was that no one fell overboard, but it was a close thing.

Of course sooner or later boredom would enter the party, just watching the bank drift past (and not at a phenomenal speed) was not good enough. So now came the time to liven things up a bit. Someone would start rocking the boat (I am not talking metaphor here either). From side to side, they'd sway, water splashing over the gunwales, totally ignoring the fact that there weren't many of us who could swim at that particular time. The boat would be awash in no time, but I must say those old boats certainly were seaworthy, they stood the test of boy delinquents in those days.

These boats were shaped in such a way that even we could not overturn them, which was possibly a good thing looking back. As a matter of fact I even considered it a 'very' good thing at the time. Brian Soer (Kiddo), who had by this time taken his turn at the oars, somehow contrived to drop the rowlock overboard. Nearly in tears he said, "I've dropped the buddy oarlock."

He always did struggle with the 'l' in 'bloody'. As the rowlock had now become the star of the show, it should have had some reverence attached to it. Unfortunately, it was that word 'buddy' and the fact it was not a rowlock or even an oarlock that took centre stage. Everyone just curled up laughing except Kiddo, he was about to have a seizure. His brother Kenny would have shown a great deal of sympathy I feel sure, the only problem was he and Terry lay in the bottom of the boat killing themselves with fits of laughter. We all understood the gravity of the situation but we were in fits of laughter too.

We finally got the boat back safely and, apart from the rowlock, mostly intact. We reported the missing rowlock but they were just glad to see the rest of the boat back dry, well more or less and still afloat.

Chapter Six

In my youth I had a contradictory relationship with fire. Were I to strike a match in the woods, it seemed that with immediate effect it would bond with the resident leaves and suddenly half the woods would be cheerfully blazing away. My friends, while calling me certain names from which I have never recovered, would, armed with boughs and branches, flail into submission those offending flames. After all the excitement they would remove from me the box of matches, feeling well assured in the knowledge that they had saved Thorpe Hamlet from annihilation. Maybe their actions had even saved the city. After this, play would resume as normal, they in their self-satisfied 'holier-than-thou' attitude, me in my 'up yours' attitude.

Now we come to the contradiction. Later in life when I was perceived to be less inclined towards random arson attacks, more stable as it were, I was left in charge of lighting the fire at home. My mother was at work and didn't arrive home until later, whereby I became the guardian of the whole entourage of the fire lighting experience, so to speak. My mother, although well aware of my many faults, now believed that I knew roughly where the appropriate place to light a fire was located.

From that same woodland, which in former years had been inclined to burst into flame as soon as it was even shown a match, I gathered the sticks for kindling the fire. I assumed that, as they were so anxious to leap into an inferno then, there was small chance they could have forgotten the routine. They would be little trouble now. The fire I laid in the time honoured way. A goodly amount of paper, then the fire-knowledgeable twigs I placed tenderly on top, the coal would be gently and with tender loving care balanced on the twigs. From the box of matches, now back in my more mature and reliable hands, I would select the most efficient one I could find, strike and apply it to the paper, expecting the whole issue to burst into flame, but I must say I was bitterly disappointed.

I had my aspirations distressingly unfulfilled. Although I did not wish for something which could not contain itself to the grate, something which would become unmanageable, a thing to which I would need to call my fire fighting friends of yesteryear in order to preserve the house from becoming a smouldering pile of ashes, neither did I expect this apology for a fire. It (I call it 'It', because I'm loath to call it a fire), smouldered and then fizzled out completely. I cursed It, re-laid It and re-lit It. Although 're-lit' is a misnomer considering its disobedience toward being lit in the first place. No matter how much coaxing or cajoling I did, this 'It' would not light. In desperation I applied an amount of paraffin to 'It', struck a match, stood back and threw it at the heart of where the fire should by now be blazing. With a great flash the paraffin ignited, lasted about 30 seconds and then vanished leaving a cold charred mess. All would need to be removed, re-laid and the whole ritual begun again. As I explained earlier, when Sooty Sid did the same thing to clear the soot from the chimney he nearly started a civil war, almost got divorced and had his old lady confined to the madhouse. My fire just petered into obscurity.

Dampers and airways were fully opened, and a sheet of paper held over the fireplace to assist the draught. There I stood both in awe and trepidation waiting to see what mode the 'It' would now don. Anyone still awake and with a modicum of perception will by now be well ahead of the game. Of course, cantankerous and as controversial as ever, 'It' set light to the very thing it should not have set light to, the draught enhancing sheet of paper! Whether it was sheer stubbornness or blatant disobedience, I will never know. In blind panic with hands and arms waving and flailing frantically, and with some assistance from the draught, I managed to confine 'It' to some sort of order. With manic contortions I clapped and harried the fiercely burning but half-charred remains of the paper up the chimney. After which I stood there amidst muck and mayhem, cold and disillusioned, in fact a broken man bowing to the superior will of 'It'.

That which I was, and in fact still am, confused about is this: how is it that with very little assistance fire will destroy buildings, woods and even things you would not expect it to touch if it shouldn't, but given things it should be at, 'fire' strikes out on an agenda of its own. In an area it is not required, it will devastate all with relish, forever expanding, yet if you try to encourage it a fire can be the most obstinate and infuriating element known to man. I think fire must have a mentality close to man. If something is illegal then that's the thing it will passionately battle with and excel in its enthusiasm. Should the exercise be legal and helpful to the human race it will demonstrate great reluctance and a good measure of indolence will take over. Anyone with any thoughts on this matter, please send to: J Bennett, Home for the Mentally Disturbed. SAE will be required. In my search to discover the reason why fire behaves in this way, I have uncovered one extraordinary fact. The great fires, such as the Great Fire of London and that which left Rome a charred mess, are fires of substance (or maybe it would be more accurate to say those that destroy substance) and had one thing in common, they have all become famous. My own Wellesley Avenue Woods fire, although not documented up until now because of the thirty-year secrets rule, was also a mammoth event in its own right (not the thirty-year secrets rule, that was not the mammoth event – the WAW fire was the mammoth event).

Books have been written about such fires, studies have been made on their attributes and their idiosyncrasies. All in all they have reached world acclaim by just being controversial. Therefore, on reflection, I wonder if it is always down to outright rebelliousness that fire works in this disruptive manner! It could be its quest is for world recognition. If a study were to be made on the common 'fire in the grate' I am not sure it would reach too many intellectuals.

In the early part of the twentieth century domestic heating was low on the priorities of householders. It was not until later on in the mid 1900's that people really started to think of methods to heat their premises efficiently. Prior to this places were heated more by convenience of resources with not much thought as to how economical they were. There were in fact not many alternatives available: coal and wood were the most common sources of fuel burnt on open fires. Kerosene oil, along with candles, was used for home lighting. When gas began to be manufactured it revolutionised the way that people illuminated their homes and the way they cooked their food. The streets also became lit by this new medium. It was made from coal and it was easy to light and easy to burn. However, coal gas was a toxic and a very volatile medium. Many a good soul was removed from earth's pleasures *and torments* by foolish antics involving this substance. Anyone wishing to, could put their head in the gas oven, turn on the gas and leave the world quickly and conveniently. Accidents were also quite the thing, by this I am not referring to a vogue thing but regular occurrences. Coal gas was well accomplished at accidentally conveying people to their next existence. Even those who would in the natural course of events have wished to stay awhile could find themselves trying to explain to Gabriel that it was more by foolishness than desire which now found them there twenty or so years earlier than need be. When electricity was introduced it took over from oil and gas as the means of lighting. Electricity was immediate, throw the switch and instantaneous illumination. In America it became the main way of dispatching the odd wrong doer, throw a switch and you had instantaneous elimination. All of these different lighting and heating methods took their time in becoming established. From the beginning of time hardly anything moved in that direction, then suddenly, from the nineteenth century onward we had this immense surge forward in all of these life's conveniences. Some of the improvements and discoveries were due to man's ingenuity, some due to natural progression, but many were due to accidents. However they came about, most of them have resulted in easier ways of life for quite a lot of the world's peoples. Unfortunately, there are still many miles to travel before all the people can benefit from the discoveries of the nineteenth and twentieth centuries. We can only hope that the will is there to bring these technological advantages to everyone.

Chapter Seven

At school I was always a bit of a dreamer. Going round the veranda throwing a rolled up handkerchief into the air, mumbling as it dropped "Hold it," on catching it I would congratulate myself by saying "well held." This little charade would continue until the next class was reached or a severe prod in the back from an irate teacher returned me back to reality. Most boys live in this world of twilight and fantasy. See a boy, see a dreamer. This brings me on to comics. Comics are for dreamers. In my youth the most popular comics were The Beano, The Dandy, The Film Fun, The Wizard, The Champion and The Rover. The last three were mostly boys' adventure stories, The Beano, The Dandy and The Film Fun were picture comics. Kenny and Kiddo's family took The Dandy comic each week. On Saturday mornings I would go across to Kiddo's (his back garden was just across from my back garden), but he was never up when I called. Always I had to wait for him to get up. It's not easy for young boys to just hang about with nothing to do. I would read their Dandy to while away the time waiting for Kiddo to reintroduce himself into the world. Had I stuck to just reading the comic, the next bit of trouble may well have been averted, but, idle hands, retarded brain, etc, etc.

Now! Kiddo's mother and father were a lovely couple, always friendly, never grumpy; well not without a bit of provocation, and that was my job. His dad's name was Arthur and I must admit that there were times when I sorely tried Arthur's patience.

Arthur's job allowed him to get hold of certain things that were in the main pretty useful. On this particular Saturday morning I noticed he had managed to acquire a set of golf clubs, but he wasn't about to take up golf so he'd used them to make a fence. There were a couple of golf balls lying around. Well! Kiddo wasn't up so I thought I'd pass the time by having a few practice golf shots. This game was coming to me new and untried, as this was many years prior to my becoming acquainted with Tiger, the clean cut young man, winner of vast fortunes and mammoth cups. I know now it would have been better had I awaited Tiger's instructions, or possibly just stuck to waiting, period.

However, here I was: club, ball and enthusiasm, time on my hands, so the thought occurred, 'give it a go'. Placing the ball on the ground I addressed it (you see, all the right terminology, unfortunately the wrong direction - had I considered the direction the folly I am about to relate would not have occurred). Ball in place, club at the ready, I gave it an almighty 'thwhack'. Unfortunately, the ball flew off in the very direction I least intended it to fly. Not to the safe part of the garden, but straight through the window. There was a terrific crash and the ball landed in the living room. Luckily it never did much damage once it got in, in fact it settled quite quietly which was a relief.

Arthur came rushing out and his whole attitude, plus his language, told me of his displeasure. At that precise moment I couldn't quite take it all in. I just stood there with the golf club still clutched in my hand, absorbed completely in the ability I had just shown in hitting that golf ball. There was no way I was going to be distracted from my euphoric moment. Had this been on a golf course I would have been hailed as the next Arnold Palmer. Once the moment had passed, Arthur cooled down and became more rational. The club was replaced so once again it became just a part of a mundane old fence. After a bit of a wigging I was forgiven, and things returned to normal, but I will never forget that shot, straight as a poker it went. I'd had my moment of fame but never again did I get the opportunity to show off my golfing talents. After this Kiddo and I departed with our football to play a safer game and the incident was consigned to history.

About two weeks later the same routine occurred, I called for Kiddo and he wasn't up. Arthur was in the kitchen cooking the breakfast serenely oblivious of the events which were about to unfold. Once again I had to wait.

As I stood around I noticed that the golf clubs didn't look too perky, and on closer inspection I could see that they had been bent in halves. On posing a tentative enquiry, it transpired that only a much shorter fence was required and that was the reason for their ultimate demise. Well! That seemed pretty plausible. At this juncture I must relate that they also owned a dog. I say *they* owned a dog, but this dog belonged to all of us, or so it seemed. It was part of the gang. Wherever we went, the dog followed. It was a gentle, friendly, faithful old boy and we all loved it dearly. Unfortunately, on this particular day, when I opened the living room door the dog ran out. For some reason (and he usually had the run of the district) he had been confined to barracks so to speak, I believe this was due to some canine strumpet, living in the area, of whom Arthur disapproved.

Seizing on the opportunity he decided to leg it down the street (the dog that is, not Arthur, well, not immediately). It took a few seconds to consider the dog's action and his own reaction. Arthur, assessing the situation, rushed past me in what I can only euphemistically describe as a hurry and in passing he shouted, "Now look what you've done!"

Arthur then hotfooted it in pursuit of the fleeing dog. About five minutes later back he came accompanied by the dog both looking quite disgruntled, but that wasn't a patch on just how disgruntled Arthur was about to become. During Arthur's frantic outing around the unaired streets of Plumstead Estate the cooker had been getting on with that which cookers usually get on with, namely cooking the breakfast. Under careful scrutiny cookers take about three times as long to cook anything than they take when not under a watchful eye. Arthur's cooker was no exception to this rule. Maybe there are some cookers that will behave themselves when not under supervision, but as I say Arthur's cooker was not of that ilk. Almost at once, when returning from his enforced early morning jaunt, he discovered that the sausages were burnt and, as he succinctly put it, "Now you've made me burn the bleeding sausages."

To the best of my recollection, yes, I did open the door which contained the dog, but it was the dog who escaped, it was Arthur's negligence that left the cooker to its own devices, it was the bloody irresponsible cooker that overcooked the sausages. On reflection, I feel the burden of the entire debacle could, and should, have been a bit fairer in its allocation.

In the first place, I believe Arthur overreacted to the situation, and in the second place I'm sure that the punishment (you honestly do not want to know) Arthur recommended was far too severe to accurately reflect the facts as I understood them at that time. Finally, as a magnanimous gesture he too considered that to be a bit drastic, banishment from the country maybe, eventually however I was reprieved, on condition that I touched nothing from that day onward.

The never-ending quest for excitement led us into many scrapes, and it also made us a few enemies. As we passed away the hours, days and years, usually 'gainfully' employed, every so often we would find ourselves at a loose end. One such occasion, I recall, and not without a good measure of trepidation, was as four of us were idly drifting into an afternoon of boredom after suffering a morning of tedium. We were wandering down the passage that connected all our back gardens, when one of our number spotted an old knife grinder.

He sat on a tricycle with a grindstone attached to it. He was beavering away at his work, sharpening and grinding, whetting knives and scissors, as serene, calm and tranquil an old soul as ever you set your eyes on. And so he would possibly have remained. Unfortunately, someone saw this old grinder as some kind of quick fix to disperse monotony. The first few insults were ignored, but this seemed to spur us (I say us, I really mean the others) into more taunts. Suddenly this benign tender old man took on a persona of such magnitude that could only be created in nightmares. From a seated position I would have estimated his height at five feet ten or so inches, as he arose he grew to enormous proportions, and at ten feet I stopped guessing. Sheer panic set in. Then he spoke, the voice came from somewhere near the soles of his socks, his demeanour was not of this world, he pointed a long bony finger, which was attached to a long thin gnarled hand, this in turn was joined to this great un-human body (which incidentally was still growing) and uttered four words "Once seen never forgotten." It was at that precise moment that I decided that the once seen was the last sighting he was ever likely to get of me. The terror that had invaded my brain, turning my legs into boneless wobbly things, was replaced with an immediate necessity for self-preservation. A sudden wish to face another day of boredom suddenly became quite desirable. If only I could convert this desire into useful energy I would be on my way. The other three were by now in full control of their limbs and were legging it to a safer domain. Then to my immense relief my little white legs started to work, and work well. They delivered me from that spot at a rate of knots only Ben Johnson on speed ever came near to. The other three never spoke of that episode again and I was always loath to broach it. Although even to this day when the wind is moving and whispering in the trees' boughs, I am sure I can hear those four words uttered on that fateful afternoon. In my prayers I always finish by saying "God bless my three friends and all lovely old knife grinders." Well! It might help. If he still exists and a strange feeling tells me he might, I would just like to say sorry and hope sorry is adequate.

There were two other people who were good for a bit of fun on going-nowhere-days. They were Ted the gardener who worked for Miss Harboard, and the park keeper who was employed by the local council.

Ted not only tended the needs of the flora but also guarded the woods within the confines of Mousehold House's grounds fervently. He took his work very seriously. If any children were seen trespassing, Ted would violently inflict pain on them. First he would send out a gentle warning by saying, "If I catch any of you little buggers, I'll stick my foot up your arses." Ted would be up for consideration in any arse kicking team and could eventually become the captain, later on he might even aspire to national coach. He had all the attributes required, he had a murderous attitude toward children, wore great big hobnailed boots with potential for serious anal damage that could only be measured on a seismograph, on top of which he regarded his malevolence as a pleasure as well as a duty. Just thinking about it brings my eyes to a state of dampness.

Ted could be brought to a *state of readiness* by just sighting a boy, his hackles would rise and off he would set hot foot in pursuit of any child he could catch. He was an awesome sight when in full flight after his quarry. He was not a man to take chances with. Bravery was not the order of the day when meddling with Ted. Fleetness of foot was an attribute not to be sniffed at if serious anal damage was to be avoided. Even in my dreams I could see Ted in full flight about to deliver a blow which could gravely restrict any likelihood of sedentary employment within one's lifetime. Although any likelihood of life's longevity would come under serious threat should his boot register a direct hit. Even a glancing blow could preclude too much comfort for the foreseeable future. Ted had a wheelbarrow, which he protected with his life. It was his constant companion, but occasionally he would leave it unprotected and Ted's unprotected wheelbarrow was sufficient to drive small boys to mischief. On these odd occasions it had a habit of disappearing, but after a few hours Ted would search it out, swearing his loyalty to its safety, and death to any small boys encountered within a mile of his beloved barrow.

Parky, although having an occupation roughly on the same lines, did not have the same fanaticism. Never mind about inflicting pain on others, he was quite content if he had managed to complete the day by not having us inflict too much pain on him. As I explained, the woods were divided into two by a valley which ran their length. These wooded hills either side of the valley would permit us to get Parky moving with a bumbling gait in order to protect the flora before too much damage could be imposed. Parky had no barrow, but he did have a bike that he pushed around with a loving devotion that most people would consider went a touch beyond that which may have been termed as platonic friendship. Parky's movements were ponderous in comparison to Ted's which were more sprightly. We always felt that Parky's bike was more of a hindrance to his cause than a help, but then pushing his bike was far more sensible than leaving it unprotected and to the vagaries of vandals who might or might not treat it with the same reverence as he himself was wont to treat it.

Parky, not being as frivolous as Ted with his wheelbarrow, never let his bike out of sight. He would push it all the time, at no time was he seen astride his beloved machine. Although Parky never rode his bike, he did wear cycle-clips. We assumed the clips were worn to prevent little uninvited creatures from scaling his legs.

On days when we played Robin Hood, it was necessary to have bows, arrows and lances, and trees, by the nature of being the raw material required, would come under the knife. For some reason this did not please Parky. A position could be gained at the top of one side of the valley that provided a vantage point for observation of Parky's movements. When seeing us cutting his lovely trees he would push his bike up the slope. On his reaching our position we would abandon our ground and run across the valley, digging in at the top of the opposite slope, and there we would wait. Sure enough Parky would come trundling down pushing his bike and up to the new position we commanded, and off we would go again. This little ritual would go on until we got bored. Parky would never get bored, on the other hand he never got (as did Ted) maniacally excited. Parky, on reflection, must have been a fairly phlegmatic character. This worked well in his favour, the lack of a killer instinct, the absence of bite, and the dilution of the danger element meant that the chase became a bit stereotyped and ponderous. The fact that we were not in a life-threatening situation seemed to reduce the adrenalin rush to but a trickle.

Unlike Ted, Parky could not be spurred into frantic efforts, even rude verses had no effect on him. It was never clear as to what elements, when concocted, would set Parky alight (metaphorically speaking), but then is that not the case with all or most council employees? Personally I think it is all the tea they mix with the bromide. In the heady days of my youth my friends were supplied with unlimited fun, brilliant antagonists, and all that was required was the know-how to activate them.

On a good day, if there was nothing more pleasurable to do, we could upset Ted, confuse Parky, have a stone fight with some kids from a rival gang, cadge ninepence off mother (decimal equivalent is four and a half pence) and go to the pictures (Theatre de Luxe, or cinema), to see Roy Rogers or Gene Autrey.

Come out, jump on an imaginary Trigger (Roy Rogers' white steed) gallop home, cram some tea down our throats, go out and play rounders, cricket or football and finish up completely exhausted with eyelids the weight of lead ingots, we would sleep the untroubled sleep of angels.

By this time Ted and Parky would be just distant memories. Having finished their duties they would be home reminiscing, Ted with some homicidal thoughts and new plans for physical violence, Parky, his innermost thoughts unknown (well, who knows!). The council would have thought for him all day long so it is highly unlikely a sudden rush of constructive ideas would invade his weary brain this late in the day. If they did he would no doubt quickly dismiss such alien intrusions as unnecessary and slip into tranquil oblivion.

Chapter Eight

In 1938 an agreement of appeasement called 'The Munich Agreement' was drawn up between Germany, Britain, France and Italy. This pact allowed Germany to extend their territory into the Sudetenland, a frontier region of Czechoslovakia. This region was inhabited by a German-speaking minority. Germany thereby gained a foothold in a country where its right was arbitrarily decided by countries who themselves had no right.

Neville Chamberlain, the Conservative Prime Minister, on returning from Munich after agreeing the Munich pact on behalf of Britain, issued his well-documented 'Peace in our Time' statement. Now established, Hitler decided he would like to travel and embarked on a crushing tour of the rest of Czechoslovakia. Hitler's insatiable desire for travel then gave him a wish to visit Poland.

Great Britain had a pact with Poland. Therefore the invasion of Poland involved British soldiers who were beaten in the conflict. This forced Chamberlain into issuing Hitler an ultimatum: he either withdraws his troops from Poland or a state of war would exist between Britain and Germany. A deadline was given after which Chamberlain broadcast to the British nation that he had not received any assurance from Hitler that German troops would be withdrawn from Poland and so a state of war now existed between Britain and Germany. That broadcast by Neville Chamberlain cleared the streets of adults much as did Dick Barton clear them of children. Mums and dads, aunts and uncles, all gathered around their little sound boxes. After the broadcast they each pronounced their theories on the best way to beat the Germans.

Aunt Ada had the best idea when after an hour of listening to what she described as 'words from where only diarrhoea should exit' she proposed making a pot of tea. The men, whose brains had been tested to the very limit, felt that something stronger was called for, and as the pubs were by this time opened for business we were privileged to witness what was to be the first great retreat of the war as the men all sloped off to the local.

65

Days turned to weeks, weeks turned to months and never a sight of a German, well apart from Gladys Albright's Dachshund called Herman. This was a rather unfortunate choice of name, but chosen more in lack of foresight than with any malicious intent, and as he was not of an aggressive nature it was agreed he could maintain his freedom in spite of the anti-Herman-lobby which would have seen him incarcerated for the duration. The Home Guard mustered at regular intervals, broomsticks were issued, knives sharpened and attached to the broomsticks, men's underwear washed in case they got captured, (the men not the underwear although of course they would probably all be caught together) and no self respecting woman would have her hubby being scrutinised by the Bosch in unclean underwear.

As children we would become the last line of defence were we to be invaded. All our tree hacking and weapon making would now become very important. Unbelievably Parky still refused to recognise our efforts in the struggle for survival. It was suggested that he should have been taken to The Tower immediately, but the Sheriff of Norwich, during a debate on the matter, added some relevance to the argument by asking, who would keep the little buggers in line if Parky was locked up? Another member suggested that the children did manage to hone their warlike skills by throwing stones at their rival gangs and although actively discouraged from doing so in the times of peace, could still be almost as dangerous as the Home Guard. Some other wag (who had been a recent victim of an errant stone during one of the many wars which erupted between rival gangs) piped up with the theory that the only danger children ever posed was to their own kin and others of the community and added that, as far as the Home Guard was concerned, his old woman posed more of a danger than them. Those with an intimate knowledge of the speaker's old woman, although loath to talk on the subject, nodded their complete agreement.

And so in September 1939 the world was plunged into a war, a war which would continue for five and a half years. It would devastate communities, cities and countries alike.

The main difference, and possibly the only one, in life before and after the announcement that war existed between Britain and Germany, was the zealous digging mania that suddenly gripped the country. Well I assume it gripped the country, it certainly obsessed the population of Plumstead Estate.

There was a drive to dig as much as possible. It was mostly men. They were digging for victory, digging for growing, digging to install their newly arrived corrugated iron shelters, some it was rumoured were even digging for pleasure; but I do find that a bit hard to swallow. Nevertheless there certainly was a lot of it going on. It seemed to be becoming the national pastime. This digging was happening everywhere and unashamedly so. This manic hobby was never going to last. Sure enough, come opening time, tired legs would haul tired bodies down to the local. Men would be convinced (either self-convinced or peer pressured) that their time would be better served in discussing the strategies of the coming events.

The drinking classes have always believed that the public house is the place to expound their views. Here was a major crisis developing, and any man worth his salt would feel accursed could he not put his point across. It is also an undeniable fact that, after a few pints of brewers' delights, the mind of Einstein takes possession of the feeblest of brains; so it would have had plenty to work with there. Not that they were all possessed of a feeble brain, why! some hardly had a brain at all. They could listen to what their mates had to say, reject it out of hand, go for double top and sit back and await the next pint, and point. An absurdity that can be heard within the drinking classes, and there are one or two, is 'go on just have one for the road'. Now, apart from the two pints already consigned to the urinal, the rest would probably finish up on the road anyway. This along with the breakfast previously eaten.

Six or seven pints later our heroes would have to give up on any decisions of strategy. Waiting at home was roast beef and two veg. Also, there was the wife, she never did take too kindly to standing over a hot stove all morning just to have the dinner ruined, she too had to be taken into consideration. Were the dinner to be spoiled, the wife would be a far sterner adversary than anything Hitler could muster.

But we must never lose sight of the fact that these were the men who would go to war, either on some foreign soil, or doing that which was necessary on the home front, faced with terrifying situations against immense odds in order to preserve democracy. Some were born heroes, some became heroes, but however they came to it they were heroes nevertheless.

Now when the Americans arrived they brought their own digging ethos with them. Yes indeed, digging was now, it appeared, world wide, there were no borders it would not cross. Fascinated, we children would watch these aliens with their peculiar looking shovels as they toiled away at whatever task was allocated to them. The Americans' digging was no more intriguing than the home fare, but it did mostly result in the offering of some gum, the home entertainment only resulted in some chore or other.

Meanwhile children who were not able to enjoy the pleasures of drink had their own pleasures. Most children spoke incoherently, fell over and became aggressive without the aid of Bullard's, Morgan's or Steward & Patteson's yeast and barley delicacies anyway.

When you reached an age where only alcohol made you fall about, from then on it was only okay to act in this way if you had absorbed the required amount of alcohol. The requisite amount was not on a scale from one pint to twenty pints, it was the amount which allowed the body to function when the brain had no longer any interest in that which the body was getting up to, and just before the body lost any desire to remain upright.

Regarding children, Herr Goering was forever trying to do us mischief, and all the adults were forever threatening to either box our ears or kick our bloody arses, and what with the slipper, the cane and the boot at the command of the adults' armoury I now believe we would have been safer in the front line of some foreign field. To our entire credit it must be said, never did we buckle under to these incessant threats of violence, and we certainly had a fair amount of freedom.

During the early months of the war my family was given an indoor shelter called a Morrison shelter, this was because I was an asthma sufferer. This was made up of four posts, one at each corner, each was of 4" angle iron with 2" angle iron joining them top and bottom. The top was of ¼" steel plate and the entire ensemble would have supported Norwich's Castle Museum with the minimum amount of effort should it have been necessary. Each side and at the head and foot of the structure were iron mesh grids. It was just about as impenetrable as it is possible to get (plans obtained from me at a nominal cost should the imagery not suffice).

Many things were adapted during the war period. The resourcefulness of people in crisis is unlimited. We had drives on saving discarded or unused materials. The children would spend hours going around collecting scrap metal. This was great fun, as not only was it aiding the war effort but it also permitted some vandalism to boot. Great mounds of scrap metal were collected. I must just say at this point, had our Morrison shelter been used and made into bombs it would have demolished Berlin and half Dresden in one fell swoop.

Great hordes of children were going round gathering metal, some not actually scrap. People's railings disappeared and they never protested that much. Maybe it was out of a sense of patriotism, or even fear of what might ensue should they have protested. Children rampaging in a good cause is something best not tampered with.

Then there were pig bins for the collection of unused edibles, potato peelings, surplus green leaves from vegetables, left over scraps, etc. There were not many left over scraps as most things palatable were gorged by ravenous children. Some things that were not particularly palatable suffered the same fate.

The pig bins also came into play with children who were looking for a bit of mischief. We would place them on a doorstep, knock on the door and hide to await the reaction. If it were a calm person they would just remove the bin and go back inside. These people would have failed the test and would never be entertained by our visits again. There were, however, one or two who would go into a manic rage and come hunting us with violence aforethought. They were the high-flyers; we would amuse them as often as possible. Another thing was that the exercise they acquired during the chase did their vascular system the world of good. Had it not been for that exercise they would have sat in a chair, read all the bad things happening in the world and probably died of a heart attack. I bet they were really grateful later in life.

One man in particular used to get so angry that he would bellow and snort in rage, but because of his build the chase would be a tepid affair. I don't believe he was too kindly disposed toward us, especially on one night, in the dark, when he fell over the pig bin. On that occasion he did display a side of his nature which was not very nice, plus a few obscenities which demonstrated that his upbringing was not especially respectable. Had he have been in any state to catch us he would have dealt out a punishment also way beyond that which was deserved. In hindsight I don't think he was at all grateful.

So it was and is, children even when in mortal danger can usually come up with diversions with which to deflect that danger.

This was vividly displayed to me one day when I was designated to pick up my grandson Sam from school. My car has installed in it a computer kind of configuration. In order to start the engine it requires a number to be tapped in. On this occasion, in my foolishness, and at his request, I decided to allow Sam to partake in the pleasure of tapping in the number. Three times he tried and each time he tapped in the wrong number. By now I decided enough was sufficient so I relieved him of the duty. Unfortunately, by now the car also felt vexed and defied any attempts I deployed in order to start it. To make matters worse, not only remaining stubborn in its pique, it kept flashing a little red light and beeping. Whether this was in anger or just a temporary sulk I don't know. My intelligence may not stretch far, but I do know when a car refuses to start it means it. This is knowledge I've gathered over the years from other petulant pieces of miserable mechanical garbage I've owned. To make matters worse, Sam, my ex-grandson, informed me he was just playing about.

With this remark he then became the recipient of my full-blown wrath. Having informed him of my displeasure and explained how he had effectively put to death, by his imprudence, my lovely car, I then made him walk to my granddaughter's school in order to pick her up. My point is this. By the time we had reached her school my (by now well divorced) grandson had managed to draw a blanket over the immediate past, and was skateboarding around my granddaughter's school playground and having a whooping old time. His erstwhile old granddad was left having a nervous breakdown with no car and requiring a course of Valium and a couch consultation with the local shrink. Children are capable of going through trauma and hurt and coming through virtually unscathed.

My formative years were spent during a period of war. We were bombed, caned and deprived of many of the goodies of today's children, yet we all managed to survive with very little permanent damage. Incidentally Sam and I are back together now, but I'm open to offers. The other thing, before I leave the subject of Sam, the car and my wrath, was the sympathy I received from the rest of the family. It bordered on very little and hurried along rapidly to none at all. The general consensus of opinion was that anyone who trusts Sam deserves all he gets.

Chapter Nine

In 1940, some eight months after the declaration of war, Chamberlain resigned and Winston Churchill took over the government and set up a coalition taking on himself the dual role of Prime Minister and Defence Minister.

Churchill was a stirring orator with such defiant words as 'We shall fight on the beaches, we shall fight on the landing grounds, we shall fight in the fields, and in the streets, we shall fight in the hills; we shall never surrender.' After the Battle of Britain, in which the RAF pilots, flying Spitfires and Hurricanes, saw off the German Luftwaffe (air force) thereby stopping them from bombing Britain's airfields, Churchill gave the speech 'Never in the field of human conflict was so much owed by so many to so few.' This was a fitting tribute to the bravery, endurance and skill of the young pilots who undertook a mammoth task. These young men faced death or mutilation each time they flew. They protected our airspace and our airfields. Although their chances of survival were low, they never flinched from their duty. Their actions ultimately ensured Britain would not be invaded. The sacrifices made by the valiant soldiers who fought on foreign fields and gave their efforts and lives towards the final victory, those men of the Navy, gallantly braving the hazards of the German surface ships, U-boat raiders, and the severe elements to ensure convoys got through with vital supplies must never be forgotten. As a child my perception was of men, as I grew older (and those defenders allowed me to grow older in freedom) I know that a great majority who flew, sailed, or marched into the insatiable jaws of death were but boys.

On the home front we had the Local Defence Volunteers (later to become the Home Guard). Then there was the Fire Service, and the Auxiliary Fire Service who also did a great job. Men who fought hard and bravely to keep under control fires that were started by the German incendiary bombs. Men scaling burning buildings using wooden ladders all amid falling masonry, fought infernos of unbelievable intensity, enormous flames licking round them like dragon's tongues, ready to devour them. We often forgot the gallantry of those men who foraged through the rubble to save people trapped underneath and all in the shadow of death from unstable walls, knowing the dangers but carrying on regardless of those dangers. In fact it was a time when everyone galvanised their efforts towards ultimate victory.

Churchill's talent for saying the right words is legendary. He roused the nation with the eloquence of his speeches. After the greatest air battle ever fought he gave our pilots the fitting tribute with 'This was their finest hour' thus leading the nation to believe that it would now pass into light. But the nation's people passed much water before any light shone through their darkness. Although the pilots had won the battle of the air there was an even greater battle still to be won, but at last we were going forward. Churchill took his oratory to the American people when he delivered to the US Congress his speech after Pearl Harbour 'It becomes more difficult to reconcile Japanese action with prudence or even sanity. What kind of people do they think we are?' By this speech he had allied the causes of the two nations.

From 1939 the lives of people would change from that which went before. Women's roles became much more important, or at least the perception would. Women as child bearers, wives, homemakers, etc., were usually classed as being of less value than the men. Their jobs were undervalued for the most part. Women were seen as an underclass, mainly there just for supporting their male counterparts. It was the man who earned the money, he who deserved the acclaim.

This was all about to change, not at an alarming rate, but almost by stealth. Those tasks that were the traditional preserves of man were now being undertaken by the 'incapable' female. The problem and the advantage was, the ladies were as capable, if not more capable. Women warmed to their new-found emancipation. They took on work in munitions, police, post office, agriculture and all the other work men once did. On top of all this new excitement they still managed to perform their other work, the housekeeping, raising children and home accountancy.

THE WOMEN'S LAND ARMY had been created in 1917 and by 1918 it had 23,000 members. In 1939 it once again came into its own. In September 1939 it was foreseen that the agricultural industry needed more people. Males were enlisting for the forces so women were then taking on farm work. In September 1939 there were already 1,000 volunteers. By December 1939 the number had swelled to 4,544 or maybe 4,545; it must have been a fairly pedantic account to pin the number down so precisely. I used the number 4,545 as it is quite possible a call of nature could have excluded at least one person from the count. However, I do not wish to dwell too long on such a piddling matter, but in moments of deep depression I do wonder (and I know it is sad) if this was an exact number 4,545 or was it 4,546 even 4,544? I had best get on as I feel a new depression heading in my direction.

Back to the Land Army girls. By March 1940 the number had risen to an estimated 10,200 (as this was only an estimate we must assume that the person who counted them was either dead, drafted or mad). This included regular workers and seasonal workers. Women were also employed in the ATS, WRNS, and WAAF. In these services and in all other instances they equalled their male colleagues. The only exception was in armed combat. Now even that is within their remit.

Women in unarmed combat were something else. In 1941 women were being employed by public transport companies as clippies (or conductresses). They were called clippies because of the way they clipped tickets to show how much had been used. One of these clippies was slapped across the face for turning away a woman because the bus was already full. The aggressor was prosecuted for her petulance.

It also appeared that the drivers (all male) were getting far too friendly with their co-working females after they had worked together for some months (now there is a surprise). The company got to learn about it and through feelings of morality or maybe jealousy, promptly proposed to split them up. It almost came to a strike. I am led to believe bus crews were required to travel with buckets of cold water after that. On reflection I suppose it was a miracle buses ever left their starting point.

Some passengers also reacted differently. The women passengers saw their sisters freed from the drudgeries of housework and little envious goblins took over. The men saw the women as either a threat to their dominance or some would see them as a target for their amorous desires.

Driving buses must have been a complete and utter nightmare. Their headlights were dimmed to nothing more than a small shaft of light because of the blackout. Signposts were all removed from roads just in case Germany invaded Britain. Now this *does* seem to be a bizarre notion. It was probably to confuse and disorientate the German army. It would have been more likely to have confused the locals. It is quite easy to confuse locals especially at closing time, but the logic of this argument was obviously missed during the edict's formulation. Now, many years later, we know that to confuse the Germans all we need to do is remove their towels.

Germany had already managed to find their way through Poland, Czechoslovakia, France and Belgium where signposts would have not been understandable, it is highly unlikely that the removal of a few signposts in Britain would have caused them too much concern. We can only put the reasoning down to too much alcohol, insufficient brain cells being applied, or a touch of inbreeding. It may have been more effective had the signposts all pointed in the direction of Wales. It's a fair bet the Land Of Our Fathers' signposts would have brought a bit of chaos to the occasion. There's one thing for sure, had the Germans enquired directions from the locals they would certainly have been bamboozled. Even when they use English I still can't understand a thing they say. The Germans would have soon come to the conclusion that a belligerent Taffy is best left alone with his sheep.

The buses themselves with their crash gearboxes were another story completely. Drivers today have more congested roads but with hydraulic brakes, synchromesh gears and power steering, the actual vehicles are far easier to drive. Power steering in the forties was all about muscle, arm and body strength, not mechanical assistance.

What with having to contend with heavy steering, difficult gear changing, darkness through the blackout, and then the strain of the physical demands at each and every terminus from his clippie, I would not think much kept the driver awake at night, well apart from their marital duties, I wonder who had the headaches then!

All house windows had to be shuttered at night to prevent light being shown to enemy planes. On opening outside doors the lights had to be switched off. Many were the times the cry would go out, 'Put that light out!' There was also a penalty for showing lights, as it was against the law.

The postal service also introduced women into their work force as not enough men could be found. This was the first time women had been employed in the postal service but they were received well, at least that was how the Norfolk & Norwich Weekly Press reported it.

After the Battle of Britain ended in humiliation for the Luftwaffe, Hermann Goering, who led the Luftwaffe, was feeling a little upset, so he told his pilots 'Hard luck boys you did your best, go and have a cup of tea, you've plenty of time, the next train to Auschwitz won't be along for half an hour yet', or words of similar encouragement.

The attacks on Britain's aerodromes were supposed to remove the threat to the German forces when they invaded. However, the plan now lay in tatters so another strategy was deployed. Also by this time in 1942 the severity of raids on Germany was being increased.

It seems that Reich Marshall Goering and a few friends were playing an after-dinner party game of I Spy when one of the gathering of intellectuals spotted something beginning with 'B'. It transpired it was a book. The book was called 'Baedeker Travel Guide'. This was a travel guide written by Karl Baedeker and listed cities throughout Europe of historical interest. Unfortunately, Norwich was one of the cities listed but, as with

Adolf's other theories, such as the Aryan race and his world-domination ideas, he then had problems with the Baedeker concept. Adolf, assisted by the mammoth-brained advisor, Herman Goering, studied the Baedeker travel guide and decided to visit our old historic towns and cities. That which they failed to grasp was Baedeker only meant to visit. His idea was to sightsee and enjoy, not to rearrange the masonry. We as a nation felt that any adjusting necessary we could do ourselves. As it turned out they really had no idea anyway. Anything which stood erect or perpendicular they just made horizontal. Now is that any way for the furtherance of good architecture?

Goering thought it would be good fun to visit Norwich. Goering was not as keen on travel as Hitler so he just sent his pilots with lots of planes and loads of bombs.

The Luftwaffe needed a nice clear night and on the night of April 27 1942 the German planes paid us a visit. It began well before midnight and it was a night of death, destruction and terror.

Chambers Dictionary of Etymology defines 'Blitz' as the German word for lightning; I think terror, fire and destruction could be added, and it would still be a euphemism for what actually happened to Norwich and its people on that night.

We lay, my sister, mother and I, huddled in absolute terror as bombs exploded and gunfire boomed all around. The high explosives and fearsome incendiaries rained down on Norwich for what seemed hours. My main concern was not my safety or my family's as we were safe in our steel and iron bunker, it was my cat Tiger. Tiger would have been a match for any single German, but this was different. He was a battle-scarred tough old bugger who slept all day and woe betide anyone who was silly enough to disturb him, he bonked all night and ate nothing but lights (the lungs of sheep, pigs and bullocks, (bullocks as spelt with a u). We had had flash raids over Norwich for quite a while, but this was Armageddon, and such a short time into my life. Within a few minutes Norwich was torn to shreds, fires raged out of control. It is unimaginable to contemplate. It had to be lived through to appreciate the horror and fear this awesome onslaught brought. Even now after a violent thunderstorm I half expect to see the city laid bare, such is the power of memory. Fortunately, for most of us, there are no enduring scars remaining, such is our resilience.

On the Tuesday we tried to get into the city. It was not until we viewed the city from St Matthews Hill and into Riverside Road that the damage became apparent. There were fires still raging, no-go areas because bombs had refused to explode on impact, buildings with damage so bad that they had to be flattened, but amid it all there was still humour. Shops with fronts blown out hung with little notices such as 'open as usual but longer' and 'if you don't mind the mess we would enjoy your company'. The tragedy was of those whose company had gone forever and that we would never enjoy again.

Plumstead Estate was hardly touched at all and Tiger returned the next morning with a twinkle in his eye, demolished his lights and promptly crashed out. I doubt if any of it ever disturbed his romantic nights and it certainly did nothing to blunt the little sod's appetite, nor did it sweeten his temper.

There were also other forms of destruction, bombs filled with oil and a nitro-glycerine charge that exploded on impact and fired the oil with terrifying power. Firemen worked tirelessly to quench the flames and many were killed along with civilians. I can still recall those blazing buildings, seeing the homes of hundreds of people either completely flattened or damaged beyond their ability to function as homes any longer. Half houses left standing, their souls revealed, people's former lives left in shreds but the dead no longer cared. As for those who were left, the homeless, the bereaved and the grieving, they had to find the courage to carry on. The strength of people's character under such distress remained undiminished, in fact their resolve increased. They watched their films which were for the most part slanted towards propaganda, and listened to their radios, drawing comfort from every crumb of good news available. They sang along to Workers Playtime, laughed at the comedians and cried at the 'weepies'. But they never lost faith in the ability to remain staunch, their dream remained steadfast in the belief that one day 'the valleys would bloom again' and 'their children would sleep in their own little rooms again', and the bluebirds would indeed fly, soar, and trim their weaving patterns 'over the white cliffs of Dover'. Meanwhile, however, there was much effort needed to bring the dream to reality.

By now American and British planes were bombing Hamburg, Cologne and Dresden on a twenty-four hour basis. As a child I remember seeing an American bomber crash on the waste ground almost opposite the Fountain recreation ground on Mousehold. We ran from Plumstead Estate all the way to the crash site. My abiding memory was of the plane covered in foam from the fire engines and the removal of bodies from the wreck. The crew, as far as I know, all died.

The terror of the Blitz on Norwich must have paled beside the raids now being carried out over Germany. It was good that Germany was now in receipt of the horror inflicted on us by their office. Unfortunately, many of the victims were innocent ordinary people. They too were the old, the very young and those who just wished to live in peace.

Thorpe Hamlet had attacks made on it and this was my home. I believe the worst incident in this area was when Raven's shop (at the corner of Malvern Road and St Leonard's Road) was hit, and the whole family perished. The site was cleared and later on a prefabricated house was placed on it. Prefabs were supposed to be temporary buildings lasting about ten years, but this one lasted for maybe thirty years. Some were so liked that a brick skin was built around them to give them permanency. However, the one on the site of Raven's shop was eventually removed and town houses are now there.

We had evacuees from London for a while and I recall a bus stopping on Pilling Park Road. From this bus stepped these little London urchins, clasping their small cases. These cases carried very few of life's chattels, but I expect to these small bewildered children they formed an emotional link with home and family, stronger than steel. They stayed for a few weeks, we suffered them and they us, but friendships finally formed and when they left it was with some mutual sadness.

There was one lad who was billeted on Wellesley Avenue and became the bulwark of our rival gang. He was one to be avoided, that is until he upset Terry Whall's brother John who was our bulwark. John promptly bloodied his nose and after that the streets were safe once again.

In the centre of the area which lies amid the streets of Brigg Street, Red Lion Street and Rampant Horse Street stood Woolworth's store which was razed to the ground during the Blitz. The rubble was removed and a massive static water tank was installed, to combat any fires from the German incendiary bombs. It remained so until well after hostilities had ceased. At one time a giant inflatable raft was floated and money was tossed down into it. This was for some charity, I don't know which. It was eventually sunk by the weight of coins tossed into it. After that the site became a temporary car park before Curls was built there, and now it is Debenhams.

Gas masks were another feature of living during the war. When worn, and this happened during gas attack exercises, we resembled aliens. The structure was mainly rubber with elastic drawn tightly over the head; a filter of sorts was attached at the base. They were most uncomfortable to wear. The mundane questions such as, have you got your lunch, money, handkerchief etc, now included have you got your gas mask? The apparatus was carried in a cardboard box with a loop of string attached to allow it to be slung over the shoulder.

It was compulsory to carry it wherever you went. Carrying it was far more preferable to wearing it. Anyone suffering from claustrophobia would have had a pretty torrid time inside it, I should think. At times I wondered if it were not better to be gassed than to be suffocated. Fortunately, the chance to explore the theory never presented itself as the Germans decided that with boys' reluctance to wash their feet there was no gas known to man at that time of day which could afford the nasal airways more suffering.

There was speculation on the reasons for the Blitz; some said it was reprisals, some that it was to break the people's spirit. This may all be true, and certainly a lot of residential homes were hit, but it may have been wayward bombing as well. There was quite a high concentration of industry around those areas that were hit. If the bombing was designed to kill off, or raze to the ground, an historic city then the main features, the Cathedral, the Castle, the Catholic Cathedral, all prominent buildings were missed. A friend told me that he was informed that the City Hall was left undamaged on strict instructions from Hitler. Hitler thought it would be an ideal place from which to administer their affairs. Norwich Council also thinks it a good place, unfortunately some of the affairs they administer are not that good. Hitler may have wanted it saved for its architectural design, in which case it says as much about his taste as it says about the place's design.

As I mentioned, we had day raids and the siren would blast off, this was the first warning, the crash warning would mean the planes were almost overhead, then the crash All Clear. Some days the All Clear would not go at all. Children at school would be underground all day. It was almost like the life of a mole.

During the raid of 1942 Thorpe Hamlet School was hit. The next day when the children found they no longer had a seat of learning to attend, they were desolate. They felt wretched. However, they need not have fretted, as another place was soon found for them. Once again the smiles returned to those saddened little faces, and dull eyes shone again. And so another fairy story ended happily.

I also remember that during the worst of the air raids voices could be heard outside our house. The comfort this gave to an eight-year-old sheltering from death was immense. Whole families were killed in the raids, nearly 250 people were killed in the Baedeker Blitz and 700 people were injured. On the Monday night, 27th of April 1942 alone, 164 people were killed. Discounting the Blitz, on other raids between July 1940 and November 1943 a further 100 civilians were killed. Gravediggers were probably the busiest people in the city. Considering the severity of the raids, it is a wonder there were not more casualties. Those made homeless numbered many hundreds. The raids touched every citizen in Norwich, I would not think there was one person who did not know of someone who had died or been injured. Now that is a statistic that would be hard to realise in a city the size of Norwich.

Through all the mayhem, the destruction and disaster no one that I can recall ever got despondent. There was always an air of optimism, a joke, and a cheerful word. It was said that no one had a good word to say about Hitler, that is a lie, I heard some very good words said about him, unfortunately they are not repeatable.

In this period of the Blitz civilians were compelled to carry out that which was termed fire-watching. Norwich's shoe manufacturers were manifold in the years prior to and during the war, and well after the war, although they have been in decline for several years now. My mother worked for one such firm called 'Bally & Haldinstein'* and even though she worked from home she still had to do her stint as a fire-watcher. That was a strange name for it, it should have been called watching to see there was.no fire.

My mother's brief was to do her time at a place called the Rubber Works in St Andrew's Street in Norwich. My sister and I used to go with her to make sure she did it properly. We had a great time charging around playing hide and seek and making sure that everyone stayed awake . . . whether they wanted to or not. It now comes to mind that had the place been hit by an incendiary bomb we could all have been bar-b-cued. This place had enough combustible material to keep the Fire Service interested for weeks, but what did we have? We had a dozen buckets of sand, half a dozen pails of water, a stirrup pump and a prayer book. Anyone who has had anything to do with a stirrup pump will realise just how handy they can be when faced with matches, cigarettes or sparklers, but when it comes to forest fires, towering infernos or German incendiary bombs they are woefully inept. I should think the prayer book would have been of more use than the stirrup pump. Luckily we were never faced with much in the way of big blazes. The most exciting thing was when a woman called Lil got her dress hooked into her knickers after a visit to the bathroom. But even that piece of stimulating action fizzled out when some party pooper told her, but not until after my sister and I had a few minutes of childish giggles. The incident had also awakened some stimulating activity in the lower regions of a bloke called Bert. This threatened to be quite a blaze. However, his ardour soon cooled when he was reminded of his true duties. I wasn't too sure what they meant, but someone said Bert's wife had been unreceptive for years and a woman's dress arranged thus could inflame passions even Bert never knew he had. The only passion it aroused in us was merriment.

Having already mentioned the Morrison shelters I would now like to divert your attention in order to say something on the other type. This was the Anderson shelter, the outdoor counterpart of the Morrison. It consisted of twelve corrugated iron sheets about eight feet in length. The last three feet curved over so that when two of the sections were placed facing each other they formed an arch. These were held together by bolts. The other six were fixed in the same way (I hope my readers are doing this at home). If a stamped addressed envelope is sent I could possibly include a plan of this along with the instructions for the Morrison shelter at half price. This is a service supplied for the more seriously cerebrally challenged, set up by the Bennett to Assist Simple Tormented And Retarded Dummies (BASTARD).

The eight sections when assembled formed a shed-like construction. Men who had a little idea of that which was needed started to cover the things with earth in order to make them sturdy. Men who had more idea realised that these things needed to be dropped into the ground. Standing above ground made them susceptible to blast and shrapnel.

Out came the earth moving implements (shovels). Large holes appeared in the men-of-ideas gardens, soon everyone caught on and so all or at least most of the shelters were sunk into the ground. Only a direct hit by a bomb could damage them now.

People did not stop there, steps leading down to the floor were made, bunks and lights were installed, provisions stored and some were even carpeted. In the future these hideaways would be used far more often than could have been foreseen then. From 1940 up until 1943 Norwich was under air attack and on some days the siren would go early in the morning but the all clear would not go all day. The day was interspersed with crash alarms and crash all clears, but not the main all clear. The main alarm was a long oscillating sound and the crash alarm was three short monotone blasts, the crash all clear was one short blast and the main all clear was one long monotone sound which trailed off in a gradual decline and finally into silence, all were distinctive. There were times when we waited so long we couldn't remember whether the main all clear had sounded or not.

The Luftwaffe, not wishing to upset anyone by ignoring them, would show women and children that they were just as important as anyone else by strafing them with machine gun fire. They were very even-handed, and it kept up our morale to know we were that important. In fact it was quite fulfilling to know that Fritz (as we called the Germans) was interested in us. There is nothing worse than feeling that you are a nonentity and children would not wish to be disregarded at a time when everyone else was given such high status as being shot at.

* My mother was in the habit of calling Bally's shoe factory Bally & Haldinstein, but a friend of mine recalls that just before the outbreak of war Mr Haldinstein handed over the reins of control of the business to Bally and it became solely Bally's shoe factory.

Chapter Ten

My father having managed to produce two children considered his life's work well done and in 1942 promptly died. At the time I thought that that which he had considered was in fact most ill-considered and quite untimely.

This left my mother to bring up my sister and me on her own. Would she be able? Would she be strong enough? In a male-dominated world could she feed us? The answers arrived within weeks. As long as I could remember she had worked. She was a forewoman at Bally & Haldinstein's Shoe Factory, she had also been a clippie with the bus company ('but her bus always left the terminus on time'), so she wouldn't be afraid of work. It was just a case of fitting her work in with the needs of two hungry and demanding children. Demanding means in no way selfishly demanding, it was demanding through life's needs. Ultimately a complete solution was found, she would take in shoe work at home.

A month prior to my father's death he had taken a job as a hotel manager in Goudhurst, Kent. Fortunately my parents had the vision to keep the house in Pilling Park Road going for that period. This was in case my father's new job didn't work out, we could then return to our former home. The hotel required a married couple and after my father's death, as my mother could not find another husband at such short notice, we had to move back to Norwich. The furniture of our former life had been sold so that the house we now returned to was like old Mother Hubbard's cupboard, and it was just as well we had no dog as I feel its disappointment would have rivalled Goering's of earlier days. We couldn't live there without furniture and so my sister and I were given into the care of the Salvation Army.

A lady Salvationist living in Coltishall took us in, fed and housed us. We enjoyed our stay there apart from the return to the outside loo. This was a hut of some simplicity which housed a large metal container. The seat provided was of some refinement that the rest of the assemblage lacked. Each week a horse-drawn cart would call and empty the container, a job that few envied.

The fellow in charge seemed a cheerful enough man, his work he did with relish, and maybe it was because his job was a reserve occupation. No other person could be found to do it. Not that the job was beyond the capability of others, they just hid up and couldn't be found. Apart from the toilet arrangements (which transported me back to my first home), everything else was idyllic.

This period was in August of 1942. My sister and I stayed there a fortnight and then we transferred to another home. We didn't go too much on the new place and tried to escape. We considered a tunnel but Coltishall to Norwich seemed an exercise of massive proportions, so we gave it a miss. Anyway all the spades were being employed in this wretched hobby of digging for shelters and victory.

The best thing was a family just down the road. The parents of this family had managed to produce twins and, although they were golden angels to their producers, they were rather less reverently received by the other villagers. These two boys could levy distress on the whole village within a very short space of time.

Now it came to pass that in this village were two little semi-orphans, or as is now termed a 'one-parent family' and all due to the father's inability to stay alive. They were only temporary dwellers and knew little of the affairs of the village, or the terrible twins. This would possibly have remained the case. Unfortunately our new locum parentis, a woman not given to too much hyperbole, related some of the lesser sins of our wayward pair. The greater sins were too heinous to recount. Had our surrogate mother been in touch with the fallacy of uttering the phrase 'Don't play with those twins', life would have been much less exciting.

Was it not Oscar Wilde who said, 'The only thing I cannot resist is temptation'? And that, broadly speaking, is the same with most people. Within minutes of banning my sister and me from the iniquitous duo off we set in search of them. Their place was a treasure trove of delight. There were things to be played with, things that would bring death if played with, and even seemingly inanimate objects which could bring life to a violent ending when not even touched.

These boys had their parents in rapturous delight but the rest of the village in rupturous (I made rupturous up so don't go scanning the dictionary) despair. They were up to anything that would bring them pleasure, but that which brought them pleasure usually managed a goodly amount of anguish for others. Whenever the twins appeared the villagers disappeared.

The village siren, apart from its normal function of warning the approach of enemy aircraft had another duty far more terrifying to the people of the village; it warned of the pending arrival of the twins. Cats were seen to flee in panic, babies hidden, washing was removed from clotheslines, girls were issued with chastity belts and two pairs of knickers for safety, and general pandemonium ensued.

When apprised of our desire to escape, the twins decided that the best mode of transport was by rocket. Up to and including this moment we had seen some pretty scary projects contrived by those two scallywags, most of which fell into the category of dodgy and ascending rapidly to dangerous. But because of our desperate plight we agreed to do the test flight from Coltishall to Norwich.

During the next few weeks we collected anything that could be persuaded to become a rocket. For sustenance on the flight we would take sandwiches and a few bottles of lemonade. We would need a compass, some books to while away the hours in flight and a parachute just in case a speedy exit from the rocket was required. As most of the parachutes were being used on more mundane operations it was decided that, as we were only light (in the head I assume they meant) two umbrellas would be adequate and easily acquired. Most of the ladies attending church on a Sunday took umbrellas. Such was their faith in God they even took them when it was not bucketing down with rain. However, their faith in being able to leave them in the lobby *and* finding them safe after the service finished was indeed much stronger. So it just goes to prove that God will protect umbrellas from the villain, but He has little control over the weather. Or it may well be He has a maladjusted sense of humour.

The twins thought we were mighty helpful and mighty brave in being the first people to travel in their new invention. That was until I suggested that it would be wise to pack some nappies. It is possible that some credibility could have been lost in that instant. But it was restored when I said that I was only thinking of my sister, and heights tended to affect her bowel movements to a certain degree that the twins saw my point and agreed. In fact when it was explained that this had no reflection on their workmanship they were quite happy with the notion and commended me on my humanity in the brother/sister relationship.

Unfortunately, by the end of August we were rehabilitated back into our home at Pilling Park Road by a duller mode of travel (the bus). The twins were distraught to think that all their efforts had been in vain. We too were distraught, but to a slightly lesser degree. Of the twins, after we left we never heard again. There were rumours around that time involving strange lights in the sky and unexplained bangs, but it was only idle gossip.

Maybe the twins became model citizens and conformed to the rules which governed all the law-abiding members of the village. Possibly, with the willing help of the villagers they did finish their rocket and emigrated to America, finishing up on Alcatraz or Devil's Island. On the other hand they may have made a bomb instead. I remember a few years later there were a couple of big explosions somewhere in, I believe it was Japan. But who knows? Too much speculation could turn the mind and having skated the fringe for most of my life I feel it would be folly to topple over the edge at this late stage.

By this time my mother had got a home together and was working hard making a living at the sewing machine that had been delivered to our house in our absence. She feverishly laboured away in order to feed and clothe us. She would get us ready for school, do the housework, and then sit at the sewing machine for hours and hours. During the air raids when my sister and I were in the shelter, she would toil away. The German bombers would be almost peering down the chimney before she would take cover herself.

Such devotion and such dedication. Even today, as I walk through memory's garden, I find it hard to believe that such sacrifice of self-interest was made. It must have been for her the most austere life imaginable. Lent lasted three hundred and sixty-five days for her, plus one for Leap Year. She never smoked or drank, her meals were without meat. Frugality was a euphemism, but in all this we, the benefactors of her thrift, never suffered at all.

My sister, who was a reader of some accomplishment, would read us books in the evenings. Most were humorous and would have us laughing almost to the point of tears, my mother would even interrupt her sewing to listen (either to her reading or my laughter). Now and then my sister would pause to quench the fire in her throat. At these unnecessary interruptions I would goad her on "Go on! Go on!" I would implore. However, I now feel her reading had a detrimental effect on my own literacy, why should I learn to read when I could be read to?

I believe the selflessness, devotion and commitment of mothers in those bleak years should be the standard of today's parents.

Women sewed patches on clothes, darned socks, provided for and tended their young children. Single-mindedness was their byword. There was also a community spirit that seems to be missing in today's helter-skelter, materialistic world.

Having often looked at photos of young boys during the war years, it has always struck me how the lengths of clothes varied. That's not to say between one child and another, but the dress of each child. The trousers were always too long and the jacket seemed too short. It took me a while to ponder on this mystery. Now the reason has become clear. With clothes rationing we were only bought one suit of clothes every year, there wasn't the casual and varied choice there is these days. This meant that each set of clothes had to last for at least two years. A boy's talent for growing is legendary, mothers would understand this so they would compensate by buying the trousers long, hence the reason for 'short trousers' being almost knee level. The jacket would have to be about the right size; after all a boy couldn't have the sleeves coming over his hands, it would impair his writing and he was quite capable of impairing his own writing without the aid of overlong sleeves. The problem is, the jacket, although a well fitting garment to start with, would fall into the sloppy habit of looking too short two years later. Also another aid to the sloppy look was the bulging pocket syndrome. This would have been caused by the amount of valuables a boy needed to carry around with him. The most essential of these would be: a penknife, a catapult, cigarette cards, stones (varied), handkerchief (in which to wrap injured frog, bird, half-sucked sweet etc), *some* marbles, but most boys would not have *all* their marbles, a packet of gum recently acquired from the Yank who'd taken their elder sisters out the night before, or for assisting them in their digging, even to stop boys from assisting; a piece of string, plus a number of nondescript items, but all necessary to ensure safe passage through the day. There would come later the obligatory patch in the seat of the trousers. Jackets, although usually split at the pockets, were left because of the regularity in stitching they would require.

Of course there were other things to concern the good people of Norwich. Feeding the family was one such task for the women who had to provide something not only edible but also palatable. This was usually accomplished in spite of rationing and limited finances. Bread was always available although it had the grey look of a corpse who should have been interred two days since, but had won its case in the face of fierce opposition to remain on earth a little longer.

There were coupons for clothes that rationed people in the sartorial sense and restricted women in their main hobby (shopping). There were points for sweets, they would secure three quarters of a pound per month. How today's children would cope I hesitate to imagine, they would devour that in a week, some even at one sitting.

Stockings were one area of clothing where women could adapt in order to lessen the misery, especially the young girls. They would colour their legs with a dye, I even knew of girls who would make a colouring agent from cocoa and water. They would then pencil a line up the back to create the impressions of a seam. This was a great idea in the sense of innovation but lacked the foresight of the disaster were it to rain.

When the Americans came to town young girls soon discovered that a sweet smile could beautify the legs, and we are not talking thick unattractive lisle, we are talking high quality, low denier, sheer silk, leg-beauty-enhancing hose. From miserable faced sisters the girls were miraculously transformed. Their faces were now cracked in smiles from ear to ear whenever a stocking bearing suspect appeared.

On top of the family's demands of cooking, sewing, housework and wage earning, mothers also found time to shop, and this nearly always necessitated a certain amount of queuing. Queues were a feature of the war years and have remained so ever since. People queued for buses, for food, for clothes, for anything in high demand and short supply. A queue would form at every opportunity. It became a national pastime. It was almost a compulsion to queue. Some queues would form and lengthen without anyone ever knowing why. It was little use asking the person in front because the chance of their knowing was very remote.

People have joined queues where two women were only chatting together. Some would join for recreation, for fun, or just to while away an hour or two. There was many a person joined a queue for no other reason than it was there, when they arrived at their turn it would be to discover they had joined a toilet queue. This was okay because by this time the toilet was in all probability urgently required.

There were genuine reasons for queues to form; for example a consignment of oranges or bananas. A notice at the door of a shop would proclaim the declaration 'BANANAS FOR SALE!

Shop will open at 0900 hours tomorrow'. This news once acquired would be revealed to none but a few close friends. However, these close friends would also have close friends who were close friends of other close friends and so on ad infinitum. By nine o'clock the next day the only person who didn't know was Hitler and that was because he had no friends at all.

Oranges had the same effect; notice of a consignment of anything unusual would entail the obligatory line of human beings called a queue. 'Queue' is a strange word and means 'tail' in French, from the Old French *'cue', 'coue', 'coe'*, from Latin *'coda'*. In English the word had the meaning of a band of vellum or parchment (about 1475). Later it came to mean a line of dancers, probably around 1500 (that is the year not the time). This was later extended to describe a line of people, vehicles, etc. It is my belief that the world had been eagerly awaiting that piece of info since the beginning of time. Stay with it, you never know what absorbing information I shall impart next.

Life was lived mainly as a pleasure, rather than a duty, and ran a course between bumpy and smooth, nothing was ideal but neither was anything too wretched. On the Plumstead Estate the children of my age could always find enjoyable entertainment.

The rationing restrictions were a bind, and now in this age of affluence and plenty the restrictions on that which could be purchased seem severe. Meat was limited to just 1s 10d (just under 10p decimal) per week, per person. 4 oz bacon; one egg (although dried egg was available), 2 oz butter – this came to the shop in slabs, it was cut off and slapped around until it formed an oblong (or got fed up), then wrapped in greaseproof paper. Nothing was pre-wrapped. 8 oz sugar per person – this was shovelled from a large container and transferred to a thick dark blue bag, its grains were meticulously measured, almost counted to ensure the exact amount was doled out. Shoppers also had to watch the fingers of the shopkeeper, you could be buying the weight of this finger without the benefit of taking the finger home, nor for that matter your sugar entitlement. 4 oz margarine, 4 oz lard and 4 oz cheese.

My mother shopped for her meat at Spurgeon's, a well-established firm of butchers, as had my father before her. After the war she still used the shop. One Saturday, after the war, on asking for 3s 3d worth of meat she was told he could only cut to the nearest 6d. Never a one to hold back, she soon, and in no uncertain terms, reminded him that during the war, and as skilful as a surgeon, he had been able to slice meat to the nearest farthing. After this, his skill returned and each week she kept him on his toes by asking for any amount, which never came to an exact 6d.

The directive on shopping for the weekly ration of meat was, the butcher had to be nominated·and once named that was where you had to shop for your meat. This also applied to certain of the week's groceries which were on ration. You had to be quite selective in your choice because before you could change you had to apply, much like the doctor of today. Once the choice was made you were stuck with it. My folks used a shop in Davy Place 'Ashworth & Pikes' and they were quite good; not only could you purchase your essential weekly groceries there, but they also sold bread and cakes so you could get your required needs for the week in one shopping expedition.

There were, however, some really devious shopkeepers around. In those days of austere and frugal existence the unscrupulous dealers were able to make fairly substantial amounts of money by double-dealing. Any consignment of scarce and bounteous fruits they received would lose a proportion as it slipped surreptitiously and gracefully under the counter. The quick lucky people would get their fair share of that which remained above the counter, the unlucky ones would get nothing. The really lucky ones; friends and those who were able to pay over the odds, would be able to acquire not only their own share but also that of the unlucky ones who had been denied their entitlement.

So even in the days of neighbourly camaraderie some people were able to obtain privileges denied *to* their neighbours because they were in a position to pay over the odds, or for returned favours. Some greedy and rich customers allied with underhand

and under-the-counter shopkeepers, all with only the self first and self last ethos being the principle and with the criterion being that they were *able* to abuse the system. Unprincipled, dishonest, and deceitful, denying other families their right to a ration of scarce goodies, but even in those days which we regard as seeing people pulling together, some were only pulling for themselves, and they didn't even have to queue.

Inside shops various items needed separate queues, but this was just for nostalgic purposes. Anyway queues were now a part of everyday life. In one of Bill Bryson's books he congratulates the Brits for their brilliant and organised queuing. He berates the French because of their concept of queuing. Apparently they get the first bit right by standing orderly in a line, but when the bus arrives or the doors open the queue disintegrates into a massive and unholy mayhem thus destroying the general notion of queuing in the first place. Is it any wonder that, with the French's screwball notions on lines, the Maginot Line failed? The Germans, being aware of the French ineptitude in dealing with the way lines work, decided to bypass it. Had they confronted it they may well have got embroiled in the general mêlée, become as confused as the French and lost the war there and then. Fortunately for the Germans they were able to miss the havoc that the French line conception would bring them to. After the avoidance of that shambles they were then able to amble unhindered into their own ultimate catastrophe.

In today's society the powers that regulate queuing decided that as the British so thoroughly relish the forming of lines something needed to be added in order to update the experience and make it even more pleasurable. Other methods had to be found quickly. So, in seeming contradiction to the idea of quickly, a committee was set up. Great men with enormous enthusiasm were gathered in order to find new ways of getting people into line. Their edict was to find original ways of raising the quality of our queuing to a greater height, or maybe more accurate to say, extend to further lengths.

Hours and hours of sittings took place (which of course is normal for such pursuits). Much hot air with little progress ensued (which is once again the norm for committee meetings) plenty of hot tea was consumed but still no solution was found to the problem. After long hours of brain searching, bum aching, head scratching, and motivated by the amount of tea drunk, off they all tripped to the bog. This they did all at the same time because as yet no one had formulated any other means of queuing, so in order to preserve the traditional means already available the grand exodus was agreed upon; up until that point this was the only thing that they had agreed upon.

While awaiting his turn in time-honoured tradition, one member suddenly cried "GERONIMO!" or maybe "EUREKA! I've got it." At which point the once organised queue disintegrated into an unholy fiasco. Aghast at what might be revealed, they waited in feverish panic. However, to the immediate relief of the rest of the assembled mass it was made known that it was not some nasty contagious disease preceded by an over zealous rash which could wipe out entire committees. Neither was it a dose of invasive crabs nipping away at the very roots of society. No indeed, it was the answer to their prayers, an end to their relentless debating on a subject which up until now was proving to be a very sticky dilemma.

"But what are we talking about here?" enquired one of the more sceptical of our fearless group.

"We will set up a means of forming a voice queue," our intrepid committee member divulged amid shrieks of derision.

"How can we possibly do that?" asked the inquisitor.

"Through the telephone, we get in touch with all the big companies and have them form a new kind of queue, a phone queue. It will revolutionise the whole concept of queuing. It will give people a new purpose in life."

So with new found enthusiasm the other members implored "Ata-Boy, onward, onward."

"Hundreds of people phone the great conglomerates for all kinds of reasons. Unfortunately, up to now they have been able to gain contact with mind-numbing ease, such is the effect of this that it is gradually eroding people's will to live. Now, form a respectable queue and once again some spice will be introduced into their little hum-drum existences." The wizard of the invention then went further by adding a few innovations which would, as he prophesied, entertain callers for hours.

"When a call is made we can give them some options to get them started, such as pressing numbers to clarify the service required. We can then have a voice telling them to 'hang on as we value your custom, you are in the queue and your call will be answered as soon as one of our staff is available'. Then some music can be played just to keep them amused. Intermittently the voice will repeat the message, then the music again." A huge three cheers was then accorded to this man of genius. Each member, made fully aware of the benefits to mankind that this revolutionary notion would create, took the foundling idea into the wider world to see who would adopt it. The concept was hailed by most big managers with words of adulation. It was accepted by the telephone company as the most marvellous idea since the truss; not to mention the most profitable. The subscribers loved it too, and now when at a loss for things to do they will phone up some big corporation purely for amusement.

Now is the time I feel for complete honesty; is there anyone reading this who has not been utterly delighted, enchanted and totally enthralled at this new queuing innovation? No, thought not. Letters of appreciation should be sent immediately to any company using this wonderful method just as a token of your approval for the pleasure and enjoyment you have incurred.

The man, to whom we now have to pay homage for all those splendid hours we spend at enormous cost and in blinding delight derived from enduring the dulcet tones of some disembodied voice while listening to some meaningless and hugely pointless music, has asked specifically, in the interest of his safety and in the face of fierce danger he might encounter, presumably from adoring telephone subscribers, to remain anonymous. Sorry about the long sentence I've given to our friend, but believe me it is not half as long as the sentence he should receive.

Enough on queues, back to shopping. The comparison of prices in early post war Britain to the present day is quite revealing:

Provision	1945	2002
Cheese, per lb.	£0.05	£1.40
Instant coffee, per qtr.	£0.10	£2.10
Potatoes, per lb.	£0.01	£0.40
Bacon, per lb.	£0.08	£1.30
Cabbage	£0.03	£0.40
Margarine	£0.04	£0.38
Brisket per lb.	£0.07	£1.50
Belly of Pork per lb.	£0.07	£1.40
Sirloin per lb.	£0.09	£5.40
Sugar per lb.	£0.01	£0.26
Whisky per bottle	£1.10	£12.00
Postage stamps (1st class)	£0.15	£0.26
Gross weekly wage average (manual work)	£6.50	£450.00

Sweets were rationed to three-quarters of a pound per month. The main night out was a visit to the picture house (referred to as the flicks). A pint of beer was about 6p, a fish and chip supper 8p a throw, a packet of cigarettes 16p for 20, the price of a ticket at the pictures was about 6p, so for less than 50p (10 shillings) a decent night out could be enjoyed. If you took a girl friend or your wife it would still be less than £1.00. If you took both you would be insane. Food is probably better value today, but house prices have rocketed. A typical semi then at £2,000.00 now costing around £85,000 is a rise of 4,150 per cent. A small terraced house could be bought for £400, larger ones cost around £700 to £800, and bungalows with large gardens for around £1600. Most of the terraced houses would only have the basic sanitary ware and hardly any plumbing. Most had a shallow sink with but a single cold tap over it. Some had old brick kilns and a copper for laundering clothes, which would have been heated by coal or wood. The bungalow would not have fared much better, although it is possible that an elementary domestic hot water system would have been installed. Usually the better type dwellings would have been provided with a bath, cold water and a gas water heater. It was not until the invention of small central heating pumps in the late sixties that domestic central heating systems became widely available.

Cars have risen in price by 1500 per cent and have become much better and more reliable. Petrol has increased from 10.5p per gallon to about £2.90 per gallon but this is mainly due to tax. As with owning your own home, only the well off could afford a car. Although cars started at around £50 in price, they were still out of the reach of most people. If you owned a house and a car you had a very well paid job.

In 1971 we in Great Britain were introduced to decimal currency, this was in order to bring the UK in line with the European nations. Prior to this we dealt in the duodecimal system, which used a base of 12 units affording greater divisibility. This meant that where there were 240d (d = duodecimal) to the pound, there were 12d to the shilling, and 20 shillings to the pound. When decimal currency came in there were only 100p (p = pence) to the pound. This meant a loss of 2.4% on each unit, as a 1d was 240th of a pound but 1p was 100th of a pound.

In the 50's through to the late 60's wages were kept fairly stable. Wage rises were increased by only 3d or 4d and, as wages were only around £9.00 to £10.00, this was quite acceptable. Unions would ask for maybe a shilling in the pound and then settle for less, they would not expect that which they asked for and the bosses would be quite happy (well not exactly happy, bosses were not a happy breed, it's the late nights incurred by sitting up counting all their wealth which keeps them liverish) to pay them the amount they would settle for. This way everyone was happy, they would all go home bemoaning the fact that they had been hard-done-by while inwardly gloating over the fact that they had done as well as could be expected. The 3d or 4d rise would give workers a reasonable increase and, as inflation was fairly stable, this was quite agreeable. Prices would rise by 1d or even a halfpenny (this was pronounced hapenny) and so the 3d or 4d rise would allow for this.

When decimalization was introduced, instead of 240d there were now only 100p to the pound. Whereas the unit rise of 2d on 50 items would only yield 8/3d, the same unit of 2p would now produce one pound. Soon after decimalization the ½p was removed, which meant that goods could only rise by a minimum of 1p. Traders were doing quite nicely, thank you, and most shoppers were in a state of confusion; they always wanted to revert back to the old currency in their minds and of course this was not practical. Prices began to rise dramatically, but to counterbalance this the Government began to raise wages as inflation reached certain percentage points. Thus wages kept pace with inflation created by this change in the system. Ultimately people did rather better than they first feared. Even so there was still an urge to try making comparisons between the two systems, mostly they were shocked by the way prices were still rising but quite happy at the way their wages managed to keep up. If only the prices could have been kept at pre decimal levels we could have all retired as millionaires within about 6 months moved to Spain and become matadors. When I was a boy my mother told me to 'look after the pennies and the pounds will look after themselves'. I have followed her advice all my life. I now have pocket full of pennies, but I'm in thousands of pounds worth of debt. I wish I'd looked after the pounds as diligently as I did the pennies.

Chapter Eleven

As you can imagine, during the war years Christmases were particularly austere affairs. Breaking up from school was obviously a bittersweet experience, almost a poignant time. Leaving my friends and mentors (or teachers as I called them . . . at times) was quite traumatic, and having no lessons was in itself something not to be taken too lightly, but I tried to face up to it bravely and contain my emotions.

The actual day of breaking up was the most enjoyable day of the year. That is, of course, once I had come to terms with the realisation that I would be without Sir's company for a whole fortnight. The morning would be taken up by drawing and playing different games, all in a very relaxed way. It may seem strange, but these things could be enjoyed without any curricular subjects in sight. In the afternoon we would have films, or pictures as we called them. The whole school would be in attendance and the film shown would be 'He Stood Alone' or some such heroic title, plus a selection of Popeye films. This of course was not my mate Popeye, as any film would have been much too violent were it to include him. The film 'He Stood Alone' depicted the theory that one man could thwart the mighty German war machine. It was one of those propaganda films designed to keep morale high.

It was about a young British sailor who was captured by the Germans after his ship had been sunk by them. He managed to escape when the ship pulled into a Norwegian fjord for repairs. He stole a rifle and stealthily slipped away during the night. Hiding in the rocks he held up the work being carried out on the German ship. He did this by popping away with the rifle at the German sailors who were trying to repair the ship. Eventually the ship was repaired. When it was ready to sail the party of sailors who were sent out to shoot him were recalled to their ship. Unfortunately, the poor boy was shot by a stray bullet as the German party left the rock. Being a propaganda film the words which rolled across the screen at the end explained how the boy's action had probably shortened the war (I'll bet anyone reading this wishes I'd shortened the story in the same fashion). I believe that this was the only film we had in the school archives because I think I saw it three Christmases on the trot, so there's no need to feel too bored, you've only read it once. I often wondered how they got him down or even if they ever bothered to get him down.

The year I left school was the last time I ever saw the film, thank goodness, I couldn't cope with the cameraman just standing by and not helping the poor little sod. Then we sat and laughed at the antics of Popeye. We cheered as Popeye brutalised Bluto, jeered as Bluto brutalised Popeye and cried as they both brutalised poor old Olive Oil. A brilliant afternoon's entertainment.

After this, I recall all the children who had lost a parent were given presents. Those whose fathers were killed in battle got the biggy, those whose mothers were killed got the next best, those whose fathers were in the forces got the next present down the line, and so in ever diminishing order. Finally it got to me; now I was of a lesser God because my father took it into his head to just plain die of an illness. He was too old to go to war and wasn't intelligent enough to get himself killed. Now I would have preferred to be allowed to leave with all the other kids who still had their families intact. Although my father was just as dead, and my grief was just as real, I felt at the time that he could have chosen some other way to die; it was not because I wanted a better present, it was because I felt somehow belittled. After all it was not my fault that he had even died at all, maybe I was a contributory factor but I certainly wasn't entirely to blame. As I got older I realised that no one has the choice of how to die. Anyway I expect he passed through the same Pearly Gates and was greeted just as enthusiastically as the others. Had my teachers been in charge I expect he would have had to use the trade entrance.

In 1944 the Americans were by now well established, and although they were viewed with some wariness in certain quarters they were very good to children. In the Christmas of that year they invited some of the children from our area to a party, and although I was not invited they did present me with a big hamper.

The hamper contained sweets (or candy as they were wont to call it) and a brand new football. However, the pièce de résistance was the pair of roller-skates my mother had bought me. I spent hours on them creating havoc, scattering old people, scaring the dogs, and terrifying the neighbours. Hurtling along at speeds I never before was able to attain, climaxing in falls that caused pain I never knew existed. On certain days when I felt benevolent and my sister was lost for entertainment the skates would be divided between us and we would each have one skate and skate one-legged, sort of mono siblings.

Once out of school my days were taken up mostly by not doing those things my mother thought I should have been doing, and enjoying the things I should have left well alone. But I usually managed to get some things right. This pleased her as she was only expecting a percentage and not a miracle. Going around and buying her presents was one thing I did derive pleasure from. Helping out with the odd chore, I did avert the usual disasters I was normally prone to. My mother was working at her sewing machine most of the day at the start of my holidays so that she would have two or three days off over Christmas; it was left to my sister and me to do as much as we could to help.

Through an accumulation of wealth, 10/6d to be exact, I purchased presents for my family. For my sister there was her first piece of real glass jewellery, of which she was very proud, well at thirteen she probably thought it to be at least part of the Crown Jewels. This was possibly because I may have hinted at something in that general direction and she got it wrong. For about three weeks before Christmas I had travelled around the shops buying all manner of small presents for my mother. On getting them home I had to sneak them into my bedroom without her knowing. As she was mostly at her machine, and although she never let on, I am sure she must have suspected that I was up to something. Once there I would keep nipping down for sheets of newspaper to wrap them up in. She either thought I was a secret paper hoarder and was possibly best left alone, or it was something far more sinister and was *definitely* best left alone. On Christmas morning my joy of receiving my presents was matched by the joy of giving my mother her gifts. However, even that joy paled beside watching the delight on her face as she unwrapped from the newspaper those things I had bought her. There was nothing too expensive but with each gift's unwrapping came the expression of elation. This was true generosity. The magnanimous thanks of receiving, the generous appreciation of the recipient toward the giver made the effort all worthwhile. My joy was complete.

We always had a Christmas tree, but the decorations were a fairly tame lot. We had a few baubles and tree enhancements, but the main thing was improvisation. There was some tinsel and to back this up we used small pieces of cotton wool. We had no lights but with a bit of adaptation and imagination the tree's appearance was quite exotic. Mind! It did need the imagination bit.

In the days of my childhood, children stayed mainly in the same crowd. The same gang would play together and stay together. I always considered my friends to be the tops and even now, looking back through the years and decades, I still believe that to be so. Down the end of Pilling Park Road lived the Barons, there was: Mr Baron (Hector), Mrs Baron (Lily), and two children, Brian and Barbara. Every Christmas they would hold a party and all the friends of Barbara and Brian were invited to attend. These were wonderful do's. There would be loads to eat, jellies, blancmanges, cakes, drinks, everything the times would allow. After we had scoffed our fill there would be games, Blind Man's Buff, Musical Chairs, Pass the Parcel, and then a strange game. All the children were consigned to the kitchen, the hall or wherever they would be least likely to do any damage when left to their own devices. The set-up was that Mr Baron and one of the bigger boys would stay in the living room and obtain a sturdy tray or board. One child at a time was then allowed back into the room, they would then be blindfolded and guided onto the tray, the tray would then be raised some two or three inches and wobbled to give the impression of being lifted. The person on the tray would be tapped on the head with a book (yeah! OK, I know what you're thinking – no, not tapped in the head). This would make it seem as if the head was touching the ceiling. They would then be asked to jump. Now I ask you, who in his or her right mind would leap from that height? Not for one moment am I suggesting that twelve or thirteen years olds are always completely in tune with rationality. However, they usually have some perception of self-preservation. There was no way the child was going to commit to that sort of idiocy, at least not without the presence of a priest. The next option was a slight nudge in order to get them started on the descent. The look of horror on the child's face was immensely pleasing to the onlookers as the child thought it was about to start on a downward spiral to horrific injuries or even death. What they didn't understand was the utter amusement others were getting. The one thing about children having gone through such drama is they're always reluctant to save their friends from the same fate. Of course the look on the children's faces when they realised they were only some two or three inches from the floor was a bit disappointing, but a child can only stand so much pleasure at one time.

In those days most children received only one present, the girls got a doll or a doll or even another doll. The very privileged would get a pushchair or some other girlie toy. Boys would get either footballs, train-sets or roller-skates. Other things we would get for Christmas were paints, Plasticine, books for reading and books for painting in, crayons and jigsaw puzzles. Most toys would be as much educational as playthings (although it must be said that looking at me you would never guess it). Then there were the boxes the toys came in, they were for general amusement: pierce two holes in the end of the box, attach a piece of string, and there you had a great pull-along toy. Get the cat to sit in there and you could amuse him and yourself for hours. My old cat Tiger was a bit of a challenge, if he didn't want a ride I very much doubt if the SAS could have persuaded him that it was only for his own good. The only thing that ever came from trying to make him have a change of heart over anything, would be lacerated hands, shredded shins and bite marks.

Children who were given paints for presents, were lucky, they could hone their talents as almost certainly did Leonardo da Vinci. Leo probably got only half a box on occasions, as he didn't always finish what he started. He did manage to paint a woman called 'Mona Lisa' (and ever since the world and its uncle has wondered why she keeps grinning). He also finished 'The Last Supper', painting it not eating it.

Then there was Michelangelo, he must have been given Plasticine *and* paint. He became a sculptor as well as a painter. Goodness knows what else he got, but it is a fact that he finished up floating toward the top of the Sistine Chapel and painting the ceiling.

It is not inconceivable that Picasso's dear old Mum and Dad, having heard of Michelangelo and Leonardo, would have realised (after seeing what Pablo did with his porridge) that he had talent, and investment in a paint set could in future pay rich dividends.

In the year 2001 an artist called Martin Craig won £20,000 by turning a light on and off; how Leo, Pablo and Buonarroti would have viewed this as a progression in art is anyone's guess. My efforts will come to light later as I perfect the technique of turning the television on and off.

Although we received main presents there would also be stocking fillers, these would be a penknife, some marbles or maybe a few sweets, and since sweets needed points (sweet coupons) anything that came your way was appreciated. Most mothers would save the points during the two or three months before Christmas and then use the savings for Christmas treats. There were no electric toys in those days, but there were good mechanical toys. There were also the traditional board games and of course the stalwart Meccano set. In retrospect I think the best games children had were with their friends. Football was the most popular, however, not many boys had football boots so it was mainly played in walking out shoes. Walking out shoes were made of sterner stuff than the shoes of today. Today's shoes would have lasted about a couple of hours, which would have been of little use. No one wore a watch so most games could take at least two hours to get to half time. Most matches lasted at least until dark. There were times when the ball got so seriously damaged that football as we know it today became impossible. By the end of January any football given as a Christmas present would already be in a state of serious decline. After much abuse, suffering and many patches the bladder would finally be read its last rites. An operation to remove it from its outer case would be carried out and the severely damaged bladder would be issued a death certificate. The bladder would then be irreverently discarded leaving just the outer case, stuffed with rags, to soldier on courageously. Even Beckham would have had his work cut out to bend that ball. There were times when it felt it had had enough and would lodge itself in a tree and stubbornly refuse to come down until someone had climbed up and wheedled it down with a swift boot whilst precariously dangling from a branch of the tree.

We played in the rain, in the snow, in shoes and in boots. We even played in wellies, hence the old saying 'Give it some wellie'. There were abroad at that time of day boots that came from a government department called 'National Assistance', (NA) this organisation was there to help the needy. Although most families could be classed as needy, some were more in need than others. In order to make these boots go further (in time and distance) they were reinforced with iron cleats toe and heel. Then north to south and east to west, iron studs were implanted. Any boy wearing these sort of armoured plated leather hackers, if on the opposing side, soon gained respect, not to mention great space, also he had the added advantage of being given plenty of the ball. If the boy was a bit careless about where he delivered his kicks it would be very imprudent, if not downright reckless, to approach him with anything but the utmost care. In today's games of football trainers are worn, in the days of NA boots armed with the plethora of steel, the trainer type shoe would have offered little in the way of protection. The only trainer you would have been looking for then would be the guy with the magic sponge, splints, a hot line to an ambulance and with a priest in attendance.

I got my first pair of real football boots courtesy of a Provident cheque. My mate Kiddo also got his at the same time. I remember we both went down to a shop in St Benedict's and purchased those boots along with a tin of dubbin to keep them waterproof. Those boots were treated with loving care and lasted until I finally grew out of them. Provident cheques were one way of saving up money. Each week the Provi man would call and your parents would put a little money in and when there was enough for that which was required you got a cheque to spend. Although they were only accepted by certain shops they were still a good way of financing the small luxuries of life. I never liked using them as it seemed a bit demeaning, but I had no qualms when it came to buying those boots.

Children of the forties, fifties and even into the sixties were less restricted in their movement and their play than are the children of today. No one knew what a paedophile was, it could have been a queue where you waited to urinate as far as we knew. I believe that this freedom also gave a greater perception of any dangers we encountered. We swam in dangerous waters and played in dangerous areas so self-survival was our main aim. Although most boys' games seem to produce madness, mindlessness and mayhem, there were gentler pastimes. Top and whip was one of the more gentle games. The string of the whip was wound around the top and pulled to set the top spinning. The whip was then used to keep it spinning. After the top was past its best, lost, or no longer needed, the whip was sold to the young Conservatives. What they did with them is beyond me, but the strange thing about it was, they never wanted the top.

The greatest and most exciting toy could have been the yo-yo. It wasn't of course, but if all other toys are removed it could come into its own. Although this toy has been around for many years it is still not recognised in some quarters. It is quite a colourful little number but it has its ups and downs in life, though it never gets depressed. It is these little ups and downs that allow it such gay abandon. Its main function, in fact its only function, is to travel towards the floor and then travel back again. This is accomplished by wrapping a piece of string about 2' 6" long round and round its midriff until all the slack is taken up. You then allow it to drop until all the attached string is unwound. Now this is the clever piece: at the very moment the yo-yo reaches the point where the string runs out, an upward jerk is applied. Should the jerk get it wrong, disaster! Get it right and, euphoria! If the jerk is too soon the string will quiver, this in turn will cause the yo-yo to tremble, acceleration will cease and the yo-yo will become disorientated and forget it should be returning. If the jerk is too late the poor yo-yo will not understand and remain in the doldrums until it can once again be wound by hand and re-motivated. If the proper procedure is followed then hours of fun can be wormed out of this little creature called the yo-yo. To get the maximum amount of pleasure from the yo-yo certain precautions must be observed. Exercise is required to strengthen the heart, this is because once up and running (or should it be up and down running?) this little toy can arouse in one latent desires such as have never been envisaged. In fact this could even be a substitute for foreplay. Once you feel that your fitness is adequate a spot of yoga could be tried to tone the mind. Finally a medical check and, if nothing untoward is revealed, you can then move gently into the sport. Just a few hours per day to start with and gradually increase it. When fully expert at yo-yoing it will fill your every waking minute. This sport must be kept under control. Try to get your proper amount of sleep, and learn to eat with one hand, as this will allow uninterrupted yo-yoing. Any woman intent on taking up this sport must make sure that her husband can cook, there is nothing worse than getting into a good rhythm and then having it all fall apart because HE wants his dinner. If the yo-yo belongs to your child and he/she wants it back, tell them it no longer lives at this address or that the refuse collector has stolen it. This is a sport where jerks come into their own and you can't say that of too many sports; in most sports jerks are invariably discouraged. This is also a sport whereby the seasons don't interfere. Yo-yoing can be played any time, anywhere and by anyone (well, apart from pygmies, but they can stand on a chair). It's not that yo-yos are discriminatory against pygmies, it's just that pygmies haven't the height to do the yo-yo justice.

However, I don't think the yo-yo craze has yet reached the rain forests of South America and even when it does it will be many years before they invent chairs. At the moment they eat whilst sitting on the ground (or so my researchers assure me) so this would in itself preclude them from yo-yoing (and, I might say, from falling off chairs). Anyway may I wish all past, present and future yo-yo players many ups and downs and all pygmies a very Happy New Year, whenever it is.

Most of the games had their seasons. Popguns were only needed during the autumn, as they required acorns for ammunition. These playthings were made from a bough of elderberry, cut to about a foot in length from a branch of about 1.5 inches in diameter and hollowed out by removing the pith (there are no esses in pith). Shave down a piece of wood oblong in shape to make a round piston which will fit into the elderberry leaving it about 1 inch shorter than the barrel, but leave about 2 inches unshaven for the handle. When finished, make a brush at the round end by wetting it and hitting it against a wall (but not my wall) until it splays out. There you have it, a perfect popgun, but only if you have followed these instructions explicitly. To use: get an acorn roughly the same size as the bore of the barrel, bite it in half, stuff one half into the end of the barrel, ram it as far up the barrel as the piston will allow. Withdraw the piston and stuff the other half of the acorn into the barrel. Holding the handle of the piston against your abdomen, force the other half toward the first half. This will then compress the air inside the barrel, out of the barrel will shoot the unsuspecting first half of the acorn, killing or maiming all within its path (exciting or what?). Plans of the front, side and top elevations can be obtained from me while stocks last, or while I last. There is just one note of caution. At the involuntary exit of the projectile i.e. the first half of the acorn, there will be a rather loud pop as it rushes to freedom. Hence its name POP GUN. The only other danger is of course if you hit anyone bigger than yourself. Should this be unavoidable you must, for your own good, take steps. My advice would be large fast ones.

Now we all have a rough idea of how to make and fire a popgun, plus the inherent dangers, not forgetting the safety measures required in order to survive against bad tempered recipients of the odd rogue acorn. Yes, these people will on occasions be met! Not everyone can take a joke, especially after being assaulted by an errant acorn, but now we must move on.

The other 'toy' was the catapult, now that is far too lethal to be allowed into the public domain so we'll just skip that. Anyway tree vandalising plus your sister's knicker elastic are required for this, and I have no wish to come between siblings, neither have I the wish to incur the enmity of some face in the forestry department. Cigarette cards were another good source of entertainment, not as exciting as popguns or catapults because they lacked the danger factor. A nice refined little pastime, nevertheless.

Cigarette packets carried these cards and each card had a topic of interest. Some had sporting personalities, some had fighter planes, some had warships and there were many other topics of interest. Many and varied games could be played with these cards and if your father was a heavy smoker he could save coupons and after enough were saved you could then buy an iron lung. The cards went in sets, with fifty making up a set. Most boys just played games with them, they'd flick them up against the wall and the winner was the one who landed his card on top of those already down. Another game was to flick them to see who could get them nearest to the wall. We had games of marbles, and conkers; I guess conkers is still played, and probably with just as much fervour. We used to soak them in vinegar, bake them in the oven, take them to church to get them blessed and all just to get the world champion of conkers. It was a great game, but it could also be a very painful game, small boys thrashing around with conkers are not necessarily the most careful or accurate of people. Many a good knuckle has been savaged by a speedily accelerating misdirected conker in the hands of an irresponsible and reckless boy, and irresponsible and reckless boys are always best avoided, with or without a conker.

This brings me nicely onto girls. I have mostly dealt with boys up until now, the reason for this is that not much was known about these strange little people, apart from the fact they were different from the boys. At school boys were separated from girls, each having their own seat of education. However, I feel girls merit a mention at this point, so the boys can take a rest from this next piece of writing.

Some of our games girls would participate in and some they would not. Now take fishing, girls very rarely seem to appreciate the joys of the angler and this is a shame. There is the thrill of getting up at half past five (am that is), the excitement as you go and buy your first bucket of worms, the exhilaration as you delve your hands into the wriggling mass of bugs and maggots! Then there is the challenge as you combat all the elements that nature's four seasons can throw at you. Sitting silent as you dangle your tackle in the river (maybe it's the silent bit that girls shy from). Then the competitive challenge: is yours as big as his; of course this would hardly matter in the case of girls, they are always telling men that size is of little consideration. The wonderment of life as you impale your next maggot onto the hook after some uncooperative fish has just killed the last unfortunate creature by ripping his flesh apart and then having the cheek not to become attached to your barbed hook. How unsporting, you're not there to feed him, he's supposed to be feeding you! And what triumph as you finally manage to entrap a fish, the eyes bulging, the shocked look, the writhing at the end of the line and the fish pretty well much in the same state. Almost like two spirits coming together.

After the match all the fish are weighed and the fisherman with the biggest one is declared the winner (biggest catch total, that is). And now girls for a little competition among yourselves. What happens after the prizes are awarded? Do you:

(a)   Sell the catch to a fishmonger?

(b)   Take them home and cook them?

or

(c)   Throw them back?

Answers on a post card to me. Prizes for correct answers:

1st	One bucket of maggots
2nd	Half bucket of maggots
3rd	Two mating blowflies.

Some girls will find fishing a trifle traumatic. Putting hooks into maggots can be very stressful, it could ruin your fingernails. Then there are the screams as flesh is torn on the barbed hook, the blood, the suffering, the pain, the squirming, and the wriggling, and then the relief as you are told "Why! it's only a scratch, a plaster will soon take care of that." The nausea passed, back you can get to some serious maggot impaling. Other girls may feel some sympathy towards the maggot, but most will be too concerned about breaking their nails to worry over much about some bug or other, anyway what do bugs know of such tragedies? They aren't intelligent enough to even have beautiful fingernails. I recall once overhearing a conversation with a girl talking to her friend about an ex-boy friend. This boy was supposed to be out fishing, but she had by some quirk of fortune, or you might say *misfortune* on his behalf, discovered he was dangling in places best left un-dangled in. She was explaining what action she thought she should take after discovering that this poor ill-fated (or up to that point providential) lad had been faithless. Any maggot should feel a certain amount of relief that he was just going to be impaled on a hook, there were much worse things about to invade the life of her, soon to become ex. The main point of attack was to be his genitalia and to divulge further would not be proper, suffice is to say that impaling on a barbed hook would seem like light entertainment as compared to her ex-boy friend's intended plight. So as you can see, much fun can be derived from fishing, less if you are a maggot, but the enjoyment disappears completely if you happen to get caught dropping your tackle in the wrong pond.

There is one other tale I must relate just to balance up my theory of boy versus girl in the fishing world. Sam, my grandson, you'll remember (the awkward one) decided to take up the gentle sport of fishing. My daughter Sally bought him a rod from Big W's, I believe it was, just to get him started. My ex boss (Peter Taylor) a fisherman of some accomplishment (along with myself, retired and only accomplished in a general lackadaisical lifestyle) was requisitioned in order to lend some expertise and sanity to the ancient art of maggot mangling. So armed with bountiful supplies of bugs, grubs, victuals, drinks, and tackle, off we intrepid three set, expert, apprentice and me. We visited various venues under our mentor's guidance until we finally found the very place where the fish would be quite accommodating. In fact, literally overjoyed that we had arrived in order to give them some decent land time. It's rather akin to humans having a swim so I'm assured.

All around were men of varying ages and in a variety of attire suitable for sitting for hours on end while time and the meaning of life simply drifted by, relating tales of fish formerly hooked and landed. Some even related to Moby Dick sized monsters. At this point it must be said that I never saw anything quite that big, but such was the sincerity in the telling that I do believe such monsters exist. On the other hand one or two of the more senior anglers did appear to nod off occasionally and may well have had an alcohol-assisted hallucination, but not wishing to get into any arguments with lawyers I will accept their accounts without further ado.

Anyway, after much preparation Sam was in the throes of excitement and ready to haul as many and as large fish as were prepared to sacrifice their lives on the altar of his hook. Listening to the countless tales of historical deeds, hook meticulously baited and the pond scattered with Sainsbury's tinned sweet corn (Peter explained that the fish preferred Sainsbury's sweet corn to Tesco's) and the young of accommodating blowflies, we waited and waited. Just for the sake of balance and to deter legal action, I don't like Sainsbury's or Tesco's sweet corn and can't be held responsible for the eating vagaries of fish.

Every now and then Sam would strike, heave the line, hook and bugs out of the water fully expecting to find a twenty-pounder (fish that is) on the end of his line. Alas nothing, such was his enthusiasm that several times the whole fishing ensemble finished in the tree which was inconveniently planted beside the pond. I was just thankful that there was no fish to extricate as my tree climbing days have long since passed.

Peter then decided that the rod was useless, and produced a better rod after which four fish, rather sympathetically, made Sam's day by obligingly surrendering. The first of his catch was removed from the hook, but Sam in one of his more awkward moments dropped the poor little creature. It seemed quite stunned by this sudden lapse of concentration on Sam's part and immediately went into a swoon. However, Peter assured Sam that it would be okay, so Sam returned it gently back to the pond. There it went into some emotional behaviour, pretending to be hurt. It lay on its side for great dramatic effect, but finally gave up when we pretended we didn't care and it disappeared from sight in the murky under current.

After what seemed days rather than hours, and after we had eaten most of the food, we decided that we should terminate the expedition for the day and went home. Peter said that what was needed was a more up to date set of rods and a better reel. As Sam's birthday is in December and after all this *was* late May, he decided that the appropriate action would be to advance it slightly and he would be quite content to have his present there and then.

Knowing my grandson I was sure he would be on my case until the requisite amount of fishing gear was purchased and anyway I knew him well enough to say that there is no way that he would deny me the pleasure of purchasing something else for his birthday. And so on the Tuesday after the Bank Holiday Monday off we all trundled down to the place recommended by Sally's partner (James) another fisherman of some accomplishment. This highly recommended venue was Lathams' of Potter Heigham. Armed with some sound advice and a cringing wallet we sought out that which we felt would give Sam an edge over the fish who had been too shrewd to be enticed from its habitat on our previous soirée. On entering Lathams' and viewing the plethora of goodies on show I realised that this was going to be disastrous unless we had a strategy. Unfortunately, Sam's strategy and mine never seem compatible, especially in the financial area of our relationship. He goes for the better-looking equipment where I tend to go for the better-looking price tags. I'm not mean, but Sam always seems more blasé with my purse strings than when using *his* money. Usually we compromise, he gets what he wants and I spend what I can ill afford.

After looking around to find some, what might be termed as 'hands on assistance' and realising I would need to present some facade of experience I tried to look taller and more assured. Unfortunately, I failed to look at all like Captain Ahab and looked more like Captain Pugwash. "Do you - er think this will catch many -er- fish?" I tentatively enquired, at once realising it sounded a bit amateurish. The man eyed me with that sort of look that you give to something nasty attached to your shoe.

"Well," said he, "the fish have to be worked." His air now seemed to take on a patronising manner with an undertone of 'something more intelligent than I see before me may well be required'. It's always the same, when anyone with a splattering of knowledge stands behind a counter they invariably have an urge to humiliate rather than instruct, and this guy in no way betrayed that notion.

With the corners of his lips turned up in a sardonic grin, the 'assistant' then addressed Sam, possibly looking for the aptitude he'd failed to find in granddad. By now I had become *persona non grata* and was just the means by which Sam was going to acquire some decent fishing tackle and the assistant was going to win Salesman of the Year, added to my conferred title of Prick of the Year. After much discussion and in depth debate between specialist and grandson I was finally allowed into the act, or truer to say my piece of plastic was. I don't quite know whether it was my hangdog expression or my softly murmured whimper, but for some reason our new found 'friend' seemed obliged to offer some words of comfort. Almost apologetically he said

"These things don't come cheap do they?"

In as brave-a-manner as I could muster and feeling at last we were at one with each other, I meekly replied "Indeed they do not." Grasping Sam's hand and our purchases I fled the premise before bankruptcy, depression, and finally madness engulfed me.

On the Sunday following, Sally, James, my granddaughter Jemima and Sam all toddled off to the very same pond of Sam's previous accomplishment. Now here's the rub, whilst Sam spent the afternoon teaching the bugs to swim on the end of his 'state of the art brand spanking new rod' Jemima, with Sam's discarded Mickey Mouse gear was hauling fish out by the hat full. She did expect everyone to tend her every need, but then that is Jemima. She has a great sense of occasion. On this occasion she got quite excited. In fact she got a bit too excited and at one juncture when told to 'strike', her enthusiasm took a rather manic step and she heaved a touch too violently and the fish, line and bait almost flew into orbit much to the merriment of the anglers and the annoyance of the fish. It is my understanding that they all enjoyed the day, even the fish. However, I can only see my role as assistant and no matter how many people tell me that this is a sport that grows on you I don't think there's much chance of my getting *hooked.* Except of course by an ill-directed cast and my grandchildren are quite adept at *ill-directing things,* especially Sam.

Now should that not attract more of you into the sport of fishing I can enlighten you on an even more exciting boys' sport. This is a bit more dangerous. I say it is more dangerous because of the amount of enthusiasts who have gone to the wrong station by mistake and have been run over by a speeding fire engine, or gone to the police station and been detained for loitering with intent. I am of course referring to that time-honoured sport of train spotting. This does not require the same amount of equipment as is needed for fishing, the down side is that you don't get to play with maggots or worms. All that is required is a book and a pencil or pen, anorak and thermos flask. As with angling it will need dedication, application and patience. If a doctor can be found who is willing to perform a frontal lobotomy, this will help enormously. When all the gear has been obtained you just present yourself at the station (making sure it is a railway station) should there be an absence of lines this would be a good indication that something is amiss. Check maps, compass etc and if correct station is confirmed await your first train. It is not as exciting now as it was in the days of steam and with the lack of smoke it is harder to tell whether you are at the right station.

Girls seldom wanted to play boys' games, or if they did it would have to be on their terms. Stick Release for example: the stick had to be of their choice, if it was thrown and they got hurt they'd either sulk, or seek a deadly revenge. The stick, originally and mutually agreed upon, would be discarded and a much less friendly implement would be sought. Girl and new implement would then go in pursuit of the offending boy. At this point the game of pleasure would instantly become a game with dire consequences, especially if the boy was not fleet of foot. He would have to find refuge as soon as was possible. Failure to do this and he could be faced with a very ominous and immediate threat to his existence. The rest of the gang could only watch in wonderment . . . and relief. Wonderment as Miss Sugar and Spice and All Things Nice suddenly turned into Miss Acid and Bile and All Things Vile before their eyes and malevolently chased some poor little sod who only wanted to play a game and not go to war with Attilla the Hunness. Then relief in the fact that (although we sympathised with our comrade's plight) we were jolly glad it was not us.

There was also cricket: to allow girls into this arena was madness, as not only did they not understand the rules and intricacies of the game, when advised of them they would wish to alter them. The only thing they wanted to do was to bat. That was of course great; England needed batsman, but there was no way of getting them out, they were almost as hard to remove as Geoff Boycott in later years. They would protest that the bowler bowled too fast, each delivery would have to be to their liking, or something wasn't fair. They would then dictate where they wanted the ball to pitch and how high it should bounce. They were a complete nightmare to play with (at that time and at that game anyway). The only consolation was that a girl soon got bored, or got the hump with any fielder who had the audacity to suggest she was out. He would then feel the rough edge of her tongue and be damned lucky not to be feeling the smooth face of the bat across his buttocks.

Fielding after batting was never an issue, she always felt fielding was a joy she could quite happily leave to someone else. The question as to why she would not field was one not too many of us had the courage to pursue. The end of her innings could be swift and painful if you weren't alert. The bat would be cast into the outfield with strength belying her slight frame. With luck it would miss the silly mid-off (who incidentally was the guy who had berated her for not obeying the conventional laws of the game), the flying bat would then come to rest just twenty or so yards beyond cover point (who was enjoying a quiet snooze). Miss Grumpy would then toddle off to feed her doll. That would be the last you would see of her. The last words would be from her as she left the field. "Who wants to play that silly old game anyway?" But then they always do seem to get in the last word.

Football was another game girls struggled to come to terms with. Let a girl into a game of football, and life and limb were in peril, but mostly limb. They would kick anything that moved, shins being their main target. The only thing they seemed to have trouble in booting was the ball and, if by some miracle they did manage contact, it usually went in the wrong direction anyway.

Girls were always good politicians, as I mentioned before. My sister was always as quiet as silence itself; this enabled her to be privy to all and every piece of gossip that was on hand. She knew all the family secrets, while I myself never even knew we had any secrets, much less knew what they were. She seemed to be able to blend into the furniture, a sort of Mata-Hari of the Bennett household. Any visitors and she would be there, ears like an elephant, nose poking into everything, never missing any morsel of scandal or intrigue. It was always a mystery to me why she wanted to be witness to each and every bit of tittle-tattle that went on. The reason of course is quite obvious, when girls attain adulthood they just love to gossip; whereas men just get on with their lives, women feel a need to be part of everyone else's life. As children, girls are just learning the craft of gossip, it's an educational thing. Later on in life whenever I wished to know anything about the family affairs there she was, the walking family encyclopaedia, my sister. But not only did she know all the family scandal but everyone else's too so I have long since realised that this is a special trait inherent in girls, whereas boys don't need to know. It's only the main events in family life that arouse any kind of fervour, and then it has to be beneficial to our welfare.

Christmas and birthdays come to mind, apart from those my relatives really did not enter my thoughts too often. Most of my relatives were not that memorable, but there was one aunt in particular that fascinated me and this was my Aunty Maud. On the occasions of her visits she would arrive quite unannounced, huffing and puffing, while between breaths quoting the immortal words, "She's gone, Lucie."

She always seemed in such a hurry to reveal the departure of some poor misbegotten creature, I often wondered if she enjoyed the moment a bit too much, whether she relished the role of being the bearer of bad tidings, or maybe she was just glad it was not her own demise that was being bandied about. In later years I elicited from my sister that Aunt Maud was only a distant aunt, and several times removed.

It was only about six or seven times we were lucky enough to be brought the news of someone's unfortunate end (and straight off the press) but it did seem a lot more. The reason she and Lucie (my mother) had so many common acquaintances was that they had worked together in years gone by. Another factor in this enthralling saga is that Aunt Maud was a person who laid people out after death although my perception of her was that she would probably do it for you at any time if business was a bit slack just to keep her hand in (if that is not an unfortunate remark).

It must be said that my mother Lucie was, on these occasions, the epitome of solemnity, always demonstrating the necessary amount of reserve as befitting of such sobering events. It was in all probability this sedateness that encouraged our aunt to return with such eagerness in order to advise Lucie of her latest masterpiece in laying out their mutual acquaintances. Then one day her daughter came round to advise my mother of the passing of Aunt Maud. After this all deaths had to be discovered by trawling the local rag. This not only gave everyone else the opportunity of receiving the news at the same time, but worse, it meant we were no longer, in a morbid kind of way, special. The loss of Aunt Maud carried a more personal kind of tragedy. Whenever Aunt Maud visited she was wont to leave us sixpence each, now she was gone so was the money. Now that *was* kind of tragic. It must be said that her daughter's generosity never reached such golden (or brass) heights when she visited us.

The service of laying out by the local volunteer has long since passed away (oops sorry, a Freudian slip) and is usually done these days by the funeral director, and for my part I'm rather relieved. I don't really relish any of my neighbours delving through every nook, cranny and orifice never touched by human hand before, well apart from my own human hand. I realise that by this time you're probably past caring, but it still seems a touch undignified to have your most intimate bits scrutinised by someone whom in life you wouldn't allow anywhere near the less seemly parts.

Cars were not the danger they are now, the style of living was so much more relaxed, there was no need to rush through life as though the hounds of hell were on your tail. What didn't get done today got done tomorrow, or even eventually, and that's how life was. Goals were achieved, but at a slightly slower rate without the frantic lunacy of haste adopted in today's society. I just wonder what we do with all the time we save by all the frenetic insanity that we put ourselves through. When I say we, of course I mean others, I must admit that I've never been openly accused of doing anything too energetically frenzied apart from one or two rash or indiscreet moments. Even at work I never regarded haste to be anything but the destroyer of energy which might well have been needed on other higher planes, e.g. leisure and pleasure.

Everyone seems intent on being in front of everyone else. I believe the car is mainly to blame for this. Observe when you are driving, the car ahead is always holding you up and we treat the driver in front as if he's doing it just to annoy us. He's obviously retarded, it's almost as if he has a vendetta against us. He doesn't even know us, nor do we know him, but what a plonker! Here he is preventing the progress of the nation by being bolshy enough to be sitting with his arse on our front bumper.

"Needs to take the bloody driving test again," that's the opening shot. "Wonder if he's ever taken it, wanker!" Then "Should never be in charge of anything faster than a Zimmer frame. Lethal, that's what he is, bloody lethal."

Then you attempt to drive his car as well as your own. "C'mon - the bloody lights went green half an hour ago, 'as-'e-gon-ta-bloody-sleep?" Coming up to the next set of lights; "What's-'e-stoppin-for-now?"

"The lights are on amber darling, maybe that's why."

"They're not bloody red, I was taught to stop on red, not bloody all stations in between."

Once again we question his right to be on our road, his competence, his sanity and even his right to live will be the subject of our scrutiny. No matter what he does it will still annoy us, not because he's doing anything wrong but just because he's in front of us.

Women drivers; "Christ! Shouldn't be allowed near a car. The kitchen, the bedroom, and the supermarket . . . those are their territories. They only use the bloody mirror to see how good they look."

That's got women out of the way, so then it's down to a few observations on pedestrians, or walkers as we call them, avoiding the over use of the 'n' using the 'l' instead. We will of course use the 'n' when addressing them directly as in the case of "Get outer the way you w-n--r." Then the aside "Bloody pedestrians," (loud and fierce on the horn) "Git-out-o'-the-bloody-way. See that? Silly old sod, is-'e-tired-o'-living?" Then there's the congratulatory; "Ha-ha see the bloody old bozo jump? That'll teach 'im." It's hard to put reason to this irrational behaviour, but it is only within the enclosed environment of the car that we adopt these Jekyll and Hyde characteristics. Can you imagine pedestrians behaving in that extraordinary way? Imagine, everyone chasing headlong to get in front of the person in front of them, think how chaotic that would be. It would take on the madness of an eternal London Marathon held in Bedlam with chaotic consequences, much like a rugby match between England and Australia.

Ultimately it's difficult to see why, when we get into the driving seat of a car, we leave logic, manners and common sense at home. It used to be that politeness and courtesy were extended to people, now we don't seem to have the time to wait for anything. The emancipation of women has also contributed to a decline in moral and social standards. Where men used to walk on the outside of the pavement as a courtesy gesture (actually to protect them from spray from vehicles), it now no longer happens. A man giving his seat up on a bus is very rare, although I must say that sometimes nowadays when a woman looks at me she gives her seat up. Some women get almost offended if you hold a door open for them they'll even walk through an adjacent door just to show how emancipated they've become. Some will want to go Dutch and pay their share of the night out, although not enough is done to encourage this, (personally I do all I can to make this statutory rather than optional). Most of the changes do detract from the way of life now as opposed to when I was young; well apart from the going Dutch bit and that should be rigorously pursued with verve and vigour to ensure equality and further the cause for women's emancipation.

Parents, in my younger days, could let their children out of sight and be assured they would come home, filthy dirty, ragged and torn, but safe and sound; of body, that is, maybe not of mind, but you can't have perfection even in children. And more crucial was the fact that there were no drugs. There were cigarettes, but as injurious to health as they were, they never had the evil effect that the present day drugs have.

So the dangers inherent in today's society were not there when I was a child. The main dangers were of the children's own making. In the games children played they would have to carry a survival kit. There was a game called stone release, or releaso. This was a risky game, there were dangers in this game to clothes, and bodies. It relied on speed and skill of thought both in its playing and in its explaining. The skill of thought came when explaining to your mother how you came by the rents in those new trousers. The speed was required if she did not believe you.

The game was something else. I think that the health and safety people would utter a few tut-tuts at the stupidity and pandemonium that this game offered. You don't see it played now, it is probable, rather than possible, that the NSPCC and the Health and Safety committee, chaired by Kate Adie, got together and in the interest of child safety banned it, although I would imagine it did irreparable damage to the rag trade, especially in children's clothes. Releaso relied on science, inventiveness and creativity, but with a liberal sprinkling of thuggery, brutality and savagery. However, it was a good game, but not for the weak, the feeble or the delicate, it was more for the foolish, the rash and the injudicious, but most adolescents fall into the last three categories, while their brains usually fall into the first three.

Although there were no real rules on how to enjoy this game, the best way I found was to get into the side where most of the psychos and future serial killers were. It was safer to join them than oppose them, although we are not talking hugely safer, just marginally so. It was also a more likely way you'd 'enjoy' the game. When I use the word 'enjoy' it may have misled you; it was exciting, frenetic, at times brutal, and more for the suicidal than the rational. The enjoyment was when someone else was being ripped apart, so more a relief thing than an enjoyment trip. It usually finished in a scrum-like ruck with bodies piled high and the top layer denying air to those who were seriously suffocating at the bottom. To extricate and separate, limbs would need to be untied, blood flow staunched and teeth braces snapped back into position. Anyone receiving one of the NA cleat-enhanced boots in a tender spot could say hello to pain for some considerable time into the future.

Stick release, formerly mentioned, also relied on one's ability toward being quick and nimble. The idea was to get a stick and, as we lived near a woods, there were plenty to choose from. Then the participants would gather in a circle, someone would toss the stick in the air, the person nearest it when it landed would be the catcher. The catcher would pick up the stick and chase after anyone he felt he could hit with the stick. This was all right until the street madman got to be the chaser, then somehow the nature of the stick would be changed. It would take on the appearance of a branch, rather than the twig it originally was. This had its advantages, it carried a bigger incentive not to get hit, because getting hit was somewhat painful. If you were the one to start off the game the ideal tactic would be to get the stick as far away from yourself as possible. Another good ploy would be to make sure it landed near the boy with the poorest eyesight or the poorest aim, but the ultimate strategy was toss it up and run. These were some of the games of my boyhood days. There were fewer dangers, or appeared to be, especially from traffic, and so we had more areas in which to bask in our freedom and enjoy each other's company. Richmal Crompton, the author of the Just William stories, was probably writing about all boys; their dreams, their hopes and their play. I expect there is something about William Brown in the makeup of every boy to whom foolishness and imprudence is a natural phenomenon, so that doesn't exclude too many of them.

Chapter Twelve

By 1944 Norwich had changed some of its architectural make-up, and of course, Herr Adolf's contribution must take most of the credit for providing plenty of open space on which to build. His demolition party did a magnificent job in opening up the city. In fact his bombsites were its main features rather than buildings. The bombing was over, at least bombing by piloted planes. But there was now an even more terrifying evil that was invading Britain's airspace. This new evil was raiding by rocket, the weapons were pilotless and known as doodlebugs. They were missiles loaded with high explosives and filled with enough fuel to reach a certain point. As the fuel ran out these bombs would fall indiscriminately on innocent people. When overhead they made a bloodcurdling whining sound, they also emitted flames from the arse end. When the buzzing stopped and the flames went out, down came the rocket. On hitting whatever was below, it exploded and created extensive damage. These things were fearsome because of their ability to fly un-piloted and this gave them an air of mystery, this in turn heightened the terror.

The doodlebugs had little to do with the destruction of Norwich, this had been caused by the Luftwaffe. This was when Norwich was blitzed and extensive damage was done to the Dereham Road area, Barn Road, Vauxhall Street, Heigham Street, Old Palace Road, St Benedict's, Westwick Street, St Stephen's, Rampant Horse Street, Bethel Street and St Giles. Also along the river were the heavy industries that attracted the Luftwaffe's attention, Colman's mustard factory and Read's flour mills, together with King Street, Carrow Hill, Bracondale, City Road and Hall Road. These places were left either blazing, burnt out, or skeletal outlines of former buildings. The bombings from the Luftwaffe left roads impassable, buildings perilously unsafe, and lives devastated. Many believed that the intensive air raids were used to destroy the morale and lessen the resolve of the people, because of the massive destruction visited upon the residential areas of the city. But most of that damage was inflicted on the places where there was a high density of factories and also in the vicinity of the rail system. This is not to suggest that the Germans would have agonised too much on the plight of the ordinary citizen, but had the Luftwaffe's intention been solely the demoralization of the civilian population I'm sure the housing estates would have been shown greater interest. In the case of Plumstead Estate my old cat Tiger's reputation might have been the deterrent, he certainly deterred his nearest and dearest (namely the Bennett family) on many occasions.

On May 5th 1945 the war in Europe finally ended. On May 8th 1945 the lights went on again in Norwich. It is hard to describe how this felt after five years of darkness, no streetlights, no car lights, shuttered windows, all now freed from the restrictions which the blackout imposed. The destruction had been horrendous, the grief was both personal and communal, but the relief at the deliverance from the evil that had encompassed the world was intense. The joy was unbridled. This was the end of a nightmare, a five-year nightmare. Millions of lives lay forfeit before the altar of greed, hate, bigotry and conceit. The conceit of arrogant people who thought they could murder and pillage with impunity. The strange thing was, even though millions of human beings were being murdered and tortured, burnt and disposed of, no one knew it was happening, or at least never admitted they knew. The moment was now, the weight of war was erased and people were left to enjoy the day. The future was as yet not to be contemplated. This was a time for celebrations. Ordinary people normally given to sobriety and solemnity were carried along with this wonderful euphoric atmosphere . . . some are probably still at it.

The public houses filled, the streets overflowed with elation and a great celebratory ethos was upon the land. Members of the armed forces were returning from a bitter conflict, a conflict that had changed the world, not only structurally but also within the mentality of the people.

The Americans were still here in some numbers - over paid etc, but they did a wonderful job, they cleared the rubble from the bombsites, kept some of the ladies happy and supplied me with chewing gum, what more could be asked of them? Never mind

Tyson v Lewis, tickets at £100.00 a throw, we had Brits v Yanks at loads of venues, and all free, in fact you could even join in. How on earth these people managed to get through the peace is a miracle.

There were people who suffered far greater misery, especially those who fell into the hands of the oppressor. Through daily correspondence we knew how those at the front were suffering, how they were being killed and injured, but we had no idea of the torment being endured by the prisoners of war. It was an ordeal to be captured by the German forces and not knowing when, or how the end would come, but this paled beside the way those prisoners of the Japanese were treated. They never knew when the war would end, neither did they know from day to day if their lives would end. Stuck in a violent, unforgiving and brutal environment they were lucky to survive at all. They were starved, beaten and driven to the limits of endurance, yet through this man-inflicted hell some still survived. Through dysentery, malaria, jungle fever and four years of unimaginable torture, torment and hostile conditions they strove, and some survived.

There is a book by Eric Lomax entitled Ghost Road, brilliantly written and delicately understated which brings to light the total subjectivity and futility of war. Lomax describes how he feels about progress in technology and how it was perceived, prior to his experiences at the hands of the Japanese, as offering only good for mankind. It becomes quite obvious that progress used for the wrong reasons, e.g. in the manufacture of arms and the deployment of those arms to oppress and kill can also be evil. Through evil men with use of this 'progressive technology' the world was plunged into a nightmare. In the case of Singapore, where Lomax was captured, although this was the citadel of British rule in the far east, it was given up with hardly a shot being fired in its defence. Thousands of British soldiers were just left to the horrors of captivity in the hands of a regime so brutal, inhuman, and insensitive that it would be, and still is, too awful to contemplate. This was also the end of the massive warships that once guarded our seas and coastlines; the battleships and cruisers were now obsolete. The aircraft carrier was now the main strike force, the big guns of the carriers were replaced by planes, their range and accuracy was further and far more efficient than the gigantic guns of the battle wagons and they could strike faster. However, the corvettes, frigates and destroyers still had their duty to perform in the protection of the convoys which were the lifelines bringing food and supplies to Britain, and taking much needed provisions and materials to Russia.

Ultimately it is governments and the greed of man that prevents the advancement of decent standards for all peoples of the world. In 1914 until 1919 the world was embroiled in a conflict in which millions died and millions more were maimed and injured. By 1939 the world had learned nothing. The apathy of the many allowed the few to drag the world's people into yet another disastrous conflict using even 'better' progressive technology. Now people could be killed indiscriminately without physical contact, and even more 'progressively', in far greater numbers. In fact you didn't even need to see them. Then the definitive weapon was discovered; the atom bomb, at least definitive until the hydrogen bomb made its debut and that can destroy far more effectively. Hopefully these technological nightmares are too destructive to ever be used, at least we can but hope, but then again you can always rely on the stupidity of man to do the unthinkable.

At the cessation of hostilities a great celebration was called for. With initiative and ingenuity, the women organised street parties for the children The spreads of food defied the shortages but the clothes proved them. Life through the preceding five years had brought rationing of clothes as well as rationing of food. Make do and mend was the order of the day. Rationing was not only the coupon restriction; it was also the shortage of money. By today's standard life was frugal: the 'throw away buy new' precept of today's society is far removed from yesteryear's code. Darning, sewing and patching was how things were.

Patches in boys' trousers usually occurred after about one week's wear. Holes in socks were quite the thing to have, that is until one's mother could get around to darning them. To darn socks, a thing called a mushroom was used. It was called a mushroom because it looked like a mushroom (subtle eh?) in fact it quite resembled the effects of an exploding nuclear bomb but of course less harmful. It was made from wood and placed in the sock, the hole would then be criss-crossed over with strands of wool until within a short time the damage was repaired. Unlike the other mushroom spoken of earlier, quite a bit more time was required in that instance.

Men returning from war seemed to be stuck in sartorial fetters. All or most wore grey pinstriped trousers and wore them as a uniform, maybe it was to conform or just that there was nothing else available. Whatever the reasons, no one appeared to mind. Women, on the other hand, would be aghast at such uniformity. Women's clothes when purchased could be a trifle drab but a little deft needlework would soon enhance their attractiveness. Most clothes items purchased had a small utility mark, this mark looked like two little fat c's and although utility goods were not too elegant, they were durable.

One strange occurrence happened on the food front. Just after the war extra sugar was released, but this had to be used for making jam. How on earth this edict was monitored is a mystery; unless the Ministry of Food actually sent people round to make sure you weren't using it to put in your tea.

After the announcement that the war had officially ended great bonfires were lit. Why? No one could tell. Over the five years of war I would have thought enough fires had raged for even the dimmest minds to comprehend the mechanics of how fires worked. It was hardly likely to be a learning curve. Although I must admit my grate at home could certainly have done with a few tips, considering the antics it put me through at times trying to get it to do what it should have done through a natural process.

There were also fireworks. These were pallid attempts compared to today's colourful pyrotechnics. They made much show in the smoke department, but the bang tended to be a whimper. Hitler's fireworks were much louder, and their entertainment often brought the house down.

In 1945 my political education began in earnest, only to stumble into dramatic decline and finally teeter to a stop a few weeks later. The whole process consisted of my taking my mother's dustbin lid and hammering it shapeless while hollering at the top of my voice the merits of some prat I didn't know; in fact I'm not too sure whether he had any merits at all. What I do know is that I too would have joined the dustbin lid in the being hammered shapeless had my mother been aware of how the indentations arrived in her bin lid. Half the kids of the neighbourhood would be doing the same thing. The other half would be expounding the merits of the opposing candidate with the same authority and about as much intelligence, which was not a great deal. I believe my loyalties were with the gang that sported the biggest boys; now that was not necessarily good politics, but at least it was good policy.

As history now records Labour, under the leadership of Clement Atlee, won by a landslide. A landslide, I can now reveal, that I and my mother's bin lid helped to achieve. Not once during Mr Atlee's time as Prime Minister did he thank me, or my mother's dustbin lid. I believe it was an oversight due to the pressures of government. Winston Churchill once called dear old Clem (I believe the exploits of my mother's dustbin lid and I have earned our right to call him Clem) a sheep in sheep's clothing. However, I think he proved himself to be a sheep rather than a lamb.

Arguably, the greatest leader Britain ever had was Winston Churchill. Churchill led us through the cruellest war the world had ever seen, a war in which the winning preserved democracy for the western world.

After the war Churchill was considered to be a warmonger and in 1945, the first general election after the war, he failed to gain power; he had not started the war, neither had he been in the government in 1939. His only contribution to upsetting Hitler was that he stood against appeasement and this had kept him out of government until 1940. On the first day of the Second World War Churchill went back to his old post as First Lord of the Admiralty and there he remained until May 1940 when he was called to the premiership as head of an all-party administration. On 30th May 1940 he presented himself to the House of Commons with his 'Blood, sweat, toil and tears' speech.

In 1951 Churchill did get back into power but although he was still a great orator his standing in the House never reached quite the same heights again. However, he was still seen as a great statesman on the world stage. In 1953 he won a Nobel Prize for Literature. He died in 1965.

For many years my interest in politics was, to say the least, only a 'nodding in passing by' kind of affair. Since my bin lid abusing days it has slowly gathered momentum. In my observations I've noted a certain reluctance within society to participate in the democratic process and to give it a chance to flourish. Maybe this is because people don't trust their politicians, or maybe not enough importance is given to the way the system works, whether it works well, or even if it works at all. People are less and less inclined even to be bothered to vote, much less find out for whom they are actually voting. The choice we make in picking our politicians is not a very cultured one, neither is it a very considered one. It is almost certain that were we picking a suit, a pair of shoes, a dress (I'm not speaking from experience on this last item, you understand) or even a tie to wear for one night out, we would give it more thought than we give to people who are about to govern the country over the next five years.

In the main, during the periods between elections, that is after the dissolution of the government until the next government is elected, prospective candidates will unashamedly solicit votes from all and sundry and at every chance available. They will contrive meetings to get their faces shown and by all manner of means try to project a high profile. Apart from the flood of pro party leaflets that will invade people's premises, all babies will be at risk from over-enthusiastic candidates trying to curry favour with the mothers by sucking the poor little mites' faces off. Babies are at risk not only through infection, but also they risk being swallowed by over-zealous candidates and should be locked away for their own protection. All photo opportunities will be seized upon, senior citizens will once more become visible and given celebrity status, or promised the earth and all that therein lies. Ordinary folks will, should they pledge their vote, be assured of eternal love and friendship ad nauseam. Take good note of these people as some of them may never be seen again, *never* that is until the next election. They will vanish without trace. Neither tracker dogs, Miss Marple nor Sherlock Holmes will be able to find them. On one occasion the Salvation Army were ordered to find one. Out they went armed with Geiger counters, Indian trackers and Boy Scouts' compasses, but not a sight of him was there. Finally they gave up, joined the Jehovah's Witnesses and now search for converts. Came the next election and wondering what all the fuss was about there he was, best shiny seated trousers pressed and ready with more promises and rehearsed excuses, grabbing babies whose mothers had been too negligent to hide their little ones, and issuing more casual and useless promises as fragile as granny's bones.

This is a brilliant time for the voters, they can get promises made on an Olympian scale, but be very wary of these Greeks bearing gifts because the trick is getting those promises fulfilled. In this time warp you will be able to observe that which is termed the party faithful, worker or activist. Even activist is an understatement, these people chase around going to any lengths to ensure a few more votes for their candidate. Maniacally they rush hither and thither, frenetically delivering their pro party literature, defying mutilation from rabid dogs and even more rabid opposition supporters. They will contort their bodies in order to push their pro party papers through letterboxes only designed for decorative effect. Lessons in limbo dancing just to reach them will be required, periods of osteopathy will be required after using them. Some of these letter boxes are almost inaccessible, some are so stiff that fingers of Herculean strength are needed just to open them; get it wrong and amputation could well be on the cards. Of course all the leaflets will have to be delivered before hospitalisation - it is expected.

The dangers don't end at rabid dogs, maniacally motivated opposition supporters or intransigent letterboxes. Consider next the 'banal old man' our intrepid party worker has encountered. Having been approached to solicit his view on his political hue, he changes into a raving old know-all from hell. He becomes an irksome, irrational bugger who has eccentric views on every subject known to man. From the state of the universe to the miserable amount he gets as a pensioner he will pontificate for an hour. After wasting our poor worker's valuable time with his ranting and moaning, he will declare in no uncertain terms his intent to vote for the other lot anyway.

The party workers will turn their hands to almost anything in order to get their candidate elected. No matter how menial or how demanding the task their willingness to ingratiate themselves with their boss needs to be witnessed to be believed. It is a fact that party workers could not be persuaded to change their beliefs even on pain of death. Mainly the party workers will be visiting that which is termed the floating voter or making sure that their own supporters turn out on election day. This is a trial indeed: get a pleasant day and they may be coerced into a stroll in the general direction of the polling station, but on a rotten day it will be slippers, fireside and telly.

The polling stations used for elections are frequently schools, so this means that children are forced into a day of no maths, science, English etc. This deprivation really upsets them, or should it be rarely upsets them? Although this could distress the children, in my observation of the situation I find they take it extremely tolerantly, but then such is the fortitude of our brave little ones.

At most polling stations voters will encounter people who are called tellers. These tellers are people who stand at the polling stations in order to see who has voted. There is nothing sinister in their presence and there's no need to tell them anything but, if you supply them with the number on their voting entitlement card, it is then passed on to the party's committee rooms; this could save you from an interrupted evening later on. Having been a teller, I have found that some people will tender their number, some will if asked, but there are a few who will recoil at the very thought of giving away such classified information.

Turnouts to vote are lower in the UK than in many other democratic countries. There are some countries where it is a legal requirement to vote (Australia is one). This does not necessarily mean a person will vote, they could just turn up and register their attendance or despoil their voting paper by marking it with something other than the correct cross (such as a rather rude comment which challenges the candidate's parentage). However, I do feel that once there people are more likely to vote in a democratic manner. I suppose in a way to legislate for compulsory voting could be construed as contrary to democracy anyway.

Voting is good for the vascular system. It is possible to meet the opposition, have an argument and, for the younger more energetic, a good old-fashioned punch-up, work up an appetite, go home, listen to the results and, if your lot have lost, cry 'It's a bloody fiddle!' The polls open dead on seven am and close at ten pm. After this time excuses such as: gran's funeral, late train, late bus, wife's shopping, (no not swapping) unable to get to the bathroom etc, will not be accepted, your fervent ambition to vote will have to wait another four or five years.

After passing the fated 2200 hours, the ballot boxes containing all the votes will be rushed to a local counting place and under strict conditions as befitting this revered event, the votes will then be sorted and counted. Once the count is complete the standing candidates will gather around the returning officer (this is the person who announces the result) and listen to hear their fate. After the winners have been declared as duly elected to parliament, being very grateful to all their supporters, they will thank them. They will then thank all those who voted for them, the returning officer, their long-suffering wives, their adoring mothers who bore them, their devoted dads for siring such a clever offspring, their cats, their hamsters, and the dog that bit their opponent at a strategic moment causing him to lose his cool, kick the mutt and lose the dog's family vote and - whoops, nearly forgot the faithful party workers without whom none of this could have been achieved.

It is of course good manners to thank the losing opponents for putting up a pathetic performance, thereby allowing the winners to spend the next four or five years sitting on their rumps, smiling victoriously and being paid handsomely. Babies can now be released back into society assured that the danger has passed, at least for the time being. Rabid dogs will once again be tethered and letter boxes exposed. In this well of emotion even the most hardened campaigner will have a tear in the eye, Auld Lang Syne will be given an airing, backs will be slapped (after the removal of knives). The newly elected member will then buy drinks all round (providing of course there aren't too many around). The party workers will be left to reflect on how wonderful it was to allow them the honour of serving such a pillar of society. The new MP will disappear for the foreseeable future, only to reappear some four or five years hence to explain why promises weren't kept and of course to make a few new, better and entirely false ones.

Just before the winner dashes off he will commiserate with the opponent, the opponent will shake the winner's hand and with a smile akin to a baby with severe gastric problems and in need of gripe water begrudgingly congratulate the winner. By now our gallant loser will be regretting the parting remarks made to the boss and hoping forgiveness is human as well as divine and will then hurry along to the chemist's and purchase some anti-depressants.

The country will once again return to some semblance of normality leaving the people to wonder if it was folly to elect another government. After all, the civil servants who had to run the country in the absence of politicians seemed to be doing quite well without their interference (sorry! of course I meant 'help').

After the general election is over and the House is back in session the democratic process then diminishes, especially if the incoming government has a large majority. The lack of an effective opposition allows the ruling party to run its own agenda regardless of any manifesto, in the light of which they were given a mandate on which to govern. The opposition must then come from within the dissenters on their own backbenches. The backbenchers can vote against their own party if they feel the policies being put forward are too radical, but only if they are indifferent to a blighted career.

In conclusion I would suggest that the British people are less motivated politically than most of their counterparts in other countries. In Britain we have, in the main, had good representation from our governments. We do not have much civil unrest or corruption coming to light. It takes quite a jolt to spur us into action. It is more likely to be laziness, apathy or a feeling of well being that allows us such contented minds. Any feeling of outrageous dissatisfaction is usually quelled by a moan down at the local, a visit to the bookies, or a boot at the cat. However, when it comes to voting, people fought long and hard, suffered and were persecuted in order to get the vote; no blood was shed in order not to vote. Therefore once the right to vote was won then it should be everyone's duty, as well as a right, to vote.

Chapter Thirteen

In 1945 rationing was still affecting and limiting supplies of goods which had to be imported. Not only were commodities rationed by the government, but money also still limited people's ability to buy, or rather the lack of money would be more accurate.

Cigarettes had brand names such as Nosegay, Blue Tenner, Red Tenner, Players, Gold Flake, Craven A, Woodbines, Players Weights, Passing Cloud, Marcovitch Black And White, and later on came a brand called The Strand. This was advertised as the cigarette you would never be alone with, but the guy in this advert was always alone; sad isn't it! to class a fag as company. I suppose its intellect was not compelling but at least it was warm at one end.

Plenty of other brand names were around in those days and have travelled through time with hardly a scratch. Stork margarine was available, Kellogg's cornflakes, Colmans (with their famous mustard and a great diversity of other products) founded and situated in Norwich but with global outlets. Captain Kettle's Grill Sauce seems to have disappeared (I wonder where he went!) along with other brands. A few still exist, Smiths Crisps, Windowlene, Vim, Finnons Salts, Lux soap, Persil, Bournville cocoa, McDougall's flour, Marmite, Birds Custard, Kiwi boot polish, Hovis bread, Schweppes, and Gillette razor blades.

At this point I would like to interrupt proceedings with a story of razor blades that changed my life. It happened long after the war, some time in the sixties. I was working in Cambridge for a plumbing firm based in Norwich. On this particular day our boss had decided to be in Cambridge with us. Normally he would stay in the office and tend the administration side of the business, like counting the money we should be earning him, and worrying if he was paying us enough. Mostly he decided that to pay us more would be profligate and we would only waste it. This was something he could do himself. As long as he worried about it, reckless action was unnecessary.

Unbeknown to me, but waiting just down the road of life ready to ambush me, was a certain question that my-then boss would pose and my life would be changed forever. Up until lunch break all had gone along quite normally, apart from the work progressing more quickly than when boss was *not* there. There also seemed to be a few more beads of sweat than was seen on most days. We arrived at lunchtime (12.30) when the boss, not usually given to frivolous actions like spending his hard-earned money (or nearer to say his money *we* had hard-earned), suddenly asked if we would like him to indulge us in a drink at the nearest pub. There was myself, three others and boss. Now boss didn't normally do loose ideas, we on the other hand did spot opportunity whenever it arose and were not mean enough to allow those freak and infrequent opportunities to go un-rewarded by refusing his benefaction.

Even though I have said that things seemed normal, on looking back boss did seem in a pensive mode. At the time I thought he might be concerned that we were overworking ourselves. At the pub we stood sipping our pints and chatting about various topics of the day, like Jane Russell's acting ability and whether her large eyes were her main features. Just as the conversation was about to degenerate from the mating habits of *homo sapiens moronicus* to Einstein's theory on the Gravity of The Earth's Pull on Barbara Windsor's knockers, boss asked, "How many strokes of a razor does it take to shave in the mornings?"

The pub, to a man, went silent; as there were only two old gentlemen playing dominoes, other than the five of us, it was never a noisy scene anyway. There we stood, each in our own way grappling with the enormity of that splendid question. I glanced at my companions and realised that although very little was going on in the pub even less was going on in their heads. The fringes of intelligence were unlikely to be penetrated or crossed or whatever one has to do to penetrate fringes. No solution was being reached, nor I fancy sought. Minds I would consider, by looking at faces, had already returned once again to the assets of Jane and Barbara.

My eyes then met boss's eyes and I knew the question was not just a throwaway remark, neither was it rhetorical, and as I watched boss's face I knew it required an answer of some deliberation. The thought struck me, from whence did this question come? What seed of thought germinated to produce this flower of intricate beauty? Such complexity, a definitive query if I ever heard one. Where did he find the time to construct this quest for delving into such intellectual minds now confronting him? Glancing once again at my friends I could see no sign that they were prepared to offer any insight into the dilemma, and were by this time wondering whether they were going to be the benefactors of more of boss's benevolence.

Having adorned, in sarcasm, my three compatriots with the title the three wise men, I was about to learn just how wise they were and how unwise I was.

Before I could stop myself I heard my voice say, "Forty-two." It was not a calculated figure and the wisdom of voicing it even less so. Although we were in Cambridge, which is arguably the greatest seat of learning in the country, or even the world, I would guarantee that very little work had ever been done on this subject. Boss's face contorted between anger and disbelief at my stupidity. Had the question been, how on earth do earthworms mate or even, when alcohol goes down to the basement why does it have such a disastrous effect in the attic, then a true answer could have been reached.

In the dimness of the inn's lights there I was consumed in my own dimness. The three wise virgins were by now standing four square behind boss and mocking me for my foolishness. All wise now, they knew my answer to be irresponsible and to do the question a great injustice, not only that, but the spectre of the next free pint was rapidly disappearing down the metaphorical drain along with most of the first one already consumed down the actual drain.

It would have been far better had I remained silent, or better still committed suicide. Through clenched teeth I heard boss say, "NO!" I thought for one moment he was going to elaborate with "you bloody fool" but he showed at that moment the leniency and self-control that you would expect from a boss, even under such provocation.

The number he was looking for was far in excess of the miserable forty-two I had proffered. By this time my brain was fast turning into a substance I can only describe as wet jelly. My self-esteem had dipped into a trough from which I feared no escape was possible. The others, who in their ignorance of any answer and their wisdom in not offering an answer, all felt buoyant and brave, and poured scorn on me. Those sages were all toadying up to boss assuring him that they were in fact pondering the equation. It was such a good question that they were not going to rush into any ill-advised answer. It didn't take much to realise that those morons were about as capable of working out an equation as was a boar of suckling a piglet. These budding Einsteins were far more suited to pondering the size of the barmaids' bosoms and dodging the next round's purchase.

Although the theme soon changed from shaving to less absorbing topics, like brain transplants (especially mine), there still remained a smugness in the others' attitudes, a superficial glow. I think they all felt great relief that their lack of knowledge on the subject of shaving (or any other subject apart from brewers delights and sexual desires) and their silence had saved their shame.

Now, after about thirty years, I still try to count the number of razor strokes it takes to shave. I have never managed it. After forty-two I get bored, but mostly I get embarrassed and my drive for the answer to that vexing question is exhausted. The number as yet has never become clear and concise. Although boss was by now gloriously exalted into the realms of expert, he never actually divulged his wisdom, well not to me anyway. It is possible that by now he was of the opinion that as I was retarded to overtax me cerebrally might impact on my manual working capabilities. While my ego may be scratched, my optimism is such that I believe even now great minds are at work, and while the mountainous assignment may seem beyond the wit of man, one day an answer will be found.

To try to prevent it from ruining my life, I have grown a beard, changed its shape, refused to shave at all and returned again and again to the Full Monty (beardwise, that is, before anyone gets over excited). It is heart-rending I know, but I have never been able to shake off the long-term effects of that awful but glorious mind-provoking question. If anyone arrives at an absolute and unequivocal answer, I do not wish to know, just try to get out more. Any solution gifted to me at my time of life would change it yet again, and no change is far better than any change at all.

Should this story every reach the masses, it could change the world and possibly not for the better. Also, I would like to warn anyone of an unstable nature not to read this, it might just tip the balance toward Valium and periods of restrained confinement.

Chapter Fourteen

In 1945 my education was put into the hands of the teaching staff of Crome secondary modern school. Although the war had ended the country was still under numerous commodity restrictions. Rationing would be in place for several years. Men were now returning from a World War to a country that had changed, and nothing would, or could ever be the same again.

In the thirties Norwich City Council had begun a policy of building new housing estates. The mid and late thirties saw the construction of estates at Larkman, Mousehold (Plumstead Estate) and North Earlham. These houses were of a decent standard and had much better facilities than formerly was the case.

Apart from a few misdirected bombs these estates went undamaged through the war years. Unfortunately, the terraces near the city's industrial hub fared much worse and temporary accommodation was supplied until other suitable housing could be built.

The country would be settling into a more stable situation but heading into a world of rapid evolution (if that's not contradictory). Its progress and evolution would be faster than any progression since the world began. With men now returning from the hostilities, work had to be found. The building trades would need an enormous influx of labour; Herman Goering saw to that, but workers other than building trade workers would also be needed.

The demobilisation and rehabilitation processes would take time. There was also a need to retrain men from demolishing buildings, which they had been doing over the past five years, to building new premises. Many men, who before the war were employed in non-trade work, were now given crash courses in plumbing, bricklaying, electrical work, carpentry, plastering and glazing. All the skills that would be required were now being taught. On completion these men would be given a certificate and sent forth as trainees. Trades, prior to the outset of war, employed men who had undergone a five-year apprenticeship, but these were desperate days and time was of the essence. Five-year apprenticeships would be resumed, but these trainees did a good job and filled an immediate need.

The war had removed most of the young men from the educational system, and so the education of children in the early and mid forties rested with women teachers and older men. Their teaching methods relied on their experience and gaining respect. Physical pain was only used in extreme circumstances. When used it would be administered by the Head of the School. This was usually in the form of six whacks with a thin cane, three on one hand and three on the other. To break the monotony the six could be applied across the backside, I don't believe anyone had a preference; both methods were designed toward discomfort and to that end were quite successful.

After the 1939-45 hostilities we saw the return of young male teachers. Their skills had not been honed in the atmosphere of the classroom, or if they had it was only of short duration. Their skills were learnt in a vastly different environment. These men had just come through a period of violence, of armed combat, of hate and danger. Much like teaching, now I think about it.

This new breed of teacher needed no Head of the School to control small children, they'd soon sort them out. Had they had the full SP I feel most would have become building workers. A lot of the children came from poor families, homes with barely enough income on which to exist. In seven houses on Plumstead Estate lived families totalling forty-seven children. Some of these children came from homes where they faced violence on a daily basis; unarmed combat was a way of life for them. They needed all their strength and will to survive at home. Teachers were not about to have an easy ride.

The teachers I remember were Mrs Pratt, Mrs Bullen, Mrs Hill, Mr Chilvers, Mr Green (Reggie), Mr Killingbeck (Killy), Mr Gotts (Giddy), Mr Fernley, Mr Farrow (Polly), Mr Clifford (Crabby), Mr Hastings (Pop); Crabby and Pop were metalwork and woodwork teachers respectively. Then there were Mr Snelling (another Pop), Mr Sellex, and the Headmaster was Mr Bond (Owen). The headmaster of Thorpe Hamlet Primary was a

143

Mr Thorpe, but before we had time to get acquainted he quit in a rather dramatic fashion, he decided to die. By so doing he was deprived of my company, but I don't think that was a consideration.

Mrs Pratt was my last teacher at Thorpe Hamlet Middle School. She was a sombre woman but a very good teacher, and was strict but not physically violent (unfortunately). In the year I attended her class I never remember her hitting a boy. Her whole demeanour made a statement, it said 'mess with me and you'll lose'. It was a respect that she commanded, some teachers had a certain presence and you knew that there were boundaries, which were not tangible or defined but they were there, and you crossed them at your peril.

Mr Farrow, whom we called Polly, also had this indefinable quality. It was not fear; in fact to be taught by those teachers was pleasurable. Calmness reigned and work would proceed in a harmonious way.

Other teachers, however, seemed to have a need for violence. They needed to inflict pain. One in particular was Mr Fernley. His favourite little quirk was to slap pupils' faces, but to achieve the effect of absolute and maximum distress he would use two hands. As this method was honed and perfected by him, he was known as ham sandwich, small faces being the meat within the sandwich. This method was new at the time but although it was innovative and exciting it never really reached much popularity among the boys. Most other teachers preferred the tried and tested ways and the children while being quite involved were quite ambivalent on the subject, unless of course they were the immediate subject. Being the subject certainly created more interest in the whole affair, physical pain mostly helps to concentrate the mind.

One specific event I recall occurred just after lunch, the whistle had blown in order to call the school to assemble. On the first whistle we had to stand still, we would have to be still for about 30 seconds. To boys whose ages ranged from 12 to 14 this would have seemed more like 30 minutes. Fidgeting and whispering would have occurred more than stillness and silence.

Often during this period of enforced orderliness could the dulcet voices of teachers be heard to plead: please be quiet children or other phrases of a similar nature. On the second whistle the whole mass would run and form lines reflecting which class they were in. But as with all things which are designed to be orderly, this operation seldom was.

On this day Mr Fernley (Ham Sandwich) was in charge and the line uniformity did not quite meet with his approval. It was not unusual for this man to deal out the two handed slap across the face, but on this occasion he really celebrated. It may well have been his birthday or his wedding anniversary or even the day he had discovered the identity of his real father, whatever the cause it certainly got him excited.

He began with the first boy on my row and with very impressive force clapped his hands, or would have had not the boy's face intervened. He then made his way to the next boy and repeated the action, continuing on until he reached me. Whether each boy was deserving of it, or if it was just an even-handed thing, I don't know. It might have been he was just getting a momentum going and the enjoyment could not be resisted. However, he missed me out and then continued with the boy next to me and on my right.

At this point I thought, 'Maybe he likes me,' although he had never revealed it prior to this. A better explanation was, he hadn't seen me or I had become *persona non gratis*.

I stood pondering the matter. Could it be hated me and felt I was unworthy of his attention? He then came back and while I was trying to decide how my gratitude should be expressed without making it too obvious to the others that I was indeed the chosen one, he hit me. One handed he fetched me a fearful smack, my head lurched to one side, the bells began an orchestration which on recovering I could not recall, (had I been able to it could have sold millions). I must admit the day had a bit of a chill to it and Mr Fernley's action certainly warmed *me* up.

In my class, and standing just behind me, was a boy we called Popeye. Now Mr Fernley had not been at Crome School long enough to become acquainted with Popeye, and after the

145

treatment we had just received we were not about to do him the honour of introducing him. He got half way down the row behind, assaulting boys as he went, until he arrived at Popeye. He was about to deliver unto Popeye his measured punishment when I heard Popeye say, or rather spit out, his terms of retribution. Popeye said "If you hit me I'll kick you in the fucking shins so fucking hard you won't be able to walk." To my utter amazement Mr Fernley broke off hostilities and looking wan walked back to the front. As we were not in Mr Fernley's class we heard nothing more of the incident. I knew Popeye very well, we had come through the system together, and I know Mr Fernley did the right thing. The tone of the voice had convinced Mr Fernley that Popeye's threat was not an idle one.

Mr Clifford was called Crabby not because he was old but because he was odd. He was the metalwork master and also the woodwork master until the role of woodwork master was given to Mr Hastings. Mr Clifford got his nickname because he had an unusual way about him when he taught woodwork. To gain a boy's undivided attention he would hurl a piece of wood in the boy's general direction. This would ensure complete concentration not only from that particular boy but, from every other boy as well. After Mr Hastings joined the staff he was left with the metalwork teaching only. The powers that be probably figured out that only a madman would resort to throwing metal about, although I rather suspect even that was a calculated risk.

Mr Hastings was not mad like Mr Clifford. He was only a borderline case. He would take his wrath out on that which was made rather than the maker. Many were the handiworks of some budding Chippendale that would end their existence under the censorship of Mr Hasting's hammer. Mr Hastings could be a very mild mannered man but with occasional modes of manic action displayed surprisingly suddenly. He was only a small man, but then again the atom bomb is only small in relation to the damage it is capable of inflicting. He also had a rather bad habit of digging boys in the spinal area with his knuckle. If you happened to be the recipient of the swiftly delivered prod you would have to be very silly to transgress again for a while, or at least until you recovered the use of your legs in order to give yourself a fighting chance of escape.

Then there was Mr Killingbeck, who was the sports master (Killy when on the sports field, Mr Killingbeck or Sir when in the classroom). Mr Killingbeck also took classes for science and hygiene. He was as a respected master as we had. You could have a laugh with him, but you knew exactly how far to go, and when work began it became serious. To the best of my knowledge he was liked by all.

Mr Gotts was nicknamed Giddy and at times tended to be so. He took us for most subjects, and was also the stand-in sports master. He was quite excitable and often clashed with my old friend Popeye. When this happened it was good entertainment; they would start as a warm up with a few verbal exchanges, get rapidly on to some light physicals, and then into a few violent actions. It all would end acrimoniously with Sir licking a couple or so bruises and Popeye being shown the door and given a map to the Head's room. Popeye's sense of direction was not too good and he usually went in completely the opposite direction. After this we were all then allowed to get down to some less entertaining but self-fulfilling work.

I must just say at this juncture that Mr Gotts was a smashing teacher, and he was also a very respected member of Thorpe St Andrew. He did sterling work for that community, it was just that he and Popeye were not terribly compatible.

Mr Chilvers, or Chivvy as we called him, was strict at times, comical but unaware of it. He took handicraft and scripture (now I believe called R E). Mr Chilvers could be very insensitive and play on boys' defects, even their poverty. It was always best to stay below the ramparts and not become too adventurous when dealing with this Sir. Chivvy could embarrass, and this would work for him when he would need to discipline a particular boy. The pain of shame was far more effective than any physical punishment, and Chivvy was master of that ploy. He also had his favourites, and even though he treated me kindly enough, I could never agree to this type of control. A friend of mine still cringes when he relates to me his treatment at the hands of this master.

As mentioned previously, boys were very lucky if they owned more than two sets of clothes, one for Sunday and the other for every other day. Chivvy would think it good fun to haul out one of the poorer boys, put him in the sun's rays and smack him on the back. This would release clouds of dust and the boy, although he would not show any emotion, must have felt humiliation way beyond the physical pain of the stick or slap. This was also an insult to the parents who were trying their hardest anyway.

Mr Bond was the head teacher during the entirety of my stay at Crome secondary modern school. He was indeed a gentleman, a credit to the school and to his profession. He was, however, a bit absent-minded. He would be talking on a subject, glance out of the window, and with immediate effect forget what it was he was talking about. Mr Bond was always ready to help and always available. Even after they had left the school he would welcome pupils back to visit. On two occasions when I needed a reference I went to him. However, I do not feel he can have been totally honest, because on both occasions I got the job. I had nothing but admiration for Mr Bond.

Mr Green was the music teacher, we always referred to him as Reggie. This man was a good athlete. He was a very fine footballer with a great turn of speed. I recall one particular day at assembly he spotted a boy just about to fall over, this boy was prone to epileptic fits. Mr Green who must have been about ten metres away from the boy's position dashed through the ranks of the assembly and caught that boy before he had moved more than 30 degrees from the perpendicular. This was a very impressive piece of athleticism, not to mention the observation part. I must admit that I learned very little about music, but that was due more to my stupidity than his teaching ability.

And that is how I viewed my teachers. I was privileged to spend one year longer at school than had been so for pupils prior to 1947, as the leaving age went up from 14 to 15 years. We were always being told that school days were the best days of our lives, but we thought it was just a ruse to get you off your parents' hands for a while. Having tried working, I am now of the opinion that parents knew a thing or two.

Children of the forties had a wonderful time. The war years had of course been petrifying, loved ones being sent to foreign parts and never knowing their fate, when, or even *if* they would return. As children we were in the main protected from all those worries. I do recall one poignant moment. I was sitting on the top deck of a bus and from my vantage point I was able to see clearly a news vendor's fly-sheet. It read 'Stalingrad under siege'. At that precise moment, even as a child I became very aware of just how critical our survival was in relation to that of Russia's.

Once the Luftwaffe had failed to command the air over Britain, in order to mount an invasion force that could attack Britain almost unopposed (at least unopposed by air), the German high command gave up the idea. Then, in spite of the fact that Germany had what was called the 'NAZI-SOVIET PACT' and were on Russia's side, Hitler's forces set about the occupation of Russia. In Russia they were victims of their own success. Their progress was far too rapid and logistically they were found wanting. Their supply lines could not keep pace with the advance rate set by the spearheading forces. The front line became seriously under-supplied and with the Russian winter fast approaching, disaster was already confronting them. The Russian retreat was fast but organised. Ultimately the German forces finished up advancing over a vast amount of land but with no advantage. The lesson being, never ask a corporal to do a general's job. The Germans were now faced with the prospect of terrible weather conditions and a ferocious enemy. Halted at Stalingrad, Adolf, the little corporal, had masterminded a great defeat.

The air-raids apart, life had been just great fun for the children. The only blight on our horizon was school, but in the early days there was always the added excitement of nipping off to the shelters. It may seem strange, but at no time do I recall panic or fear, people just seemed to accept that this was the way of things. That which could not be altered needed to be endured. Whenever a German bomb landed near it would give you a jolt. The biggest fear in all this was your family. How would they fare? Were they safe? You were indestructible, but they were merely flesh and blood. After all, you had only just begun your life and you weren't about to allow a little turd like Hitler to deprive you of it. The fruits of life needed to be tasted before you were ready to abdicate this world. Adults who had been on earth a lot longer than you were determined to survive. If you could stay, maybe the delights that were driving them with such enthusiasm to survive would soon be yours.

Although it was difficult to see what those fruits of life were, surely it was worth a little effort on your behalf to find out. It couldn't be a desire to join in your games. For the most part older people seemed to resent your enjoyment rather than partake of it. And as for joining in our ball games some of the older biddies would become really aggrieved should a ball go anywhere near them. And should it actually and accidentally enter their gardens they would show umbrage way beyond what was necessary. There were times when I think they loved their flowers more than they loved children.

Nine doors up from my house on Pilling Park Road lived a friend called Michael Catchpole, (nicknamed Porky). Porky was some months younger than me, but quite unwilling to benefit from my greater experience. Apart from this he was an intelligent lad and a churchgoer, but whether the two are related I don't know. The religious zeal I rather suspect was more due to influences of others than any personal desire for eternal salvation. His father was a large man and ruled over his domain with something less than the velvet glove.

Porky was a member of the choir at St Leonard's Church and his voice had all the velvet qualities his father's glove lacked. He sang like an angel; unfortunately anything angelic about him terminated at the voice, from there on he was about as angelic as were the rest of us. At school he would on special occasions be requested, and with an offer he couldn't refuse (coining a phrase), to give a rendition of 'Oh for the Wings of a Dove'. There were some rough diamonds at Thorpe Hamlet School in those days, but his singing had the whole of the school entranced. My problem with Porky was not his wings but his horns – together we never seemed capable of keeping out of trouble.

One day we decided that we would take a sabbatical. We didn't understand what a sabbatical was but we would take it anyway. Later the Head Master gave it another name, he called it truanting, but that was just playing with words.

It was a coincidence that earlier we had discovered the magical effects of carbide. Carbide is a tricky and exciting little compound with marvellous entertainment properties. It is ideal for a few hours of pleasure mixed with a certain amount of danger. We had found out that if you were skilful enough to mix the right amount of water with the right amount of carbide in a bottle and screw the top tight onto the bottle it would create a pressure and explode the bottle. Looking back in time I can't even begin to imagine why this tactic was not used against the Germans at Stalingrad.

It did have its drawbacks: if the cap was loose the pressure would not build and no bang would ensue. However, if you were slow in retiring you could be hospitalised for weeks, or even in the need of my Aunt Maud's services, hoist by your own petard, so to speak. This carbide was sold at a shop on Prince of Wales Road in Norwich called Willmotts. It came in tubular cardboard containers and cost 1/3d a box (7pence).

Now neither Porky nor I carried this sort of money in ready cash so we had to reach some solution as to where to get it. Had the shop accepted a dead headless mouse we could have obliged. The very week before, Porky had visited me with his pet mouse which, with hindsight, we foolishly left unattended for a brief period. During this time my cat (you will remember Tiger) had stealthily entered the bathroom in which the mouse was happily playing, although I don't think his play would have been quite so happy had he have known that which my readers now know about Tiger. Suddenly this poor little sod's life was snuffed out. Tiger had decided on a change of diet and went quite irrationally from his usual victuals and mouse had become the variation. I don't think he was too enamoured with it (the cat I mean not the mouse, I shouldn't think the mouse was a bit enamoured with it) as he only ate the poor little mouse's head and then reverted to his regular lights.

151

When we returned to the bathroom we discovered the poor little headless carcass; this left Porky absolutely distraught. I comforted Porky with words like "Bloody hell! He's eaten your mouse." But there were no words that could soothe his grief. We cursed Tiger, I tried once again to console Porky, and we, with great reverence befitting of the occasion and with buckets of tears, buried the remainder of the mouse (we never found the head). We actually buried the mouse with soil, not with tears, the tears were there just to mark the solemnity of the occasion.

We could have dug up the mouse but felt it would have been somewhat irreverent and, although the cinema would accept rabbit skins as entry payments to the pictures, Willmotts were adamant that they would not budge from their policy of payment only in hard cash, so Porky's Mickey lay undisturbed. The general consensus of opinion was that the poor little creature had been disturbed quite enough already. Incidentally, Porky's name was really Michael, or Mick for short, so you might say the mouse was Mickey's Mickey mouse, giving it a sort of cartoon connotation, although it was more like a Pantomime, looking back on it.

So now we stood Gormless and Gormlesser, day off with ideas of enjoyment but, pecuniarily embarrassed, financially defunct, monetarily mangled, in a word, *broke*. Although this could have been a major stumbling block, an insurmountable obstacle, a snag for most, it was but a minor glitch for us. We racked our brains (and that didn't take long considering the material we had to work with was quite limited) and came up with a solution.

In the main people (or at least the people we knew) were very cautious when it came to opening their purses, so in order to extract some of their contents we needed a strategy. We realised that to just ask for money to buy some carbide in order to explode some bottles didn't seem too hopeful. People just weren't that generous . . . or gullible and they'd just ask silly questions like, "Why aren't you at school? Do your mothers know you aren't at school?" Then the threat, "I'll tell her when I see her."

It just wasn't worth the aggravation. A strategy had to be formulated. The strategy we arrived at was simple and clever, some people may say conniving, devious or even underhanded, but simple and clever'll do me. Anyway it sounds much better and less tacky. Clever may seem a touch too much to accept, but simple; we'll not get too many arguments in that quarter and why deviate from nature's course? Do that which you do best, that's my philosophy and we definitely did simple in a grandiose manner.

At that particular time the Russians were being irritated by those bloody annoying German soldiers at Stalingrad, so we colluded and thought that enough was enough, it was time to sort them out and get some money into the bargain. Having decided on our approach it was only a matter of deciding what action we needed for maximum money extraction. We then agreed that our problem was how to remove the money from people's purses with as little pain as necessary.

And so we arrived at an idea to suit all parties. On reflection (and this is what it's all about) I rather feel it may have been a suit that fitted us better than others who were about to become (all be it unwittingly) involved. We would hold a raffle. It would be for the widows and orphans of the Russian resistance movement. We knew very little about that particular movement, or in fact if there was such a movement, but here we had to rely on the ignorance of the 'willing' donors. If *we* didn't know, the chances were that no one else would know either. Who would refuse to give to a cause as worthy as the one we were then presenting?

To accomplish our undertaking the method agreed on would need a prize. It would be naive to try to sell tickets without any thought given to the form of reward the winner would be getting. But what to raffle? That was the question! It needed to be something that appealed to the recipient, definitely not vulgar, or cheap. Also it required to be attractive enough whereby the proceeds would have to be able to: defeat the German army, allow Wilmotts a fair profit, permit the winner an air of exhilaration and support a day of leisure for us to boot. After we had removed the required amount for our day of pleasure from the proceeds of our enterprise, the remainder of the money would be sent by courier to Russia. We would then await the news of the defeat of the German army by Russian forces. At the centre of the Germans' downfall would be our raffle prize, assisted in part by the Russian army. But what was this prize going to be?

When we thought it safe we went to my house and rummaged through an assortment of toys until we found the ideal one. It was a toy that, whilst not being in pristine condition, was not too broken either. It was a hoop-la game and virtually intact; well almost, admittedly there were only five rings instead of the original six, but a minor detail as compared with the saving of Russia and possibly the world. We believed the other one was chewed up by Tiger in a fit of pique, but it would take a brave man to approach him about it anyway. After we had found the box, which incidentally had not had a visit from Tiger so was still in fairly good order, the whole ensemble now looked pretty well presentable and well capable of the task it was destined to fulfil.

Together, Porky and I touted this wonderful prize round the neighbourhood as the prize draw of the age. Tickets were sold at 3d a go and strange looks soon turned into understanding as we assured the prospective ticket buyers of the great Russian need for our help in order to repel those awful German Panzer divisions from their thresholds and comfort the needy. One woman in a fit of inquisitiveness asked how the money was to reach Russia and could the Russians spend English pound notes; not that there were many of those in the offing. After we had assured her that there was a courier ready and waiting to take it as soon as we had finished collecting, and that Russian women were as skilful at spending money as were English women, she agreed to donate a rabbit's skin. Unfortunately, the skin looked as if it had been in a *no-holds-barred* ruck with Tiger, even Porky's Mickey looked in better condition than that bedraggled little mite. After thanking her for the thought we hurried off in case she delved into another question and answer session, or even worse offered some other misbegotten creature to protect the Russians. But here was a woman who needed to be shunned in any of our future enterprises as she was quite obviously a thinker and thinkers needed to be avoided. We were never quite sure how to deal with thinkers as they were few and far between in the world we inhabited, or as Shakespeare would have offered it 'Not in our philosophy Horatio'. (Thought I'd put that just in case a person of culture picks this book up mistaking it for a classic, and in avoidance of wasting their time completely.) Anyway! we must press on, can't afford too much time devoted to culture it will only confuse those of us who have none.

We sold the tickets at 3d a throw and after collecting 8/6d got bored, so we then held the draw. Democratically we decided to give the prize to the young mother of five children in order to keep *them* in order because when we were round there they were noisy little buggers and were running their mother ragged.

We then searched for someone who would be visiting Russia in the not too distant future, but with little success, in fact no success. So with the proceeds we went and bought our box of carbide, some sweets, five fags and a box of matches, and had a jolly good time. It did little to help the Russian cause but it certainly made our day. In any case it was well intended and that's what counts. I remember my Mother, whenever she needed to emphasise one of my imperfections (and she certainly had a fair selection to emphasise) she would say "You had no intention of doing that" whatever 'that' was at the time, or whatever was her particular gripe of the day, so I've always paid good attention to intention, if you see what I mean.

There is a saying that God does not pay debts in money. This means that He may at some time extract some retribution for acts committed in the past. Now I'm not absolutely convinced on that piece of folk lore, but what I do know is that the next time Porky and I decided on a day off the result was spooky.

We had managed a day off before with no hardship either to ourselves or to our teachers; why not go for it again. Surely the school could struggle on for a day without our company, they had before with no disasters, so 'Yeah! why not?' This was going to be a BIG mistake, but would have probably gone unnoticed if Porky had listened to me. We had made it through most of the day without any tragic results and were quite proud of our achievement. We were now in the woods and amusing ourselves, nothing spectacular, but just having fun as boys do, and had this been earlier in the year, say before the apple season came around, I believe we would have been ok.

The time was right about the apple ripening season and we had sighted a garden full of apple trees. These trees were laden with apples just ready for picking. Had Porky listened to me we would never have placed ourselves in the position we ultimately did. Having spied the trees and their lovely hangers on, there was no way we were going to ignore them. In order to get them we had to go into the garden. Now I'm always suspicious of men who grow apples; from past experience I must say I have never as yet met one with anything that I could say would pass as having a sweet temper or a sense of humour. Maybe the apples' acid turns their tempers sour, maybe they are born with violent natures, but whatever the cause of this strange phenomenon it is still a fact that apple growers growl and bite. They are particularly bad tempered when it comes to children in the vicinity of their beloved apple trees.

On planning a strategy I suggested to Porky that we first go to the apple grower's door and ask for a glass of water; that way we could ascertain whether he was out and we would be safe, or if in, give it another shot on our next irregular day off. At this point I didn't realise that not only would our irregular days off become less regular, they would in fact become a thing of the past, in a word, extinct. At that precise moment the saying 'famous last words' was born. "No!" says Porky "There's no one here at this time of day." This time of day was the time when school (of which we should have been a part) finished. We were now, having ignored my own instincts, merrily gathering the apples.

Suddenly from out of nowhere came this raucous voice. Out of the window goes Porky's theory on apple growers being at work at this time of day and into sight came my theory on irate apple growers. This man was no exception to the rule, his face taut with anger he hurtled up the garden as fast as his legs could carry him. Fortunately his legs were designed more for standing on than chasing thieving little apple scrumpers. We escaped with bodies still intact, but with very little to see for our exploits. We congratulated ourselves on the efficiency with which we had avoided the apple grower's boot up the backside and thought ourselves quite clever.

The next day we decided that we would honour the school with our presence and so we did. At assembly I had no feeling that anything had changed from the last time I was here. All seemed well and going to plan, as it might be termed. Prayers were said; at this point I must relate that my prayers might well have been a touch more devout had I foreseen the events that were about to unfold. The Head said his little piece, but then instead of sending us back to our respective classes he diverted from the normal course. To my utter amazement he requested the pleasure of my company; now not many people have requested that too often. I then became suspicious when he also required the pleasure of Porky's company. At first I thought that he was about to ask Porky and myself to sing, but on second thoughts I knew that Porky only did solos. No one in their right mind would ever ask me to sing.

What finally came to light was not our singing at all; it was someone else's singing. Our angry fruit grower from the day before had locked onto some boys who were coming out of school at a very opportune moment as far as the fruit grower was concerned, but a very inopportune moment as far as we were concerned. He had latched onto these boys and they had obliged him with our names. I bet he gave them an apple to make them sing; twenty pieces-o'-silver, ok, but I ask you 'an apple'- phoo - and it certainly wasn't an apple that we got, well not unless we ignore those we had already helped ourselves to.

After the long diatribe delivered to the rest of the school on the sin of theft, with the two of us standing there looking foolish, I can remember thinking that I would rather have had the cane than to be put through this kind of humiliation.' At that moment what I didn't realise was that we weren't going to miss out in that direction either. Following the lecture and the shame, I was quite willing to forgive and forget. Unfortunately, it seems that to complete our rehabilitation into society a goodly measure of pain also had to be inflicted. Our Head Master was normally quite a decent sort of-a-bloke, but I believe he had forgotten this in his haste to appease our mutual friend the apple grower. His generosity knowing no bounds the Headmaster invited us to inspect his office; when I say invited, it was not an offer that was open to negotiation, or of requesting a time more mutually agreeable. This was a Don Corleone type of request and there seemed little chance of offering, or even considering a plea for clemency on the grounds of diminished responsibility. The Head was more focused on our irresponsibility, and being a Principal with principles (if you see what I mean) bribes were out of the question, anyway all of the money destined for 'Russian Aid' had evaporated into the mists of a profligate, but intensely satisfying afternoon some days earlier, so any kind of inducement would have had to have been in the guise of an IOU, and with trust at a minimum I don't honestly believe it would have turned the forthcoming events in our favour.

After standing outside our Head's Office for an indeterminate length of time (I expect this was just to complete the disgrace) we were then invited *into* the office for further offerings, but this time in the pain department of the rehabilitation store. I'd been here on other occasions, and in far more convivial circumstances, but this time it felt quite sinister. From a rack our mentor selected a cane which looked a bit severe, then he replaced it and selected one that looked just about as spiteful. I thought, 'I bet that will hurt,' I was in no way disappointed. After a couple of practice swishes that disturbed the air with an alarming onomatopoeic (whoosh) we were asked to hold out a hand; we did, however, have the choice of which one we held out. I thought that was jolly decent of him, allowing us to choose which hand he was about to abuse. Three times that nasty little cane landed, each time seemed to hurt more than the last. I wondered whether the hand would become immune if more strokes were awarded. Just as I was wondering this, I discovered that another three *were* awarded, but I was not going to be allowed to test the theory of immunity because the next three were administered to the other hand.

We hear much about teachers and parents having the right to chastise a child with the odd smack or the cane, and I can assure anyone that lessons are indeed learned by this method. The lesson I learned from it was, if I get caught sinning it will hurt, and it certainly aids the memory on the occasion when temptation next comes calling.

Chapter Fifteen

By 1946 people were getting used to peace and restrictions on travel were being relaxed. Also shops were showing a more varied selection on both the food front and the clothes front. Over the next few years improvements of supplies would continue especially with imports beginning to reappear.

The urban spread would become more pronounced and with it shopping habits would change. In a gradual process, and accelerated by the ownership of cars, the supermarkets would become the main weekly shopping venues. Small villages, hamlets and other communities would begin to lose their convenience shops. Small retailers who catered for these communities would soon begin to disappear.

Norwich had a thriving shoe industry in the 40's, 50's and even up until the 60's. It was not just the original manufacturing, but also a high proportion of boot and shoe repairers. Shoes manufactured in the city were of a very sturdy nature, maybe not quite so elegant as they are today, but far more durable. After much abusive wear they would then allow repairs to be made which would give them a new lease of life. The whole fabric of the boot or shoe was much stronger, thick leather was used, and nails were applied to keep them together. For this reason footwear lasted longer and could be rejuvenated. The repairs would be effected by using thick leather nailed to the existing worn sole, then cleats would be nailed heel and toe, even studs would be added to ensure a longer life. They weren't the most elegant of things, but they were purposeful and they were mainly working shoes that were treated in this crude way. Sunday shoes or, as we called them, walking out shoes, were treated in a far more reverent way, they could be repaired but without the ironware.

There were dozens of these little entrepreneurial boot and shoe repairers plying their trade and making a living from that which may be termed a cottage industry. Some men even tried to do the work for themselves, all that was required would be a last, a sharp knife, a hammer, a good piece of leather, a competent surgeon for the inept knife user and the address of a more skilful repairer to put the work right – and there were plenty to choose from. There must have been a hundred or more of these repairers scattered around Norwich but for the most part I think they would have by now vanished. Those remaining are the bigger shoe repairers and even they have had to diversify, they mostly now have the facility to cut keys among other things. Today's shoes are of a less sturdy nature and their repairs are with purpose made thin rubber, or similar synthetic materials.

There were also a number of leather shops in Norwich and, to keep all these cobblers happy, one would think they were well patronised. Norwich also had its own tannery. Although the cobbling trade is now much diminished from its former glory days, the word cobblers is still widely used, in fact I'm willing to bet even as I write someone somewhere will be uttering that very word and it could become even more extensively used if anyone reads this.

With the disappearance of these small enterprises would also go a certain spirit of community friendliness. The great drive, however, was for the building of residential properties. There were the big estates erected on sites not previously used for housing, and also the clearance and reuse of land following the bomb destruction.

With the need for more dwellings, land was now being conserved by building upwards. Flats of two, three and four storeys were now being built and were becoming a bigger feature of housing complexes. It is also a fact that the more people's residences there were, the fewer the facilities. In Thorpe Hamlet there were many properties springing up, both private and public sector built. At the same time many small businesses were going.

Mousehold House mentioned earlier a grandiose building, standing alone in its own grounds and surrounded by woodland became a victim of the 'build anywhere' ethos. This house was occupied by a Miss Patience Harboard. It was held on a 99-year lease from Norwich City Council. Once the lease was up NCC could hardly contain their enthusiasm to remove her. At this time Miss Harboard was suffering in the grip of cancer; but in spite of this she was still required to vacate. One year's extension to her lease could have been granted, but wasn't. Within that year she died.

While in residence all through the war years Miss Harboard did marvellous work within the community and was a true lady. After Miss Harboard was moved out of this beautiful old building it was turned into flats. The grounds are still kept in good condition but other properties have been built in the surrounding wooded area.

The woods adjacent to the Mousehold House Estate known as Lion Wood woods have remained untouched. These woods have grown thicker and wilder. The main reason for this proliferation is due to the absence of children retarding its natural growth. In the 40's up until the early 70's Crome School was the main teaching institute for children residing on the Plumstead Estate. The route to school was through Lion Wood woods, so hoards of marauding children challenging the right of nature to produce its flora and fauna kept the growth down. With the closure of Crome School this was no longer the case. We now see the squirrel is well established, which was not so before.

In the 40's, 50's, 60's and up until the early 70's this woods was also the main playing area for children's activities after school. The trees were always being pared and trimmed in the children's attempts to keep it well groomed, although possibly quite inadvertently. Children were not allowed chain saws but could do an efficient job with sheath knife, penknife, or even mother's bread knife. Although their work was not always appreciated in certain quarters they enjoyed it.

Football, cricket, Cowboys and Indians and a plethora of other games helped to keep an overgrowth of unwanted undergrowth at bay. A pursuing bike-pushing park keeper also helped the cause. I wonder if he claimed extra money for his efforts in landscaping!

The Cowboys and Indians games were a better grounding for dramatics than was RADA. Boys would run around with a funny gait pretending to be horses, they certainly had the mentality but were short of other things, noticeably two legs, a mane and a tail. There were discrepancies in other departments, but those were the main ones. To pretend to make these pretend horses go faster the boys would smack themselves on the side of their rumps quite vigorously. Had it been anyone else doing the smacking I'm sure they would have protested most loudly. There is a limit to the speed at which a two-legged horse can run, and no amount of self-brutality will alter that fact.

The guns, when nothing else was available, would be the fingers. The index finger and the next finger would be pointing straight out and the next finger plus the pinkie would be bent toward the palm, the thumb would then act as the gun's hammer. A right-handed gunman would use his right hand and a left…well! I'm sure you get the drift. Now there is no need to try this at home as I can assure you it works perfectly well for eleven to fourteen year olds; after that age it looks a bit silly, not that it looks too sensible even at that age, but it is more sociably acceptable. Now having acquired the right equipment we can begin to play the game. The next requirement is a boy's imagination, nothing too realistic can be achieved without a goodly dollop of this. To make the whole thing come to life as it were, we now need sound. The sound of a gun is made by the throat, it's like the death throes of an asthmatic or, to be more accurate, the croaking of a frog with the after-effects of 'flu. As bad as this may seem, it was certainly a cultural advance on shouting bang, bang, and with this huge step forward bang, bang, was never heard again.

On hearing this dreaded assimilated gun noise, the boy aimed at should in theory have dropped to the ground. The theory mattered not one jot, mostly whoever it was would be in complete denial and all the shouts of "You're dead" could not stop him, a few slaps of the bum to spur him on and he would disappear into the thick wooded area replying "No I'm not, you missed." There were a few boys who were never in the need of RADA training at all. They would clasp their chests in the most dramatic way, go through the most convoluted contortions and, after boring all and sundry to the point of suicide, would slip away into a pretend death. You would then gallop away, portraying a horse, once again abusing your hindquarters in search of another Indian. It then could be your chance to be shot. There was the choice for you to make, do you run or die dramatically? This could be a choice made for you depending on the condition of the ground. If the ground was muddy, you needed to be indestructible and run; if it was dry, you could then lend yourself to a piece of acting, it may come in handy one day.

There were Cowboys and Indians who were never willing to die; although they could be a bit of a pain, they were not half as bad as those who always wanted to show off their skills at dying dramatically. I believe these boys found a great spiritual fulfilment by dying occasionally, well, even often! The best way of coping with such a boy would be to pretend to miss. "Oh! Blast, I missed" you would shout.

Unfortunately, before you could finish the sentence our budding 'Sir Larry' would already be clutching his chest and knocking at the Pearly Gates. It never ceased to amaze me how boys when shot would hold their chests, it must have been the only part of the anatomy which allowed a sure death but a nice slow one.

Of course Cowboys and Indians created a fantasy in death, but death could well have become a reality in other activities. One was our abiding desire to hurl stones at each other. Gangs were usually formed according to the road on which you lived, or the area where you lived.

By the age of twelve and a half, or thereabouts, a consensus of opinion arrived at by the intelligentsia (boys of twelve and over) decided that a more mature way of conducting these sorties should be on a less puerile basis. Thus it was agreed to conduct them on a friendly footing. All stone fights would be conducted in an affable manner, and so smaller stones with no rough edges would be used. Sharp flints were to be outlawed, as were stones likely to cause more brain damage than nature had already inflicted. We would still be on opposite sides but with warmth and consideration given to our adversaries.

The first stone fight entered into produced the first disaster. Prior to this and during our vitriolic confrontations hardly anyone got injured; now, at the beginning of this new format, we encountered our first casualty as bravado overcame caution on the assumption that friendly stones would be less likely to inflict as much damage as hostile stones.

The boy privileged to have the honour of becoming that first wounded warrior was a boy called George, although at that precise moment he seemed too traumatised to realise just how lucky he was. George was the son of Parky and a very brave boy indeed - even to be taking part. George was unfortunate enough to interrupt the flight path of a stone, in fact it was one of the first friendly stones ever thrown. It seems he popped his head up to get a better look and nearly lost an eye.

This brought proceedings to an abrupt halt while friends and enemy-friends alike gathered around to assess the injury, commiserate and offer considered advice. It didn't help the situation when someone suggested that the eye may have to come out and then be replaced by a glass one. Someone suggested that a glass eye was not a bad thing to have, but the look on George's face seemed to indicate that in George's eyes or eye - no pun intended - as it was likely to turn out, was not a particularly *good* thing either. However, apparently this lad had an old uncle with a glass eye and to amuse everyone at the different functions he attended he would remove it. This entitled him to great acclaim from his audience and also produced a few pints of beer. Unfortunately, we were reminded that George didn't like beer, but he might settle for a few sweets or the occasional homemade toffee apple Mrs Watts concocted.

Unfortunately for George there weren't too many confectioners in the area, which meant that even those who would fork out their wares would only do it once, so the benefits in that direction seemed quite limited. Mrs Watts would obviously be struck the first time George flopped his eye onto her table, and it was just likely she would reward him for the entertainment, but every trick has its day and this one, once seen, could well have reached this point after the first showing.

Also, related the lad with the glassed eyed uncle, his uncle was a particularly friendly person with a happy disposition and at that exact moment George looked far from happy. The process from his present demeanour to anything like happy would need a good deal of work.

As a boy called Ginger commented, we should get him to relax first as he did seem dreadfully dispirited, then we could work steadily towards happy.

Another spectator who had done fairly well at history during the previous term's exams spoke of a bloke with one eye who joined the navy and sunk hundreds of enemy ships. This potential professor of history also recalled that the man only had one arm as well. Another remarkable coincidence was that, like George, he also came from Norwich, or just outside at a place called Burnham Thorpe. At this point George seemed on the verge of tears until our guru of historical events assured George that the revealed story didn't necessarily mean he would *have* to lose his arm.

We now needed a medic to wipe away the blood and generally administer some knowledgeable assistance, but no one of that ilk could be found so we had to go with anyone who had something suitable to clean up the wound. This brought to light an unlikely candidate called Red; this was just a nickname he had acquired due to his head being in a permanent state of red from the use of lice repellent. Red was the only boy with a handkerchief. In this George was deemed to be lucky - had it not been for the dreadful cold Red had latched onto some weeks earlier, Red would not now be carrying it. Red ceremoniously removed from his pocket a thing which certainly could have been a handkerchief if a bit of imagination was applied, and after a piece of over used chewing gum had been extracted plus some little specks of things that were best not too closely analysed, the work of cleaning the eye began.

George's protests were noted, but disregarded, and the eye was cleaned. From this point the story becomes rather flat. After the removal of the blood it was discovered that the eye was in perfectly good order, the only damage was a cut above the eye. This was a little disappointing for most of us but I think George was quite relieved.

As I say, we were a bit disappointed but we never let on to George, as we didn't want to spoil his day. He did happen to mention that he was averse to the idea of going to sea. It appears that his mother took him to Yarmouth once and during a trip round Scroby Sands he was violently seasick and wished he could have died. After his encounter with Red's handkerchief I suspected his wish, although belated, might well come true. People reading this for the first time and not being aware of just how steeply boys' stupidity can climb will be amazed to know that our friendly stone hurling continued.

By this time catapults had come into the equation. But now they had shifted out of the weak knicker elastic, seized from your sister, of former years and had moved into the quarter inch vulcanised, stone propelling, death dealing monsters, 'only to be used in emergencies' type of weapon. The preordained edict of 'only aim to miss and terrify' was issued. This would prevent injury and death (hopefully). Unfortunately, injury and death are not too acquainted with boys' edicts and, although death got the general idea, injury completely ignored it. One lad, aiming his stone roughly in the direction of the friendly enemy and not allowing for the wind, found his stone to be of a slightly wayward nature. Before anyone could say 'Bloody hell!' or 'Look out!' the stone had smacked into a vulnerable hand. With no more ado the hand became quite crimson, as soft flesh tends to do when in conflict with granite travelling at speed, and promptly swelled to the size of an egg (and we are talking ostrich not bantam). Once again we all gathered to see the extent of the injury and to administer comfort, advice and such remarks as "Does it hurt?" "Can you walk?" "What will you tell your mother?" I think the last one had a self-preservation connotation inbuilt, well, no one wanted an irate mother on his case!

The best news he received came from a person far more in touch with this kind of situation than anyone else in the visiting group when he stated that he did not think an amputation would be called for. At this news the injured lad displayed an air of gratitude, conveyed through a veil of tears and a look of, what can only be euphemistically described as, pain. There was no blood on display in this incident so Red's handkerchief was not called upon. This must have been a great solace to the stricken lad and a measure of relief to the spectators.

Soon after this Red's head (excuse the assonance) was declared a free zone from the infestation of lice; some said it was the effectiveness of the red dye, whilst others swore that the lice had glimpsed the handkerchief and fled in terror. I am happy to report that George recovered from his wounds within a week or so, but is still having psychiatric treatment on account of the effects of Red's handkerchief. It was decided that, in the light of past events, competitions between rival gangs should be confined to sport. So, to everyone's relief (including the tenants of the area), hostilities became a thing of the past.

I was indeed fortunate to live near Wellesley Avenue woods, as I still do, and now as I walk through them I marvel at the way they have grown. Young saplings are now full-grown trees but the gales of 1970/80's took their toll on some of the older ones. Paths and walkways that were once clearly defined are now no longer. Overgrown because of the drop in activity but still a wonderful walking experience.

The council set up a trim track on the west side of Lion Wood woods. At various points they introduced differing get fit tasks and when first devised it was used, although not extensively. Now it is never used at all; neither is it maintained.

Moving up Pilling Park Road past Mousehold House we come to Pilling Park. This park was set up when Plumstead Estate was built. In the park were tennis courts, a swing field and a grass playing area for cricket and hockey. Most of the park was available to all, but the grassed playing area was hallowed turf. Woe betides any child who even looked at this piece of land. There was also a pavilion used for changing in and for tea at the interval during cricket matches.

The swings have gone, along with the pavilion and the tennis courts. The grassed square is no longer the well-tended pièce de résistance of former years. In the year 2000 some idiots drove a car onto the middle of the square and set fire to it thereby ruining the square for the rest of the season.

Moving back down Pilling Park Road and turning right into Wellesley Avenue, then left into Wolfe Road, there on the right is Wellesley Avenue Infants School. Its confines are Wolfe Road and Wellesley Avenue. This was my first school after moving into the area. It is a sobering thought to ponder on how many children have passed through this seat of learning since the 1930's. I know it has produced and furnished the country with a vast number of characters and its influence through this diverse richness of personalities will be seen all over the world. Most probably in Australia through deportation I rather suspect.

Continuing on up Wolfe Road was an old piece of ground we called the dump. Later it was built on and a building firm named Westgates occupied it for offices. There was also a dry-cleaning firm in occupation on another part of the site.

Just to divert for a moment. When the dancehall called the Samson and Hercules was built it had a swimming pool beneath its floor. In the 50's this was owned by Mr Geoffrey Watling. When the Samson and Hercules was renovated in the 1950's the swimming pool was made into underground cloakrooms and Westgate was the building contractor. I know this because I worked for the firm sub-contracted to do the plumbing work and as an apprentice I was implicated . . . sorry . . . involved! It was quite a project. Just in case anyone is still upset about the disappearance of that particular feature and wishes to extract some sort of retribution; please! I swear my involvement was very small. In fact, my boss would have preferred it to have been a bit more, but then again he always wanted more, had his requirements leaned toward less I feel we would have met at a point of mutual understanding.

Returning to the Thorpe Hamlet area. Running parallel to the dump was a swing field/playground. On the playground, the surface being made up from cinders, were various pieces of contraptions designed to maim or kill but purportedly for pleasure. In the far bottom corner of this play area was a slide, at the base of which was a concrete pad. This was designed to break your fall should you be imprudent enough to fall. The slide was high, although the top was quite visible on a clear day. To reach the top a set of steel steps was provided, but it was vastly more exciting to risk death by climbing the steel structure. I am led to believe that it was designed by Isambard Kingdom Brunel as a prototype for some sort of bridge in Bristol. Today slides are mere pussycats in comparison to this brute.

At another corner of the playground was a swingboat. This was designed to support the undertaking business. When used properly it was moderately, if not entirely, safe. However, as no instructions were issued, all manner of suicidal antics took precedence over common-sense. In fact, common was not a word one could associate with sense, as sense far from being common was usually conspicuous by its never being there. This piece of apparatus was created to train kamikaze pilots. Two children, one either end, holding the metal stays that held the swingboat in suspension, could work this evil piece of 'amusement' up until somewhere just beyond the perpendicular was achieved. I firmly believe it had been donated by the dry cleaner's just across the fence to hype up trade during slack periods. Neither bright boys nor brave boys would ride it, only those either very naïve, ill-informed or dull-witted. Unfortunately, we could have all been in at least one of those categories and some boys were able to surmount the entire list. Apart from the two child volunteers working the thing up, four others could sit and ride this boat. I am of the opinion the height reached was about 20 degrees beyond its safety point. Only the reckless, suicidal or insane would consider embarking on this journey. Again the base was made of concrete and I can only assume this was to deter anyone from falling off. The ride was so white knuckled that had you have fallen off your hands would probably have remained attached to the holding bars.

There were also swings and they were only dangerous if you walked in front of one as it swung to and fro, or if you fell off one. At least your destiny was in your own hands with the swings.

The fourth and final piece of apparatus was a swingboat that travelled back and forth. This would not drop you from a height, but as it reached an alarming speed it could propel small children on an air-flung excursion. The good thing about this was that at the point of release, which would be after reaching its optimum forward movement, it would hit what we call the jolt and your body speed would be quite rapid. The momentum and, if the wind was favourable, could encourage you way beyond the concrete pad. The cinders that you would land on, although quite abrasive, were much kinder to young flesh than was concrete, and less bone shattering.

The children who revelled in the business of working those rides were the sort of psychos you would not entrust with someone else's life, never mind your own. The Health & Safety people of today would certainly tut tut. However, the mere fact that danger lurked gave children a street credibility that would hold them in good stead when encountering future dangers.

Moving on. Beyond the dump and playground was a piece of grassy land that was unused and would have made a good football pitch. Unfortunately, we were not allowed to play there. Once again the old disobedience theory worked. Because we were not supposed to be there, there we always wanted to be. It did not matter that we were chased off, we would still return, in fact the chase became part of the enjoyment.

On to the opposite side of Wolfe Road, just after the school was Clarke's fish and chip shop, behind which was a pickling shop. Willis's was next to the pickling shop, in fact Willis had two shops, one was a general store the other was a butchers. The whole complex has now been bought for the development of houses.

Clarke's fish shop was owned by Benny Clarke a Norwich City Councillor and at one time sheriff of Norwich. He lived on Quebec Road with his wife and family. He also did great fritters as well as fish and chips and Friday night was always fish fritters and chips night.

Heading along Wolfe Road you come to Montcalm Road on the left. Montcalm Road sported a sign that declared it to be NOT ADOPTED. Isn't it sad this poor little road was so unwanted? Immediately opposite is Britannia Road. Further on was Fiddy's confectionery shop. Mrs Fiddy was a rather larger than life woman whose language was a trifle risqué but she was a very lively character. The shop and the lady have long since gone, the shop is now a terraced house.

On the corner of Wolfe Road stands the Quebec Tavern. This pub has served the area of Thorpe Hamlet for many years. It has oiled the bodies and revived the souls (even possibly sending some to damnation). It has fortified the bad, refreshed the good and inebriated the weak. During the war years it entrapped a few GIs making them almost susceptible to the wiles of women of ill repute.

When I was a boy my mother told me not to hang around such places, so there I was each night furthering my education on the seamier side of life. Unfortunately, all I learnt were a few new words set to Jerusalem and some choice French phrases. It was a friendly little pub mostly, except for the occasional altercation when a girl friend or a wife was considered to be taking Anglo-American relations a bit too far. It was all good fun, well! For us anyway.

On the opposite corner of Wolfe Road and Quebec Road stood Money's fish shop, and this was where we all gathered to discuss the more important things in life such as: who had the biggest conkers, most marbles etc, it was a great place to congregate and get a fish and chip meal, amid convivial company, after it became too dark to play football or cricket. It is a bookie's now and no children are ever seen around there; in fact you don't see kids gathering anywhere these days. On the corner of Quebec Road and Camp Road was A Yaxley, Barber. The shop was a men's only as were most of the barber's shops in those days. This shop is gone now and in its place stand three-storey flats. After cutting a man's hair the barber would be heard to say "Would sir be requiring of anything for the weekend?" If yes, a small packet would be passed across to sir in exchange for a few coppers. I often wondered what it was that was so quickly received and pouched. It was too small to be an inflatable dinghy, so how on earth could such a small packet contain a whole weekend's entertainment? It must have been something to do with gardening as once I heard a customer say, with a wink,

172

"No thanks, I'll just have to get on with the digging this weekend." So it was likely to do with setting his seeds.

Children were never asked if they required anything for the weekend; I expect the barber thought we had entertainment enough as it was.

Wickham's shop, on the corner opposite, was another general store, bakery and confectioner. The Wickhams also had a haulage business further down Camp Road. The haulage business has now moved to Frettenham and the shop is owned by Dillons. Shops were built where the haulage business was and there have been numerous attempts at various sorts of enterprises, but none seem to have been too successful. I believe it is now being run for some council project.

Further down Quebec Road on the right was a small greengrocer's, the owner was a Mrs Miller. At one time in the 40's my mother used to shop there. Mrs Miller was a stout woman with a face which seemed to be sucking a lemon without much enjoyment at doing so. She always appeared to be the recipient of bad news acquired from some dubious source, but was only too delighted to pass it on to someone else. The imminent invasion, the rising price of vegetables, nothing was too sensitive for her not to relate.

She had a great problem with weighing vegetables, especially potatoes. She would treat this operation as a goldsmith might when weighing out precious metal. Many-a-good Saturday afternoon could be spent watching her manoeuvre varying sized potatoes on the scales in order to reach an exact balance. She would perform her art as carefully as would a painter filling a canvas with some masterpiece, and no less dedicated. The woman was obsessed by the need for perfect balance. A preoccupation only appreciated by those chronically devoted to exactness. In the 40's and 50's potatoes weren't washed so with a stone (about 6.3 kilos) of spuds you would probably get 5ozs of earth. As there was no discount for the measure of earth I rather suspect an entertainment tax was incorporated. This was probably for the pleasure of viewing her prowess with the scales.

After suffering long hours of monotonous time-consuming potato manipulation and being a woman possessed of a short patience, my mother decided that the world held more worthwhile and diverse enjoyments, so she decided to find another greengrocers. Just about one hundred yards up Quebec Road was Provident Place, and a few yards into Provident Place was a small market gardeners run by a brother and sister named Alex and Cissy Peak. Cissy did the selling whilst Alex saw to the growing side of the business. Cissy was a delightful person with a very agreeable nature. Most of the produce was homegrown so it was always fresh. There were times when Alex would go out and pick it while you waited. Cissy weighed her goods with gay abandon, if the scales went bump and flatly refused to return that was the weight you got. There was never any hour-long potato shuffling to endure. Mother was obviously pleased to have discovered this new place, but I often wonder if she missed her Saturday matinees.

Further down Providence Place was another small convenience shop, this has also gone.

The new St Matthew's Church now stands on the site of Peak's former market garden. This new church was a replacement for the old church of St Matthew's. In Thorpe Hamlet in the year 1852 we were constituted a separate ecclesiastical parish from the old parish of Thorpe, and this is in the deanery of Norwich. The old St Matthew's church was built on the slope of St Matthew's Hill. It was built in 1851 on land given to the Hamlet by the Dean and Chapter of Norwich. It stands just up from the River Wensum and has a good view of its ancient relative the Cathedral. Although it still stands it is no longer a place of worship. It is a beautiful old building in delightful settings. It is built of Kentish rag stone in the Norman style. It has an apsidal chancel nave with an octagonal broach spire, which contained one bell. There were several stained glass windows and it had the capacity to seat four hundred people. (I'm beginning to sound like an estate agent, someone had best stop me there before I offer it for sale.)

The Church of St Leonard's was at the junction of Quebec Road and Ketts Hill. This church was built in 1907 as a chapel to ease St Matthew's. It was a structure of brick, roughcast and wood. It consisted of a chancel, nave and two porches. The church would seat 350 people. St Leonard's Church was the church I attended as a child; it had a community room that as children we used for games, but it has long since fallen out of use.

Thorpe Hamlet must have been a thriving little area even in those days back in the late 1800's to have had two churches with a combined seating capacity of 750. Either people were more pious or expectations outstripped reality. I would imagine the new St Matthew's Church now built beside the old Roman, East Road would be delighted to attract that sort of congregation.

Returning to the bottom of Quebec Road, this is where Ketts Hill adjoins Plumstead Road. Turning right towards the Heartsease is Britannia Road, Britannia Road carries right through to Plumstead Road. Further up on the right was another grocer's called Laddimans, now a plumbing shop. Laddimans also had a wool shop further up on the left. On Plumstead Road going on up to the Heartsease there were but a few bungalows, and hardly any shops at what is now the Heartsease shopping complex. At the junction of Plumstead Road, Harvey Lane and Heartsease Lane there was just a crossroads.

At the other end of Plumstead Road and entering Ketts Hill, we find Ladbroke Place on the left. Further down on the right is Whitwell Road, on the corner of which stood another small shop. But further on down Ketts Hill was the shop of shops. It was called Trory's. Trory's shop was a shop to delight any small boy, it sold everything. Things you could eat, things you couldn't eat, things you shouldn't eat, things that only small boys could digest and a mixture of all those things. Sweets nicely sun-tanned through a life of too much sun. Sweets mixed with an assortment of little creatures that only David Bellamy would have been able to name. Sweets with little brown specks, the origin of which could only be guessed at.

There were sweets in tubes, sweets in bags, sweets unwrapped, and all with a flavour of their own. Children whose health was of little importance and whose wealth was even less would be able to purchase Trory's marvellous offerings at wondrously affordable prices. The chances of food poisoning were minimal provided you never submitted them to your digestive system in any extravagant quantity. Much better though you ate more wholesome food and saved those sweets to curry favour with friends, that is to say if you had any friends left to curry favour with.

Trory's also sold other objects, some of a nondescript nature, but some which could be termed either useless, worthless, nameless, harmful, life-threatening or merely mundane. Just after the war Mr Trory came into the possession of some fireworks. Prior to this we were only familiar with his out-of-date sweets, dolly mixtures, gobstoppers, liquorice allsorts, pear drops, hundreds and thousands etc, all sprinkled with a goodish selection of insects which had come to grief for whatever reason. However, these newly acquired pyrotechnics were far more exciting. It must be said that to look at they were not giving off the appearance of danger, in fact just lazing there they seemed quite innocuous. If any kind of menace was their intent they displayed a great talent in concealing it, and at least you could buy them without the fear of salmonella, unless of course you were foolish enough to eat them. As we were foolish enough to eat other things bought from this establishment, I guess the possibility in some cases could not be ruled out.

However, these fireworks were okay unless you erred on the side of indiscretion and lit them. After some time they all went, but where no one knows or, I suspect, cares. It was rumoured that a man called Arnie bought the last batch. He said he needed them to kill something he called a predator. Unfortunately, they became unstable and destroyed a Russian town called Chernobyl. This was hushed up and another reason given to explain the catastrophe.

Leaving Trory's shop, assuming you were still well enough to do so, you then come to a crossroads. There was no roundabout in the 40's and Ketts Hill was much narrower. It also had a quite defined bend in it but this was straightened out when the road was widened.

Ketts Hill led on to Barrack Street, another narrow road; it was called Barrack Street because it contained Nelson Barracks. Nelson Barracks was used in the Great War of 1914-18. It was used for the artillery to stable their horses, which were used to transport heavy gun carriages across rough terrain in France and Belgium. The heavy terrain in Belgium and France required these animals as in that era they were better than any mechanical tow.

Entering Barrack Street, on the left hand side was the old mortuary, this is now Zaks restaurant. Also there was Steward & Patteson's Brewery. Then William George & Son's Tannery Works. There was the Prince of Wales Public House, the Marquis of Granby PH and the Horse Barracks PH. There was also a barber's where the young lads were always welcome. This was owned by George Nelson whose able assistant was brother Sid. Most boys from the area had stories to relate about this establishment or about George and Sid.

So although Barrack Street was not the busy thoroughfare it now is, it was a still a decent little community. There was no roundabout and no flyover, Barrack Street ran from Peacock Street to Ketts Hill. There is one other place worth mentioning and that is Burrage's Fish and Chip shop, which was renowned for its good fare for years, but which has recently been forced to close through lack of parking facilities. There was St Paul's Church at one end of Barrack Street, the fish shop in the middle and the Windsor Castle PH at the other end. You could imbibe, feed your stomach, have your haircut and then find absolution for the soul. Not bad for a day in one street, eh! And all this for less than 10/- (50 pence).

Returning to the bottom of Ketts Hill and turning left into Bishop Bridge Road there was William Arms & Son Ltd sawdust contractor. There was an upholsterers owned by Arthur Chase, the Duke of York PH, and Charles Hipper, another barber. Bishop Bridge Road ended at Egyptian Road. Going back on the west side of Bishop Bridge Road there was a little shopping complex which included Valori's Fish Shop, Southgate the newsagent's, Sam Ellis, Fruiterer; Albert Valori, Ice Cream Manufacturer; Charles Nice, Butcher, and the Lord Raglan PH. There was also a cycle shop run by Arthur Ridgway.

Ridgway sold bikes, repaired bikes and hired out bikes. The latter for the most part were poor, wearily exhausted animals, much disinclined to further exertion. Had there been an RSP of Cruelty to Bikes these contraptions would have surely been put down.

However, most families could not afford to buy all their children bikes so Ridgeway did provide a cheap recreational service. Some would go quite a distance before they collapsed with fatigue. It was best to stay around the vicinity of hire, the walk back would be less exhausting. During the summer holidays these machines must have been ridden, pushed, dragged, cajoled, wheedled and coaxed over many miles of rough and bumpy terrain by rough and bumpy children. But Ridgeway certainly provided a lot of joy at an affordable price.

There was also another small shop at the corner of Weeds Square, also gone as is Weeds Square. After Bishop Bridge Road there is Bishopgate on the right and Gas Hill on the left. Both are part of the old East Road, which was built by the Romans. On dark nights you can still hear the tramp of the Roman legions as they make their way for their fish supper at Valori's, or so I have heard. This road carries on through Telegraph Lane West and Telegraph Lane East, passing two schools on the right. The first school was Stuart, which was a girls' school and is now a First School and a Nursery; and the second was Crome School, which was a boys' school.

When education moved on from secondary modern to comprehensive, Crome became a Leisure Centre. The council had, at great expense, installed a ten-pin bowling alley at the centre and there was also a diverse amount of activities for the entertainment of the citizens of Norwich. Unfortunately, in the 1990's Norwich City Council, under Labour, decided to use the leisure centre as a political weapon, sell it off for development and move even more people into the area. An action which I'm sure they regret because it's a gaffe for which they've never stopped apologising.

The East Road continues down Telegraph Lane East, Lion Wood woods is situated on the left and on the right is the Rosary Burial Ground. In one of my less sane moments I decided to purchase a plot there in which to be planted after my demise. As this is possibly going to be where I will spend my eternity I thought; 'Lets find out a bit about it so that I will know what to expect on my arrival'. There's nothing worse than arriving at some place, knowing you will be there forever and then not liking it. I discovered that this was the first private burial ground in the country. A Presbyterian Minster by the name of Thomas Drummond bought five acres of freehold land just off Rosary Road in 1819 and donated it to the burial of the deceased of the area (who else I ask if not the deceased? That's a rhetorical question before you start making silly suggestions) simply because he came to the conclusion that other places of rest were becoming too congested for any quality rest to take place.

Incidentally, there is also a small chapel built just up from the main drive off Rosary Road where all those who read this book will be welcome to come and wish me bon voyage when the occasion arises. Tea and cakes will of course be provided and you can all stand around (no! simmer down, not 'stand a round' as in 'buy a drink') and sing my praises, that should take a couple of minutes. Then you can all go home wondering who next will afford you a good old nosh up, hoping of course it isn't you.

The first body to be interred at the Rosary was Thomas's own wife Ann, but she had to be disinterred from her original resting place in order to be buried at the Rosary. I hope no one digs me out just after I get nicely settled in.

From the date of Ann's burial, on 22 Oct 1819, many have found their eternal abode within the grounds of the Rosary. In fact it is recorded that in the first eighty years of its opening 18,000 interments had taken place, by my reckoning that's about 3.5 per week, but as there are no half graves I guess they just buried three one week and four the next. In 1903, Thomas, who, as I first informed you was not a great believer in overcrowding, then purchased another eight acres up near the area of Telegraph Lane, and once again it is rapidly filling up, but now it comes under the administration of the local council, so anything is possible.

Occasionally I wander the grounds of the Rosary weaving between the little mounds in order to make sure that all is well and no one of a disquieting nature has been allowed to infiltrate its hallowed turf. After all is said and done (now there's a term not as oft used as once was) we don't want too many miscreants drifting in and spoiling the tranquillity. Just to put everyone's mind at rest (with rest being the operative word) things seem to be drifting along agreeably well,

Of course, buying a piece of land in which to be interred is probably the most inept piece of nonsense I have ever undertaken, and looking back at a long history of nonsense to which I have readily contributed I can but cringe with embarrassment. In hindsight I believe it would have made more sense to buy a green plastic bag (green because I'm bio-degradable) tipped the dustmen regularly and regally each Christmas and relied on their judgment to make sure that I reach the tip as discreetly and reverently as possible).

Returning once more to the bottom of Ketts Hill is Gurney Road (returning that is whilst I am still able) so named after the family of Quakers. This was where Robert Kett's body was left to rot after his execution. Kett was hung drawn and quartered and his body was placed and displayed for all to see in an iron cage. There the remains stayed for many years. Ketts Hill was named after the aforesaid Robert Kett who led the rebellion of peasants in 1549. Although Kett was himself a landowner, he still saw fit to make himself the rebels' leader. Gurney Road snakes its way through Mousehold Heath and up to the junction of Mousehold Lane to the left, Salhouse Road straight over, and Heartsease Lane to the right. En route it has the company of the Fountain playing field on the right and the Pavilion on the left. The Fountain is now used mainly for football games, but it also has a rather attractive little bandstand, restored from the Victorian era, where on certain advertised Sunday afternoons a local band will swing into entertaining and melodious action. There are also other things going on. A few boys perfecting the art of kicking a ball around, or a good healthy run can be enjoyed, trying to keep some distance between yourself and some over-zealous dog is good fun, well! at least for the dog. A dog's excess zeal can be in pursuit of romance, play or an irrational feeling that he is being ignored, so it is most advisable to let him stay ignored if possible. Others may get a certain amount of amusement out of watching some canine Romeo trying to hump your leg, but for myself I find it unfulfilling and quite embarrassing.

For sustenance there is the Pavilion on the left opposite the Fountain. This used to be the ranger's residence. In his days of occupation one could purchase tea, cakes and light refreshments, but now it is owned by Zak's and you can get a full meal. There is also an ice cream vendor who parks his van just on the right past the Fountain football field, who sells a plethora of refreshments: ice cream, ice-lollies and all kinds of cold drinks.

Moving on through the leafy confines of Gurney Road, there is the Valley Drive, a footpath restricted to pedestrians. This will take you to about halfway along Heartsease Lane; I find 'a road that will take you' to be a strange phrase, all the roads I've ever travelled make sure you trudge and slog along them under your own efforts. Some of them even make sure the journey is as painful as it is possible to be. I've also noted that they contrive to get steeper once you embark on the excursion, not to mention much longer than you ever thought possible.

At the top end of Gurney Road and to the right, but out of sight of the road lurks a golf course, or rather a pitch and putt course, council owned. Turning right at the traffic lights you will be on Heartsease Lane. On the land to the left where the Heartsease housing estate is now situated was an aerodrome. It was a private airfield and I remember as a boy going to see an air show on that field in the spring of 1939, prior to the outbreak of the war. Heartease Lane was very narrow with large hawthorn hedges intermingled with brambles. The blackberries were huge, although the passage of time and the trick of memory may make them seem larger than they really were. A crooked stick such as a walking stick was a good implement to employ when yanking down the brambles in order to get at the topmost brambles where the best fruit grew. As I was too young to own a walking stick I had to improvise with a broken branch. It was felt that anyone entrusting me with a walking stick would qualify them for an immediate visit to a psychiatrist culminating in shackles and fetters for some considerable time into the future, release only on proof that sanity would never again allow such irresponsible behaviour.

Most of the Heartsease area was still countryside, and not built on until the late 40's, but now it is quite a prosperous area with its own shopping complex which sells a diverse selection of goods from edibles to alcohol and even automobiles. There used to be a rollerdome and a ten-pin bowling alley situated at the back of the shops.

Further on to the east of the city there is a health centre where the broken limbs of the less clued up or more extravagantly inattentive skaters could be patched up before rejoining the more accomplished, less reckless members of the skating fraternity. Of course, rejoining would have largely depended on whether the doctor considered that rejoining would have been an act of needing the exhilarating experience, an attempt at suicide, or just a foolish endeavour at self-mutilation. As we can see, that from being almost a rural scene back in the thirties the Heartsease had taken on a rather rounded little existence. 'Rounded little existence' that phrase just popped into my head. I think when I finally depart that will be my epitaph, on my gravestone will be chiselled:

'HERE LIES THE BODY OF ONE JOHN BENNETT
HE HAD A RATHER ROUNDED LITTLE EXISTENCE'

That should suffice to lend purpose into a hitherto mundane un-rounded little life.

Chapter Sixteen

In 1947 England had its coldest and longest winter in living memory. It started in mid January and continued through until the end of April. The snow began to fall on the 14th of January and the ground was not seen again for three and one half months.

But despite this during those wintry months the schools seldom closed and we were allowed to attend (I'm pleased to say). The teachers believed school should have been suspended, but they were out voted by the children, thus our desire for knowledge was not impaired. Although there were times when *I* felt school should have been suspended but wasn't, I believe there were times when the teachers thought it was the *boys* who should have been suspended. On occasions I did explain to my mother that a boy's brain could hardly function to its full capacity in such cold conditions. No child should be made to go to school, it should be a voluntary thing.

My mother then pronounced the theory that boys' brains rarely functioned to capacity in any conditions, in fact to get them working at all was a remarkable feat of considerable guile by the adults. Also, was it not true that my teachers would be most distraught were they to be deprived of my presence? In my experience of how my teachers felt about my presence, I must say that were they sadder at my absence than at my attending, they would have been a sad old lot, and I am glad I would not be there to witness their sadness.

Fortunately, at the end of school I discovered that it was only the school hours which caused such a blimp. I think the cold deactivates only the academic section of the brain. The part given to play was never affected, in fact if anything it became more alert. Come adulthood the cold causes everything to seize up except the brain, and that, seeing no possible chance of future advancement, will have given in years since.

That 1947 winter was great fun for the children, but for the people who needed to travel it was a nightmare. The frost was upon the land both day and night. It was ceaseless and relentless. Rivers froze over, water pipes burst, transport was unable to

183

function, buses were either late or never made it at all, and confusion reigned (not much change there then).

At that time there were no gritting lorries and roads were never salted, side streets especially were hazardous places down which to walk, or even drive. Many goods were still being delivered by horse and cart, but the deliveries that came by motorised transport had extreme difficulty in making it. The wheels of cars would slither and slide, but one method of ensuring traction was to secure chains around the wheels of the vehicles thus churning up and completely buggering up our sledge runs, or at least until the next snowfall.

After the winter of 1947/48 the prophets of doom forecast an Ice Age. This did not materialise and the summer of 1948 was one of the hottest and longest we could remember. From then on we had the mildest of winters. In 1976, we had the hottest summer on record; once again, out came the predictions. The country would be turned into a desert! Since then we have had floods and torrential downpours. Then the argument was that within a few years we would all be drowned if we didn't grow gills. However, to be on the safe side and in order to obey my pessimistic instincts, I did, remembering my youthful and traumatic ventures into boating, furtively enquire about gondolas, but was assured by a Mr M Fish (experienced soothsayer, weather forecaster and boat seller) that there was no need to worry, it would never happen. So how about the desert theory?

"No, no, it'll be just another scare, they're always promoting these irrational shock tactics; rains, droughts, winds."

"Winds?"

"Oh yes especially winds, they've done it before, but, hey! they won't catch me out."

"You're sure aren't you Michael?"

"Pooh! you'd better believe it."

"Well, thanks Mike, now I feel really assured, but what about droughts?" I tentatively enquired, "Is that likely?"

"Not a chance, and if you're considering purchasing a camel, forget it. They stink, they're covered in fleas, their breath smells like a gorilla's armpit and on top of that they spit at you with the force of an elephant breaking wind; oh! and they're bloody bad tempered."

"Thanks once again, you've given me great comfort."

"That's ok, and if, as I rather suspect, the forecasts are as crap as the dung from the camel's arse then the country will just drift from wet to dry and hot to cold for years to come, so if I were you I'd just invest in a pair of wellies and a parasol."

In the meantime, whatever those prophets of doom predicted about those cold winters they would never have spoiled the entertainment of the children who weren't about to have their pleasures marred by this nonsense. After a while the main streets were cleared of snow, gangs of men would set out armed with shovels, good humour and adorned in chill defying clothes, cheerfully shuffling the snow from one place to another and clearing the main roads only for them to be obliterated some hours later by a further untimely snowfall. The side streets were never free from snow so winter sports could be endlessly indulged in by children. Slides could be made on the road so that those without sledges could also be suitably amused. These slides were not looked upon with great enthusiasm by the adults, and slides on the path were definitely frowned on. It was true, it did cause the children some discomfort, but not half as much as it caused the adult population. Neither did it create the same amount of embarrassment for the younger generation. With the slippery conditions underfoot, it was not a pretty sight to see an adult flailing about trying to maintain balance and dignity. Once gravity has decided to embarrass someone it is not necessarily in the mood to compromise, and adults are particularly vulnerable.

Children can, in the main, retain their balance much better plus of course they don't have so far to fall, but in the event of falling will draw on wells of sympathy, floods of tears can help quite substantially in the sympathy stakes. Adults are not allowed floods of tears so they lose out on sympathy. First they come upon the disaster blissfully unaware that they are about to enter the slippery zone. They are then suddenly surprised by how fast their feet are travelling in the direction they don't wish to go, and much faster than the body wishes to journey. They next find it difficult to synchronize body and foot speed. It is because of the desire of the feet to suddenly go faster without actually informing the body that the result is eventual chaos tinged with panic, but loaded with humour; for the spectator that is. In order to achieve some kind of balance and also a modicum of dignity all sorts of contortions are entered into, all inadequate and all futile. From here on in, the inevitable must be accepted and there is no way gravity is going to be denied.

It is a strange fact that embarrassing misfortunes always encourage a sense of merriment, at such times you can also guarantee an audience. It is almost as if the event has been advertised; of course it hasn't, in fact it's a bigger surprise to the entertainer than it is to those being entertained. There is also a liberal sprinkling of kids around to enjoy such antics.

We sledged, slid, slithered and annoyed our way through the most brilliant winter. It was cold and it was frosty and chilblains abounded, but it was great. The hands froze and the feet froze into numbness, but they weren't that painful until you got home, then the pain was excruciating. I've heard women speak of labour pains as if they were the ultimate in hurt; I swear to you, the pain in my hands was like having labour pains in ten fingers all at once. Any woman who has suffered will tell you that after the event the pain is soon forgotten and so it was with those awful finger pains. As ladies are soon eager to try the same thing again, and as soon as possible, so it was with our winter games. Night after night the same ritual carried on, three and a half hours of sledging pleasure followed by ten minutes of pain bravely borne. Bravely borne because too much moaning could seriously damage your chances of pleasure the next night.

Pilling Park Road had a slight gradient for some seventy or eighty yards before turning left into the woods, then the slope through the woods became much steeper and, as this track ran some one hundred and fifty to two hundred yards further, or in metres a long way, this made an excellent sledge run. There would be twenty or more children sliding and sledging in this area. A pleasurable ride in convivial company, it was a child's Utopia.

There was one snag. The further you travelled, the further you had to walk back for the next ride. We did request that the Council install a ski lift (or rather a sledge lift) back, but as they succinctly put it to us 'Bugger off, or you'll get your arses footed.' This seemed fairly decisive, so as there seemed little point in further negotiations, we left.

In order to get your sledge started off, you would need to give it some impetus. With your hands on the sledge and in a bent-over position, you would run pushing the sledge before you until maximum speed was reached and then dive onto it. The ground beneath you rushing past, you would then be travelling at a speed designed to kill anything or anyone that got in the way. This would, of course, be another child, a stray cat or even the neighbour's dog. It certainly would not be an adult, they were far too shrewd to encroach on this sort of mayhem.

Although the school taught us subjects that would largely not be required, the street lessons were very useful. One lesson it taught me was that nonchalance was not my thing. One Saturday while sledging over the steeper slopes of Mousehold I witnessed an older lad with a different technique for getting his sledge started.

He would shove it down the slope with his foot and then dive on it, a method that needed taking on board. My downfall was failing to get on board. With my great talent for foolishness, I then tried to follow this lad's recipe for coolness. Unfortunately, as by now you will have probably guessed, I over-egged the cake, only to see my beloved sledge, unmanned, careering down the slope with an embarrassed would-be 'cool' me slithering and sliding in pursuit, credibility in tatters. After this I quickly reverted to the safer starting method, never allowing my sledge that sort of freedom again.

Later on my sledge really proved its worth. During the period of the big freeze, coal was the main source of heating. There were the small paraffin heaters, but although they were handy for keeping the room warm they did smell a bit, and also they would not heat the water. For about three weeks the coalman failed to materialise, either due to the shortage of coal or to the road conditions. For a while we managed to eke out the supply we already had and, with sticks from the woods, things were not too bad. Then we had to revert to fetching our fuel from the British Gas & Light Co. This company was situated in St Martin's Palace Plain. Gas extracted from coal was used for domestic use, hence the name 'coal gas'. After the gas was extracted it left coke (and no, you couldn't sniff it). The Gas Company sold this 'worn out' old coal for 6d (2.5p) a bag, but they did not deliver.

My mate and I trundled our sledges down to the Gas Company and got a sack each of this un-sniffable coke. We hauled it all the way up Gas Hill and back to Plumstead Estate, a trek I would not wish to embark on now. On the odd occasion I do climb Gas Hill I need six rest periods and a few whiffs of oxygen followed by three hours in an iron lung to recuperate. This is more due to a former decadent life style than to old age.

In the August of 1948 I left school, aged 15. Having been released from my academic studies I was now on the market, and ready to impose my talents on the commercial backbone of Norwich. I needed to earn money in order to fulfil a desire for the many bounties life offered to people who were heavy of pocket and light of brain.

At this point I must confess that my pockets never got that heavy, although the brain always fulfilled the second description.

As these bounties would require paying for, work (providing it was not too strenuous) would afford me the wherewithal to acquire such trappings. From here on in my life would be one round of birds, booze and debauchery. The road to perdition lay before me.

Most kids from my educational background were expected to go into factories, and there were plenty to choose from. The money was good, but I just didn't fancy the enclosed life of a factory worker, so I applied for a job working in the fresh air and with a trade. Soon my obvious talents were snapped up and I began my working life with a firm of plumbers. My employment started on the third Monday in August of 1948 at eight am (this was a shock to the system, in my former life time didn't exist before eight thirty) and by the afternoon my judgment came under some serious self-analysis and some grave scrutiny from my new employer. On that first Monday I was set before about ten thousand rusty old scaffold clips, supplied with a wire brush of many years enforced shabby treatment and requested; there-yer-are-boy clean them up. I thought; 'Yer-'avin-a-laugh-int-yer?' If he was 'avin-a-laugh he never betrayed it. I say ten thousand because to a small boy armed with wire brush, which had long since lost the desire to be abrasive, this mountain of corroded scrap iron heaped up could have reached an infinite number that even Einstein would have a problem in grasping. Later I discovered that these rusty old clips, purchased at minimal cost, (when cleaned) meant profit, and my boss never even smiled much less laughed at profit, a word he spelt GOD. However, by the Friday (pay day) I had reduced the pile by enough to satisfy him that he had found in me an asset with considerable clip cleaning ability. By now I'd settled in and when four thirty arrived I wondered why I had ever doubted my decision. Although my boss never laid tongue to it, his body language rather suggested that *his* decision may have been a trifle rash, and that a million cleaned scaffold clips never made a plumber. After that first week I was sent to work as an apprentice and with tear stained eyes left my friends the scaffold clips to the care of someone else, never to lighten their little lives again.

My boss was always reluctant to part with money. In frugality he was a legend, renowned for his 'prudence' especially when it came to paying someone as profligate as the firm's idiot. He would refuse to allow my pay packet to go until four twenty nine and fifty nine seconds each Friday. Starting off in this vein he continued it throughout the five years of my employment. Whether it was his religious beliefs or even superstition I never did find out. It was heart rending to see him agonise over the departure of his money. And it was not mine until the last second and never until, with his soul in torment, he had asked me if I thought I'd earned it? I always answered yes; well I certainly did if he was in the vicinity. Most times the money had to be wrenched from his sweating hand, but sometimes it needed ether and a surgical operation to free it from his vice-like grip. I often felt quite bad and considered handing the money back, but knowing that money handles rejection badly I resisted the temptation. I will say on his behalf, that not at any time did he enquire as to how I had used it, my answer would probably have pained, depressed, and finally destroyed him.

The reward for my loyalty and toil was £1/ 8s per week (£1.40 in today's money). Of this £1/0/0d would go towards my keep and the other 8/- was to be used on the aforementioned lifestyle. The wine was limited by the inability of the money to stretch, the women were reluctant to go out with a retard, and the debauchery never showed up in any quantity. If it did, the amount was far too small to be recognised and it was well disguised. I would say obviously disguised, but obviously and disguised could well confuse the pedant and the last thing we require at the moment are confused pedants.

The lack of enthusiasm of my boss to pay my wages never transmitted itself to me, my commitment to spending it was even greater than *his* lack of enthusiasm in parting with it. The firm I worked for, or rather (as my boss thought) which paid me, was on Sprowston Road and on the opposite side was a small confectioners called The Chocolate Box. After receiving the fruits of my weekly toil I would take my meagre wage to the shop and proceed to spend it without too much caution. Had I been as vigilant with money as was my boss, half the pubs in Norwich and most of the sweet shops would by now have disappeared and my Bank Manager would be a far happier man than he is, but heck, it's too late to think of things like that.

For five years I 'worked' for this firm and to put into perspective my boss's frugal consistency, never did I witness a smile as he parted with the wages on Friday afternoons. Looking back, neither did I see him joyful on a regular basis on any other days in the week. Having to hand over £1/ 8s to the firm's fool would have conflicted with his sentimental belief that in the main apprentices were not to be trusted with money, especially that which he considered his money. As I expected enthusiastically (but mistakenly as it turned out) that I was about to embark on a spree of drunken depravity and shameless immorality, he probably had a point.

The one bad habit that did attach itself to me was that of smoking, not as good as wine, women and debauchery (so I'm told) but okay as an aperitif whilst awaiting the main menu. It was my first pay packet which put me in touch with the habit, a habit which lasted for about thirty years. Woodbines were the popular cigarettes of the day, but Players Weights was the brand I started off with. Woodbines were spoken of, even in those days, as coffin nails, but now in hindsight I can carry the analogy a bit further. On opening the packet the cigarettes would lie in a juxtaposition like small wan bodies in some bizarre mode awaiting their final method of despatch. Each in turn would be selected and cremated and the ashes scattered to the wind. They were never seen as that harmful and were seen as a 'coolness' statement. Humphrey Bogart smoked, and all the other big Hollywood stars were hardly ever seen without a cigarette being cremated between their lips so this was the thing to do. Unfortunately, quite a few of these Hollywood stars ended up dying of cancer.

In my youth the big cigarette manufacturers had to wait until the younger generations started work before luring them into the habit of smoking, but now, with the affluence that the young ones have in today's society they catch them much earlier. Children as young as twelve and thirteen are trapped into a habit which could cause them all sorts of health problems later on. The advertising of cigarettes is much less prominent now, and carries health warnings, but still the youngsters are ensnared into thinking smoking is cool. It must be the rebellious ethos kicking in once again. Unfortunately, once embarked on the habit is very difficult to break. It is best for health and finance if kids are given intense education into the inherent problems that smoking causes. The pressure exerted by friends is often the cause of other youngsters taking up smoking, but this kind of influence leads not only to an unhealthy heart and lungs, but also to an unhealthy bank balance.

It took me thirty years to realise the damage cigarettes can cause and much stress in giving it up, but the agony was well worth the effort.

Chapter Seventeen

Coal from the late 40's began to lose its main domestic fuel status as people gradually turned to gas for heating their homes, although coal was still needed for the manufacture of town gas. Gas was much more convenient, cleaner and needed no storage space. It was far more controllable and it was instantaneous: the flick of a switch, as with the aforementioned electricity, or the turn of a knob, and immediate warmth.

In 1968 the great conversion to natural gas began. It took about six years to complete, as every household in the country had to be checked for appliances. The whole country was affected by this new fuel. All appliances had to be converted to accommodate this new phenomenon. The problem was that the new gas was twice the calorific value (CV) of the old town gas therefore injectors through which the gas passed had to be smaller. Also most of the existing appliances were governed at their own individual pressure, but now the gas had to be regulated at the meter prior to reaching the appliances. The new gas also needed to be mixed with air to allow it to become combustible. This meant that tubes needed aerating vents to allow a primary airflow to mix with the gas. Natural gas also needs a secondary airflow, as do all fuels. The new gas was now burning twice the amount of air as the old town gas, hence the reason for such stringent rules being applied to air intakes into rooms where the gas boilers were situated. Although methane gas is not a toxic gas, if incomplete combustion occurs then carbon monoxide (Ch formula CO) will be produced and CO is a very strong toxin. CO is colourless and odourless and causes drowsiness, but it is accompanied by formaldehyde. Formaldehyde, although non-toxic, will cause stinging at the back of the throat and in the nasal passages. Boilers, especially those situated in the living quarters, such as back boilers and boilers with conventional flues, should be serviced regularly, airbricks and window vents should never be restricted and it is most essential that flue ways and chimneys remain unobstructed.

Because of the primary air mixture required, gas meters were only registering half the former volume of gas passing through. Householders, mainly men who thought they knew a thing or two, would, with a wink and a nod, surreptitiously explain to anyone who was listening that they would be only paying half the price they were formerly paying, as the meter was up the creek and was only registering half the gas it should have been. This was true, well up to a point, certainly not about the meter being up the creek, that was not true, neither was it true that they would only be paying half of that which they had been paying. Had these people been told the truth they may well have had a fit. Because the gas company sells their gas by its CV and as the CV was twice that of the old coal gas the price would be roughly the same. The volume of gas burnt would be only half, the rest was made up of fresh air. It is a gas/air mixture that makes the constituency flammable or even inflammable. You could almost say they were charging you for the air you were burning. I guess it was always on the cards that someday, someone would find a way to sell us fresh air and any punter worth his salt would have certainly put a few pounds on one of the utilities, or at least something with government involvement.

Within about six years the whole of the country's gas appliances were converted to burn natural gas. Considering that such a task had never been undertaken before, I think this was an amazing feat. Many people, and from all walks of life were employed on this project. The first firm to undertake this mammoth task in the eastern region was called Gascol. They put out an advert for people to go down to Letchworth and be trained as gas converters. They then held interviews to see who were suitable to train in this demanding work. A test was devised and, provided that you had never killed, never been convicted of burglary or drunk meths on a regular basis you were ok. I myself, desiring to assist in this new evolutionary concept of chaotic household upheaval, decided to impose my considerable capacity for general stupidity on to the public at large, although they had not in any way annoyed me.

Once selected you were then sent onto a three weeks course at a training school in Letchworth. After you passed the various tests you were released onto an unsuspecting gas-appliance-owning public.

This business was arduous, traumatic, harrowing and nerve racking but, as we explained to the housewives suffering these things, it had to be done, so the sooner they unlocked the door the sooner it would all be over. When I left the training school I was put on a work van for call back purposes. Those of us on that van would visit premises that were having problems or for some reason had not been converted during the appropriate week. I was paired with a young fellow from New Zealand named Lester Barnes who not only sounded like Rolf Harris, but looked like him too. My trade was plumbing, but this converting thing was a new experience for me. These newly recruited converters came from all walks of life; there were milkmen, factory workers, postmen, in fact most of these people had probably never seen a tool kit, let alone worked with one. But they easily adapted and soon had all sorts of gas appliances in bits, and some even managed to put them back together again, and mostly in the right order. It was amazing how easily these new men adapted to the task. As for the tenants, and ignoring a few who were probably teetering on the edge before we arrived, it must be said that most were of stern stuff and bore the experience extremely tolerantly.

Being faced with someone's beautiful and adored cooker is a bit off-putting, and our first call was to a woman who looked for all the world as if she was about to be executed. When she opened her door to us she had the appearance of disbelief, as if there before her stood her worst nightmare. I don't think she had been told to expect Tweedle-Dum and Tweedle-Dee. However, I felt she appeared to have had so many disappointments in life this one just added a bit more.

"Good morning dear, we've come to repair your cooker."

Then the look of despair as she rather reluctantly said "Well you'd best come in then," and then almost accusingly "and wipe yer feet." Kiwi gave a sickly little grin as she then spat out the words which over the next three years almost became clichéd, or as one might say, 'done to death', "It worked okay before your lot touched it."

We then consoled her with the immortal words "Don't worry love, we'll soon get it working." These words were uttered with a conviction any politician would have been proud of whilst telling his constituents that he was about to cure all the worlds ills. I was so convincing I almost believed it myself. Unfortunately, it was only deeds and the restoration of her dearly beloved cooker to some normality that was going to soothe the savage breast. Not that her breasts looked too savage, well nowhere near as savage as her face.

However, when you are young you still believe in the power of your own pomposity, and you have faith.

"Don't worry love, those responsible for this lacked the expertise we possess." This satisfied her that her cooker was now in the hands of the 'competent'. There we stood side by side, Kiwi and me desperately separated by our individual theories, and deeply divorced from reality, lost in secret conversation. By now, treating the tenant as though she no longer existed, we argued our points of contention.

At one point it was mentioned that she should have had a new cooker years since, suggesting it needed replacing rather than converting. Once again, and more forcefully she expressed that "It was perfectly adequate before," but this time she added "if you can't get it to work as it did then it's down to 'your lot' to buy me a new one." I thought that at this point she was going to cry, but to her credit, not to mention our relief, she managed to restrain herself. I'm sure that at some point she must have considered murder, but in spite of the doubts she probably harboured, she saw Kiwi and me as the saviours of her cooker or the route to a new one. I'm sure our salvation was due in part to the confidence of our competence (which we had fallaciously bestowed in her). As we stood in that kitchen, steeped in our own and utter discomfiture, the immortal words of Confucius sprang to mind *('un shah flee prontus')* when in doubt depart quickly. However, we were not about to allow ignorance to keep us from our duty, and were determined that this cooker was deserving of our entire expertise . . . no matter how minute that was.

After her aforementioned remarkable restraint, our housewife now showed equally remarkable good sense by leaving the kitchen and her cooker to Kiwi, me and fate. At this point it seemed that the cooker itself got somewhat smaller almost as if it needed to become invisible, but I'm sure this was an illusion and that the cooker was only too glad of our assistance.

The tenant had hardly closed the door before Kiwi decided it was time to visit some authentic idiocy. Before there was any chance of preventing him, he negligently removed the test nipple from the gas rail ignoring the fact that the pilot flame was still alight. Now the reason we were there was because the pilot flame would have nothing to do with lighting the burners. Fire, being what it is, decided, that it didn't want us meddling in its affairs and quickly hurried into some madness of its own. As the test nipple came out, sod's law kicked in. From an obstinate standpoint of lighting nothing the pilot light suddenly realised its role in life was to incinerate everything. A sheet of flame shot out from the gas rail across the kitchen threatening to cremate animal, cook vegetable and melt mineral. It was fast and fierce as it shot into action, and just like a napalm flame it put fear into every cockroach witnessing the disaster.

Luckily the gas meter was near at hand and as panic now gripped me I leapt across the kitchen and haunted by visions of four horsemen galloping through my brain, I managed to deny the flame further enjoyment by cutting off its supply of napalm; sorry gas. In all the confusion I seemed to remember Kiwi exclaiming "Gee! shit!" in a somewhat surprised fashion. Luckily I'd stopped the flame before it got to the town. Kiwi just grinned a sickly grin before finally bursting out in uncontrollable laughter.

When sanity finally took over he said

"Gee! I think we've cured it." I doubt 'think' got too significantly involved in most of our deeds and 'cured' was more by luck than anything. The miracle was that the only thing burnt was Kiwi's hand. With great relief and divine intervention we *had* found the trouble *and* had cured it, but that was the last time that we contrived to do anything that spontaneously dim again.

After three years I left Gascol. I felt by that time the people and their gas appliances had suffered quite enough. However, it wasn't too bad as there were plenty of others left to inflict menace into people's lives . . . and their gas appliances.

There were many other changes that affected lives even before and early on in the twentieth century. After mentioning the revolution of fuel usage it would be a bit remiss not to mention the beginning of the great industrial revolution. This began in the 18th century, it was rapid and progressive, much faster than anything that had preceded it. It seems slightly off the mark to call it a revolution, a better name would probably have been extended progression. Revolution suggests something which comes back on itself, but with these revolutions they leave behind their former lives never to return, they hurry along in their own unique way creating change and disorder in all they meet. However, it is a name given to progress and who am I to challenge the sages of the past?

The world's leading industries in countries like Germany, France, The USSR and Italy were built on the earth's natural resources. Minerals such as iron and steel were the foundation on which their huge industries were assembled. Britain had its own resources but also imported materials from which it built ships, motorcars and other commodities. Iron is a naturally occurring element. Steel is an alloy and is refined from pig iron using pure oxygen that is blasted at supersonic speed into the molten iron, this burns out all the impurities including the carbon element until just the required amount of carbon remains. Steel contains about 18% nickel and 8% chromium. This process makes an alloy far more durable than iron and is also resistant to corrosion. In 1856 Henry Bessemer invented a 'converter' to produce steel from molten pig iron, cheaply and on a large scale. These mammoth manufacturers of steel, iron, copper, brass, lead, tin and all other metals have dwindled and now plastic is replacing them. Everything seems to be made from plastic. It's a marvellous invention, but how do you get rid of it? The metals could be recycled so now all that is needed is a method of either recycling plastic or destroying it. Even wrapping is now done with plastic and all that is required is for someone to invent an easy method of getting at whatever is wrapped inside the damned stuff. It takes about an hour to buy what you need and about three more hours to access the packet in which it comes. Someone suggested that a good sharp knife would do the trick in most cases, so as soon as I can get the phone number of a good paramedic I may give that a try out.

Inventions in the textile industry, inventions such as Arkwright's water frame, Hargreaves' spinning jenny, Edmund Cartwright's power loom and Watt's steam engine were at the heart of the industrial revolution. They caused much apprehension among the workers within the textile industry (this does not include Watt's steam engine, but the machines in the factories that turned out the cloth). The workers in those factories saw each new invention as a threat to their jobs. This was a grave concern to those people, for although the work was tedious and hard with the added pleasures of long hours and little pay, at least it was enabling them to have an existence.

Edmund Cartwright: Edmund Cartwright was born in 1743 and died in 1823. He was a rector of Leicestershire and he invented the power loom. In his seventy years he must have managed to advance the textile industry by many years, saved some souls, and alienated hundreds more on his journey through earth's trials and tribulations en route to his eternal home.

Sir Richard Arkwright: Sir Richard Arkwright was born in 1732 and died in 1792. He was an English barber and wig maker. Sir Richard invented the water frame. This was a spinning machine driven by water power. He was the youngest of thirteen children so it was highly unlikely that his dad would have invented too much, but he must have been a man of enormous stamina and energy. Sir Richard became one of the first capitalists of the industrial age. It was this work as a barber and wig maker that gave him the financial resources to carry on with his inventions.

James Hargreaves: James Hargreaves was born around 1722 and died in 1778. Although he was illiterate he became a carpenter and a weaver. He invented the spinning jenny. This machine allowed one person to operate several spindles at the same time. It doesn't take too much imagination to see how these inventions would upset a workforce in an area where there was very little opportunity to find other jobs.

James Watt: (1736-1819) Watt's steam engine produced a method of travelling further and faster. It progressed through the decades becoming faster, safer and more reliable, until it got to the late 20th-early 21st century. It then became slower, less safe and less reliable. Now! That's what I would call a revolution, there's not much lateral or forward progress there.

Steam travel was largely due to an inventor called Thomas Newcomen. He was a Devon blacksmith who, as far back as 1698, saw the possibilities of steam as a driving power. If the story is correct, he just sat watching a kettle as it came to the boil and saw how the steam pressure lifted the lid. He thought 'I know, I'll put some wheels on it, stick it on a track and have a dirty weekend down at Brighton.' Now I've sat watching a kettle most of my life and the only things I ever got were impatient and thirsty. So I can only take my hat off to the innovative mind of dear old Tom who saw a kettle boil and thought of something beyond the inner man. At that particular time the only real use Tom could find for his steaming kettle was to power a pump used to extract water from flooded mines.

Unfortunately, we had to wait until one Richard Trevithick and James Watt came along and got the whole project moving. Of course by this time Tom had long given up any ambition towards going on lascivious weekends. However, I have often pondered on Messrs Watt and Stevenson, both of these gentlemen were Scottish and seemed to go to an awful lot of trouble to invent, or at least improve, transport. It has on occasions crossed my mind that there was something lacking in their lives, so maybe it was the companionship of the English, or it could have been a desire to escape from Scotland. In dear old Tom Newcomen's case I suspect he, whose excitement stemmed from watching kettles boil, was quite content to stay in Glorious Devon pumping out mines. By poll, tree or pen, these are Cornish men, so it's a fair bet to say Dick Trevithick was a Cornish man born and bred and not some Johnny-come-lately who was just passing by, not that it makes the story any more exciting but it does show that Cornishmen certainly know how to enjoy life.

Richard Trevithick built the first railway and in 1804 demonstrated that his steam driven invention was powerful enough to haul around 20 ton loads at the mind boggling speed of 5 mph, so you had to be pretty smart to avoid that thing from clattering into you. Regrettably no one had come up with rails that were sufficiently resilient to support such heavy weights at those huge speeds, that is until another engineer (John Blenkinsop a Yorkshireman) came up with an answer to the frail rail impasse. And so from those humble beginnings we, through the nineteenth and twentieth century, have witnessed, travelled and thrilled to the evolution of steam. From the kettle which boiled and delighted one excitable Cornishman right through to 'state of the art' Japanese High Speed Surface Transport hurtling along at 300 mph. Although steam is no longer the driving force it is mainly responsible for our modern day rail commuting.

The industrial revolution was a long drawn-out, bloodless affair and is still going on. Every time someone invents something, technologically we advance. Maybe it is not always for the better either in life or in society, but nothing can ever halt progress.

That which I find very strange is, given the Brits' talents for attacking every country or continent south of the North Pole, and their inability to stay out of any conflict that gives rise to a bit of confrontation, here they were in the middle of a revolution and performing a bloodless coup. The French had a revolution and chopped off anyone's head who was silly enough to shove it under the Guillotine, and to qualify for this instantaneous delivery to eternal rest they didn't necessarily have to be in any way Gallic.

The Russians had their revolution and used a more reasonable way to dispatch those they considered ill behaved, they just shot them, although I'm not too sure the dispatched would have thought it too reasonable. But the Brits, bless their souls, hardly knew what was happening in their own revolution. It is a paradox that we the Brits, being as mixed and mingled a race of warlike people as it is possible to find on earth (the Huns and Mongols excluded) can't even find the energy to kill a few of its brothers in a revolution which continued for years. As soon as we hear a gun go off on some foreign field, or get a whiff of cordite, off we go, tin mug, knife and fork in hand, K rations for sustenance, ready to fight for, defend and assist all, even though they don't need our assistance.

Our industrial revolution was not in the same league as the French or the Russian revolutions. It's a pity really that we couldn't have held our revolution somewhere else on neutral soil, say in Germany or in Poland, then we might have had a much bloodier time altogether. We give a much better account of ourselves if we can march, sail or fly into combat singing xenophobic little jingles rather than indulge in our own, at home, mundane little efforts. Maybe affairs would be a better word, efforts imply a certain degree of work input and this could be sadly misinterpreted considering how insignificantly trifling, pale, bloodless, and ordinary our revolution turned out to be.

There was of course the revolution when Charles 1 of England was usurped from his throne by Oliver Cromwell and the Round Heads. A King who literally lost his head, he was beheaded in January 1649. That was a much better revolution, although Charles, were he still able, might well take issue with that notion. Cromwell, who was an English statesman and soldier, championed the rights of parliament against the claims of King Charles 1, defeated Charles's army and had Charles beheaded. Cromwell himself became Lord protector of England. After Cromwell's death his son took over. However, the Monarchy was restored in 1660 when Charles I's son Charles 11 took it back. There were quite a few bloody skirmishes during that revolution so I must apologise for giving the misconception that the English have never enjoyed themselves to the full extent in their own little scuffles.

In my short life, although the many changes which have occurred have been largely beneficial to mankind, in the advancement of our need to wipe each other out the acceleration has been truly breathtaking, or better to say life taking. Where once the ability to kill needed some close contact, and we were limited to the number we were able to dispatch at any one time, we can now kill by the thousands. This is a tremendous progression in evolution and of course we don't even need leave home. Massive weapons of destruction called weapons of mass destruction can be delivered from our own back gardens.

There is no way as yet these weapons can discriminate, but those whose children or relatives have been killed will be comforted in the knowledge that they did die for a just cause and the smart-arses who invented smart bombs are striving to make them smart enough to be discriminating, that is if there is any bugger left not smart enough or quick enough to get out of the way in order not to be discriminated against.

Most of us amble through life trying to avert disaster, seldom succeeding. Content with the small crumbs fate throws our way, happy that if, when the next catastrophe strikes, we are only spectators and not the star turn.

Childhood is an idyllic state, just waiting to be down graded into adulthood. It is a time when impending disasters are reasonably small, but with fortitude, fast brain and even faster feet you can be delivered from too much harm. Up until the age of about thirteen parental influences will normally keep you from mutilation even though the neighbours sometimes think it should be otherwise. After eighteen common sense takes over (this is of course a generalisation, in some people common sense is like Eldorado, constantly sought but never found). It is the years in between from thirteen to eighteen that are in need of vigilance. These are the years when feet are being found, although mostly out of control. Testosterone in boys is being produced in unregulated and unlimited amounts. Hormones are being replaced by even more hormones, the brain has slipped to the nadir regions, mainly to the groin which by this time has lost the wherewithal and the inclination to do anything except obey the carnal urges in other more remote parts. These parts, often visited but not truly understood, will now take control for the unforeseeable future. Common sense will be a rarity, observed only in small quantities, and will be more in the category of accidental phenomenon rather than in logical choice. Although it will flit in on the odd occasion, it will be for the most part ignored. After eighteen, young men usually find their vocation in life and then settle down to a more stable way of living.

In Norwich in the 40's, 50's and 60's there were two swimming pools. They were the Eagle and Lakenham Baths. In 1945 I was privileged to take my 50-yard school swimming certificate. I well remember it, as it was a cold afternoon in May. But this was not the only reason for my astonishing memory act. After the test, certificate assured, one of the older boys had a gathering of younger boys around him. As they seemed to be in an excited state of entertainment I thought I would wander over to see what was afoot.

I soon discovered that it was more 'what was in hand rather than what was afoot'. In the cubicle this older boy was in the throngs of stimulation, blowing hard and under some obvious excitement, or so it seemed. Around were younger boys, looking over the adjacent cubicles, under the adjacent cubicles and anywhere they could get in order to view the proceedings. The entertainer was a rather fat youth and was performing a frenetic exercise with his penis. Within moments of my arrival the fat boy's anguish became perceptibly troubling, his face first went pink, and then it went to crimson, finally he gave an agonised grunt and his body, which just seconds prior had been in the throes of some mortal stress syndrome, sank into a fleshy heap of happy self-satisfaction. At first, being of a naive disposition, I thought the lad had swallowed something nasty from the swimming pool and was trying to agitate it from wherever it had lodged. These natural baths (baths whose existence relied on being part of the river) did have a certain reputation for being slightly less than pure in content. Wisdom would dictate that most things swallowed would be far better regurgitated irrespective of whatever beneficial properties they may have contained. So much of a disquieting nature was allowed to infiltrate these waters that you had to be quite selective if you were determined to benefit from its bounties. What with the sewerage works being part of its natural charm it was not quite as agreeable as one would have wished. Fortunately the fat boy emerged from his trauma completely unscathed, nonchalantly stood up, smiled, bowed, and amid applause from the spectators got dressed and left. My own curiosity now suitably aroused I also left.

I determined that I would research the subject to find out what created such jubilation causing the fat boy to shout out with great elation and leaving him with a happy smile. At first I figured the whole episode must have been some kind of religious rite so I would, at the initial stages, offer up a small prayer. Later I heard that this kind of behaviour had very little to do with religion, was bad for the eyesight and led straight into the fiery furnaces of hell and was called masturbation. All sorts of devils were placed at the door of this hitherto little known pursuit. Hair growing from the palms of the hand, deformities of the body, baldness and blindness, all were ready to ambush the unwary. Were this the case, most boys would be hairy palmed, blind and require a wheelchair from the age of about sixteen, so not too much credulity could be placed on such tales. Nevertheless I was unwavering in my search for the truth in this matter and resolutely pursued my research (for the benefit of mankind you understand) even at times working late into the night. Earlier, as I recall, masturbation was termed self-abuse. When it became acceptable as a recreational sport, and after much study of this recreation, conducted by all sorts of authorities, it was then re-categorised as self-gratification and claimed its rightful place alongside other leisure pursuits such as football, cricket and marbles. Although it never became a team sport it was widely recognised as very therapeutic. When the name was altered to self-gratification it didn't increase its popularity, but it did remove the fear and it allowed its delights to go on with a peace of mind not previously imagined.

In the early years it was boys who were mainly attracted to the bounties of, as one of my dear friends termed it, self employment, or self fulfilment, but when girls found out about its beneficial effects it is quite widely believed that they too began to enjoy the odd finger titillation occasionally. It has been rumoured that girls are indulging in artificial aids, these I'm told are called vibrators and come in weird shapes and cause much merriment at certain house parties. However, I find this hard to swallow, as I'm sure most girls do as well.

Both the Eagle and the Lakenham baths have gone now, so where to go for extra curricular instructions I have no idea, but there must be some place where the young can go to expand their knowledge in the exciting art of hand relief. The piece preceding this is quite inappropriate for children under the age of eight as such enjoyment could seriously interrupt their education. People of a more advanced age shouldn't be at it anyway and certainly not without a doctor's certificate. People of a military persuasion should abstain from the practice mentioned, especially whilst under basic training. The occasional indulgence shouldn't be too enervating as long as the hammer and tong method (as in going at it) is not pursued. Should the practice get out of hand (figuratively speaking) bromide tablets can be obtained from the MO at his discretion. Just one word of caution, do NOT, even if approached, succumb to the temptation of charlatans or other dubious sources. There have been complaints in the past of people who, having acquired certain tablets in good faith from some malevolent dirty dealing rascal, found, after it was too late, that they had been sold Viagra. This resulted in the wearing of boxing gloves for long periods, left the pill popper with a fragile grip on reality, and made the prostrate position in bed an impossibility.

Going back to the swimming habits of our youth. There were no indoor pools in Norwich, so the only place to swim was in the river. Apart from the two outdoor swimming pools other venues included Carey's Meadow and Whitlingham. The river was an integral part of the sewerage disposal system so it would require not only the ability to swim, but great dexterity in avoiding all foreign bodies floating by (and this does not mean illegal immigrants as they were not at that time invented). The rivers in those days were quite affluent in effluence so drowning was quite mild compared to other dangers one could encounter. The railway bridge across the river made an excellent platform to dive from, but I doubt if children would be allowed to use it now, not with all the safety laws in place, but as there are less trains it is probably safer, in fact *much* safer, than it was in the days of my youth. Although I believe that children of the 40's and 50's, having faced Hitler, shot down his Luftwaffe, destroyed his tanks, taken on Parkey and Ted (even if we fled at the sight of the old grinder, God bless him; just in case he's still around) were much better equipped to deal with the lesser threat of a speeding train than are children in today's world who in the main, only have to contend with the images of danger such as Bonkerzoo and pokomondoo, or whoever the telly buttons throw at them on their play stations. They don't even have to brave the waters of the bug-infested rivers now that the sanitary society has taken control. Kids today are so hygienic that no self-respecting bug would lower itself to take up lodgings in their sparklingly washed little carcasses. Only kidding children, I expect you are all quite as dirty as you should be.

Chapter Eighteen

In the late 40's there were many small shops, the stack 'em high sell 'em cheap scenario had not as yet kicked in. The small local shops were not yet obliged to extend their prices above those of the bigger retailers in the city. The volume of trade was such that it allowed the smaller shopkeeper to compete.

Most areas had widely differing shops. There were the greengrocers', the grocers' and butchers' shops, also there were a great number of small general 'sell anything shops'. These shops were seldom on the same premises, and far enough apart to cause the walker to trundle their accumulated shopping a fair distance, but this was the way it was and it was accepted as normal.

With the advent of the car, shoppers could go to a single venue and get their entire week's needs and transport them to their front doors. No longer would the population have to haul their heavy bags around. There was a downside to this, another part of the community spirit disappeared. Neighbours used to meet up at the local shops and have a chat, pass items of news etc, friendships could build from the local shopping experience. New neighbours, people moving into the district, all and each could make friends, or even make enemies if they so wished. Even some problems could be resolved.

Anyone who has observed human nature will have realised that no one in this world needs to be alone with a problem. There are more counsellors, therapists and advisors than anyone could possibly imagine. Just the mere whiff of a problem, and every therapist, helper or agency consulted will come up with a different solution. Their own problems 'insurmountable' but given someone else's, the solution is never beyond them: woman problems, man problems, unwanted pregnancies, incurred debt, in fact anything that could possibly go wrong, and out will come the 'perfect' remedy. It's not just friends either, it can be acquaintances, strangers whom you have just met, even former enemies will sympathise. The world and his uncle love a problem and will require to be on *your* problem, immediately. Manic depressives, people with suicidal tendencies, people with enough problems of their own to sink a battleship, and all with a desperate urge to solve yours.

Since my retirement I have, on the odd occasion been privileged to watch more television than is good for me. A programme called Kilroy on BBC1 was a marvellous arena for people to air their troubles. There is no crisis that was beyond the wit of Kilroy's audiences to solve, unless it was their own. Robert Kilroy Silk was the presenter and he used to choose which set of issues to tackle each day. The topics were diverse and manifold, complexity no problem, no subject was taboo: divorce, financial, the break up of family relations, fat people who wanted to be thin, thin people who wanted to be fat, people who had had their chattels stolen, the people who stole them, you name it and Kilroy would do a programme on it. Kilroy just loved to undress people to find out if their underwear was dirty (metaphorically speaking that is). It is not quite clear why others' difficulties raise such a well of emotion, or why people have a need to address their hang-ups before an audience of millions (and me of course) but it was good viewing. Unfortunately, it was taken off the air in 2004, this was largely because Kilroy had a problem which he found great difficulty in resolving. Apparently he went too far in delving into other nations' problems and upset the powers that be, giving those powers a problem which they solved by discontinuing his problem solving. Well that's the gist of the thing and I know it sounds complicated, but it may have been less so had I explained it better. However, for a monumental fee a solicitor will sought it out. Talking of solicitors I heard a tale: a rich solicitor, a poor solicitor and Father Christmas came across a fiver laying on the pavement, who do you think picked it up? Answer: the rich solicitor, because the other two are just figments of the imagination! Isn't it a fact that solicitors can only solve problems of molehill size by charging mountain-sized fees, while everyone else solves mountainous problems for nothing?

I did like Kilroy, as he always had sad people on his show who were worse off than me. Personally I always feel much better when I realise that there are people in society who are making a bigger balls up of their lives than I am. It is a great comfort to know that someone is poorer, fatter, more useless, more inadequate, more incompetent in money matters, gets robbed more often, or has lower self-esteem, and there are paranoid people who think that the world is against them.

Dear old Kilroy gathered around him his troubled subjects and delved deeply into their souls as a skilled surgeon might delve into their bodies. He poked and prodded, sifted and separated and prospected for the smallest nugget of detail, until humiliation became a euphemism.

The whole assembly had certain insurmountable problems, but although they struggled in the depth of their own misery they each had a solution for everyone else's. The man just recently ditched by his long-suffering wife was suddenly consumed with a desire to advise someone else on their marital difficulties, which were probably only the occasional tiff anyway. However, after taking this advice the poor man would find himself paying away most of his wages in alimony, homeless, and cycling to work because his car had been repossessed. Platitudes and solutions were advanced quite unsolicited. The audience would applaud every idiotic opinion tendered, even from those people who should have been locked away in a padded cell for their own protection but were there offering such advice that only the criminally insane would act on. I have yet to witness someone with monolithic stress struggles who will not pause in order to offer some telling counselling to some other poor misbegotten sod. Kilroy's counsellors came from the city, from the country, some from Mars, and some from the dark side of the moon, all wallowing in a morass of disillusions, disappointments and disenchantments, but all armed with the sword of righteousness and the brain of a baboon, and fortified by the need to apply justice to the unfairness bedevilling their neighbours' lives. It's a mystery why this is, but it is an undeniable fact that everyone loves a problem (providing it is not their own). It could be the milk of human kindness rushing through their veins, the relief that it's some one else being mind-mangled and not them, or as in my case just bloody nosiness.

It is usually the person you would think the least likely to offer sound advice who is the very person most likely to impose their invasiveness on another of life's shafted rejects. In my youth I too, on the odd occasion, felt I had to foist my ill-formed knowledge on some unsuspecting sufferer. It was not too often, because most people knew that my knowledge would cause more problems than it solved.

In my earlier days when one disease or another attached itself to me (and there were many) especially when the weather was of an inclement nature, or even of a clement one, and medical assistance was 'necessary' in order to afford me some respite from my poorly paid, strenuous, and wholly unsatisfying labours, I would pay my doctor a visit. I recall a certain doctor (who shall remain anonymous, due to certain libel laws), who although not seeking my advice, did on one of my recurrent visits become a benefactor (if that is not too strong a word). I had waited an interminable time to see him on some life-or-death malaise that was blighting my existence and threatening my entire future when, after waiting behind twenty or so other pathetic souls, feigning anguish in order to dupe the poor doctor into giving them some time off, I finally got to see the great man. I immediately became concerned for his health. He looked far worse than I felt. An unnaturally pained expression was upon his usually naturally pained face. I said to him, "Don't you feel too good?"

"Feel too good," he griped, with an attitude of someone who was not about to let the word martyrdom stand in the way of a good grumble. With an air of one who portrayed suffering like a badge of courage and expecting the last rites any moment, or at least in the near future, he agonised, "It's my back, it's killing me, it's being stuck in this damn chair all day."

I then offered him the benefit of such advice that my limited experience would afford. I said in as professional voice as I could muster, "When you watch TV, instead of sitting in your chair why don't you lay flat on your stomach and arch your back."

He then told me in rather flowery language, punctuated with words, that someone of my tender years had no business

211

understanding and certainly no man in his position had any right uttering, that any chance of him watching television was quite limited, because irritating little sods who imagined every bug in the universe and beyond had a vendetta against them kept bothering him with insignificant problems which almost, if not entirely, amounted to malingering. It was quite obvious that here was a person who could not handle being given advice no matter how well intentioned it was. Even though I visited him quite often regarding the delicate condition of my body, never again did I afford him the benefit of my experiences in order to bring some comfort into his life. He is retired now, but anyone with that sort of attitude problem could never have featured on the Kilroy show. The last thing Kilroy needed was an ex-doctor who was not willing to take advice.

This doctor was also our family doctor, and had received on the odd occasion the request from my mother for him to call upon her, not that her requests for medical attention rivalled her son's. Now from my previous writings you will appreciate that she had in her head a rather large stick of gelignite that was attached to a very short fuse. Any time she considered that someone was being a little less than sensible she would make it quite clear that her tolerance levels were being exceeded, and in grim foreboding language would convey her displeasure. On one visit to her, knowing her potential to explode, our dear friend the doctor bounced in and in an attempt to keep her sweet and with no sign of the backache which blighted his life on my visits, asked her, "Now my dear what seems to be the trouble?" It was at this point he realised the folly of that question.

"Trouble! how on earth should I know, you're the one who's supposed to sort that out, if I knew what was wrong I wouldn't need the likes of you." Although I loved my mother dearly, it was a fact that at times she needed careful handling. Diplomacy was the order of the day, but I don't think the word 'trouble' would have been too hard for her to deal with, it was the belittling expression 'seems to be' when 'what is the trouble?' would have removed any doubt as to the genuine nature of the suffering she was trying to convey. It may well be that she saw the phrase as some kind of challenge to that suffering and although she was only about five feet three inches the poor old doctor looked as if he was facing a swim across the crocodile infested Zambezi river. It would be impossible to know if the doctor had any dealings with crocs, but he had the look of one that might relish the ordeal more than that with which he was now presented. It was a very cautious doctor who left, as compared to the flamboyant doctor who had arrived. After that I think the partnership doctors drew straws as to who should attend her in future.

Prior to the advent of television people could wallow in their tales of agony, but at a smaller venue. That is where local shops were ideal. Women (because they talk far more than men and can talk with very little to actually say) could be seen for hours discussing their illnesses and related problems. If anyone was in a hurry the thing to avoid was the neighbour who had every ailment known to medical science and then some. If this neighbour was encountered by accident the most unwise greeting to offer would be 'How are you'? This was the question that would delay any further activities planned for the day for quite some considerable time. From then on it was just an expedition through the medical journal from station A to Z stopping at all relevant and irrelevant stations in between. Personally I am a good listener, but it has cost me many of life's precious hours just listening. If I try to bend someone's ear with my problems it is a certainty that it will be the very person who is a medical phenomenon. No matter what illness I have these people have it worse and just for good measure have had it far longer. These are people I term as black cat people, if you've a black cat they have a blacker one. Of course this fanatical desire to help others is not entirely confined to illness, it can invade and attack anywhere and at any time. For instance, if you go out to buy a commodity, then mention it to someone with an air of wisdom that would rob the fountain of knowledge for months to come they will then go through an interrogative programme that will leave you dizzy.

"What! A washing machine? How much? Where from?"

"I got it from that shop in the High Street and it was only x amount."

Then an air of superiority takes over. "You should have said! That shop's a rip off, they've been up six times under the Trades Description Act to my knowledge. How much did you say it was?"

You then reiterate. "Only x amount."

"I could-a-got-cher three at that price with 1,000 free air miles thrown in." This is not an infrequent occurrence. No matter what it is, I'm willing to bet that as soon as you purchase something and your search has taken you through the five continents, someone will know of one cheaper and better just around the corner. It may have taken months even years to track down, but after success is finally gained, some irritating bugger will advise you not only of where one of these rarities is but he will inform you of where they breed and where they hibernate in winter.

On reflection it would be unwise to reject all advice out of hand, sometimes assistance is more than welcome. If, for example, anyone should come upon me in a life or death situation and the kiss of life is required to ensure my existence for a few more years, please feel free to administer such help as is immediately needed. If, however, you are a person suffering from chronic halitosis it might be best to just allow me to pass peacefully on.

These are my reflections on how I have viewed any problems that I have encountered through the years. Although in each generation people are gifted with problems to prevent them from becoming too bored, mostly they are the same type of problems that have beset us through the centuries. The venues change and in the past we had to have our nervous break-downs in solitude. But now thanks to the advent of television and the magnanimity of folks such as Kilroy, (unfortunately now shuffled to the depth of obscurity, or to wherever he has been shuffled and his passing should not be taken lightly) we can share our problems with audiences of millions and for good measure most of those millions will have a theory to offer whether we want it or not.

One word of warning, please do not assume that through my studies into the problems of other poor demented souls I am in anyway an expert. My capacity for listening to others in no way reflects my incapacity for proffering any lasting solutions. A friend of mine once told me that the next time I offered him any advice he would be asking his solicitor to be present. As I explained to him, my advice should not be rushed into with too much haste, it should be well considered before ever being acted upon. He then stated that this was the only piece of advice I'd ever given that made sense and from then on it would be the only piece he would follow. As for solicitors, my views are widely known and to elaborate further would almost certainly require the extortionate services *of* that demon profession. I have noticed in the past that people who have taken my advice have usually found themselves either in deeper trouble, in prison, or seated on a psychiatrist's sofa. However, I am not entirely convinced this has anything to do with my advice, it is more likely to be how they interpret it, and of course my advice is entirely free.

The small shops have gone into decline since the advent of the supermarket; some might say almost meltdown. There are some that have remained and even thrived. The local paper shops that incorporate confectionery and a few assortments of groceries seem to do fairly well. Then if they have the franchise for the Post Office and/or the Lottery, these shops can not only survive but flourish; this can only be good for the community. The existence of a shop in the area helps to create a sense of community.

Children were a great source for neighbours getting to know each other. Your children met their children and through these childhood meetings parents also got to know one another. Although times were hard and money was short, people seemed to have larger families; paradoxically now that people are more affluent families are getting smaller (in numeration that is, not in stature). When lots of children could not be afforded, lots were born; now they can be afforded family sizes have diminished.

Another type of business that has taken a nosedive since the late 40's, 50's, 60's and the early 70's is the small drop-in café for working men. There were many of these places just after the second world war, but since the seventies they have steadily declined. It was largely through the advent of bonus schemes and men becoming self-employed (obviously not the self-employed my mate enthused over) which caused this decline. Workers who were paid by a firm were termed as 'on the books'. This meant that their pay was regular, their tax was deducted by the employer who also ensured that their stamps were paid. When the worker went self-employed, although he may still have been getting work from his former employer, all these things he would have to do for himself. As a self-employed person he would be paid according to the work he produced, therefore he could no longer sit around in the café. The system worked well for both parties, but I suspect rather better for the employer. As for the café owner, I guess it never worked at all.

During the latter years of the war and the early years of peace the young generation were dancing to the big American bands: Glenn Miller, Tommy Dorsey, Benny Goodman and the like. The nation was laughing at Laurel and Hardy, Abbott and Costello, The Keystone Cops, The Marx Brothers and many more. We listened to Frank Sinatra, Bing (bub bub bub bub) Crosby, Tony Bennett, Dean Martin, Andy Williams and many more, all marketing great ballads. Every woman wept at 'Brief Encounter', this was a film in which a craggy faced doctor (Trevor Howard) got tied up (not literally, as bondage had not been invented then, but emotionally) with a housewife (Celia Johnson) who spoke with a voice that obviously pleased David Lean (the director) but had little in common with the way which most of the women whom I knew spoke.

In Norwich the two main dance halls were the Samson and Hercules and the Lido. Most of my mates went to the Lido as the Samson was a bit up market. If you got drunk at the Samson you got thrown out, if you got drunk at the Lido you blended in. Billy Duncan was the resident bandleader at the Lido, and occasionally he would use solo singers who came from the area. We would spend all our money, fall over because we had paralysed our brains by an excess of alcohol, vomit, then get on the big white telephone to God promising to mend our ways. God obviously believed it because as near as we were to death he would allow us to survive. He must have been a very patient God to forgive us every week, or maybe He just had a bad memory for faces, not that there were too many chances to see faces as they were usually buried in a white porcelain bog while imploring survival and redemption, or in extreme cases transcendence into paradise. The words 'Oh God let me die' were as familiar as was the weekly plight of wasteful degenerates with too much money to spend, too little brain for guidance in spending it, and heading in the general direction of a liver transplant.

Although I refer to The Lido as a dance hall it would be better recognised as a place in which to imbibe. In my younger days it would take me about six pints before I actually approached any likely candidates willing to share in my ability, and indulge me in the foolishness I called dancing. Normal sane accomplished dance-competent young girls would eye me as if they were in denial that I even existed and was asking them to accompany me. If they accepted it would result in their being dragged off to spend the next few minutes in total discomfiture followed by years in some institute trying to prove their sanity and the fact that the foolishness was only a temporary state of mental malfunction.

Although I attended these social functions called dances, it was not until a generous proportion of self doubt had subsided, assisted by bountiful amounts of alcohol releasing me from sanity and delivering me to a point where embarrassment was no longer a factor, that I was able to enter the fray. Even then my exploits were a shambling affair as I later realised. Aided by the alcohol, the feet completely free of the restrictions of the brain, I was now ready to shuffle into some hitherto untried routines. Any partner 'lucky' enough to be selected, not fleet enough to escape, or indeed foolish enough to accept, would soon arrive at the conclusion that I was either a dancing protégé or completely mad. By the time we actually arrived at the dance floor, leaving in our wake a few knocked over glasses, it was probably only a sense of duty, or the humiliation of going back to her 'loyal' jeering friends that prevented her from concluding the experience there and then.

After my experimental or improvised steps were exhausted and she was still there my confidence reached new heights. Ignoring any rhythm the band were trying to convey, my legs took on their own persona which neither of us could follow with any assurance that calamity would not ensue. Other couples, convinced that they were in the presence of genius, would allow a wide gap, while the less perceptive, unable to appreciate raw talent, could only make seditious comments.

'Watch it mate' was one of the lesser inflammatory remarks accompanied by violent threats that would have made a sober 'me' consider my actions and retire gracefully. However, my only intent was to demonstrate my dancing repertoire to its limits of ineptitude.

Most of my partners would explain their wish to terminate their experience by complaining of sore feet. I wondered why such a short period on the floor would cause them so much agony. Later a friend told me, 'Most of them were so awkward that they kept getting their feet under mine'. He apparently had the same problem.

They were great days - - as far as I remember. One of the strange effects that alcohol has is that even though it may be impossible to remember the night's events with any clarity, it is with unerring and absolute skill how, although you can't recall those events, you always find your way home.

This may seem a trivial matter to people who have never had to locate their base when it remains constant. However, sailors who, and let's face it, it does happen, get tipsy and can't remember whose round it is next, never fail to find their ship. Admittedly, some find it rather later than they should, but eventually they do manage to locate it. Drunken paralysis now invading the brain cells and taking those very cells captive will usually allow the body to function on automatic pilot. Balance, a thing that used to keep you upright, is now sadly just a memory and of course memory itself has also become a victim of the demon alcohol and is rapidly in the process of declining, hastily hurrying along to oblivion. Sailors can be falling down inebriated, but unerringly, even in foreign ports and far away lands, never lose their bearings when it comes to getting back to base. So if you lose your car and can't remember where you left it, just go and have a good old session at the local and you'll soon remember where it is. You obviously won't be able to drive it straight away, so just stick a label on it and make a note of the location so you don't forget where it is again, then walk home and pick it up when you're sober. There is another strange phenomenon with the effects of alcohol, the amalgamation of alcohol and dim wittedness seems to bring on a sense of immortality. You've just staggered three or so miles home, offended every driver who thought he was more entitled to be on the road than you, fallen over a few times, attempted antics which if tried when sober would put you in the accident unit at your nearest hospital, but here you are safe and sound at your own front door. You have pinpointed the house, the door is no problem but after having located the house and the door the biggest difficulty is finding the keyhole. You can stand outside for an indeterminable time, key in hand, encircling the keyhole without actually locating its exact position and irritated by some idiot shouting out, "Put-sum-f-----g 'airs round it mate."

To which you reply, still maintaining your dignity and articulacy, "Ya-an-up-yours you ass ole." Adding a few more sentences liberally sprinkled with words selected from the dictionary of life rather than The Oxford English version, and although it is only his behaviour that gives you a clue, you then hasten along challenging his parentage on his father's side. Luckily he's more intent on his curried supper than arguing over his lineage and ignores your remarks. But maybe he thinks, you know something he doesn't, after all he did referee a football match once amid suggestions . . . No! they were just upset because he had given what they considered a wrong decision. The next morning the operation which will please you most is not that you were able to find your way home without a scratch, but how, after about half an hour, you finally managed to outwit the keyhole. Those who were asleep just before your drunken arrival will wonder how such a simple manoeuvre could possibly cause such disruption.

In 1946 when things began to settle down, the population started to look for other means of entertainment. There were the public houses that were well frequented, but the cinema was the place where a young man could take his intended for an evening out. The children were also catered for in respect of having the picture houses opened to them on a Saturday morning.

The first of these picture houses to open on Saturday mornings was The Regal. The Regal stood on the corner of Dereham Road and Barn Road. On Saturday mornings these places were the union of bedlam and mayhem, no adult could have attended these places and maintained their sanity. The children were different inasmuch as they had only a sparse amount of sanity, if any at all, to maintain. Sanity was still a mystery to them and not to be taken too seriously. My sister and I would go to The Regal each Saturday morning where we would boo all the baddies, cheer all the goodies and get lost in a world of make-believe. At the end of the programme there would always be a serial just to get you there the next week. The first serial I remember was called 'Deadwood Dick and The Skull'. The Skull was the arch-enemy of Deadwood and would cause him much anxiety because he was always trying to kill our hero Deadwood. Each week the Skull (he was called the Skull not for his cranial expertise, but because he wore a black outfit on which was painted a skull) would set Deadwood some life-threatening problem: he would try to have him shot, pushed over a cliff, or set on fire, in fact The Skull was always devising ways of eliminating Deadwood. Each week we agonised over the fate of our beloved hero. Each week Deadwood would (a bit like Edward Wood Wood, isn't it?) escape from this life or death situation. One week you could have sworn away your eternal soul on the death of DD as he plunged over the cliff ably assisted by The Skull, but the next week he was seen to jump clear before the stagecoach went over.

Exciting! I nearly peed my pants, but this was about as good as it got not peeing my pants. That certainly would not have been too good as I only had two pairs and my cinema pair were my school pair and also my Sunday pair. I think peeing them would definitely have put a strain on the tenuous relationship I enjoyed with my mum, especially at times when my clothes got so physically abused. The short fuse of my mother (already mentioned) would almost certainly have detonated her dynamite in the event of urinated pants and possibly have caused an explosion of dramatic proportions, with me being the victim of the fall-out. No, it was the excitement of Deadwood going (or nearly going) over the edge, although it must be said I know just how that feels. Even intellectually impaired as we were, we soon began to realise that even DD couldn't be that lucky every week. However, to bring this saga to an end, Dick finally unmasked the villain. There were so many red herrings along the way to the end of this story that I would have staked even money on the skull being my own sister behind the mask. Ultimately it turned out to be some middle-aged guy making a mess of trying to look ferocious. Unfortunately, when the mask was removed he looked quite benign, more like my Uncle Arthur who wouldn't have hurt a fly, so maybe DD had misjudged him entirely.

Some time later The Regent opened its doors to the juvenile ragamuffins. Having made sure that Deadwood was now free from the clutches of The Skull, we (my sister and I) changed our allegiance. Had The Skull not have been unfrocked I, in all sincerity, would still have been attending The Regal, up until the time they turned it into a bingo hall anyway. We now took our vocal talents to The Regent. They also had serials which kept us in a state of euphoric excitement and drew us back each week. But their serials lacked the sheer grit, determination and death defiance of Deadwood Dick. I can hardly recall their nature so pallid were they in comparison.

The ABC (once called The Regent) was kind of up market, I always remembered it as the place where children had not been allowed in unless accompanied by an adult, or a dog handler; now here we were with the freedom of the place for about two hours. I think the management must have eaten some loco grass: from the banishment of all, or unaccompanied little ones, we, the unwashed, were now allowed in and anarchy ruled. My sister and I were welcomed into the brotherhood, and to be politically correct, the sisterhood (or maybe it's the siblinghood) of the Grand Order of ABC-ers.

At the ABC we were able to purchase badges for a minimal amount and were entitled to a membership card. We also learnt a little ditty that went something like this, (all together now!)

> We are the boys and girls well known as,
> We're minors of the ABC,
> And every Saturday all line up, to see the films we love
> We shout aloud with glee,
> We love to laugh and have a singsong,
> Just a happy crowd are we,
> We're all pals together, we're minors of the ABC.

After this first rendering would come the insane request, now just one more time (come on, I can't hear you). Deaf daft or what? Bugger me! they could hear you in Ipswich if the wind was right. For anyone who is not familiar with Ipswich, it's a village just down the A147, but very rarely visited by normal folk due to the danger of attack by their in-bred population which forms quite a large percentage of the community. It was once thought that they had a football team there but that was less foot and more of the other half of the thought.

There was always a kindly uncle to tend the children's needs (that's at the ABC not at Ipswich, although Ipswich does have uncles, but mostly they have cousins who spend much time kissing, or so I've been informed). I think The ABC's Uncle was Charlie, or Arthur, or something, I really can't remember, but if at some stage I get drunk it may come back to me and then I'll get back to you, or better still your whole family could make up names and then vote to see who's thought of the best name; play it at Christmas why don't you? Of course you could get out more. Anyway those were great days, you can keep your Adolfs,

Benitos and your Heinrichs, give me good old Uncle Charlie, or whoever he was, any day.

I can't remember the last time I attended the Saturday children's cinema; it's a bit like being unable to recall the last time you played a game. The last time was the time you never thought would come, then suddenly there it is, gone. However, I'm fortunate enough to remember the last time I kicked a football. It was about four years ago, I was just explaining to Sam, my grandson, that in order to kick the ball correctly, perfect balance was required. At which point I duly fell over and broke my wrist. The wrist has now healed but my pride will forever be a tragedy of circumstance and a victim to misfortune, or maybe it was an inability to realise that whereas the body has over matured the brain has gone in the opposite direction. That is another thing about the age thing; my grandson (Sam) is awkward, no one in their right mind, or has had the misfortune to be involved in his ways or had the good fortune just witness his ways, could deny it. But that is the same with all boys, I myself went through an early age of awkwardness, of which the memory now makes me cringe. However, from that age (whatever that age was) I went to a period of that which might be termed as an intelligent stable world of conformity (not that I feel young boys should be saddled with stabled conformity, they'd be rushed off to the doctors with their mothers imploring immediate attention leading to hospitalisation and intensive care) in which if I were to perceive any action that might be termed as imprudent or unwise I would avoid it. But now, as with trying to demonstrate my foot-balling prowess to my grandson, irresponsibility seems to have returned to wreak vengeance with interest after all those years of neglect. Sam was obviously quite delighted that his granddad was equally as vulnerable as himself to the misfortunes and vagaries of life. The rest of the family obviously viewed my actions as just another part in the confirmation of my ongoing trip down the road towards slops, senility and Zimmer frame and advised me that survival may well be reliant on something a bit tamer or I may well be hopping into a coffin rather than hopping over it.

Chapter Nineteen

I would just like to mention a few people instrumental in our present day well being, for apart from the changes in industry, family size and various life-changing inventions, there were also discoveries. Discoveries, such as electricity by Michael Faraday. Michael Faraday was the man who invented the dynamo, so we then had the beginning of the electricity industry. From this sprung all the joys of watching Corrie, Eastenders, Neighbours, Home and Away, etc, etc: etcetera, isn't that one of the most impressive and expedient words? Not only can it be shortened to 'etc' for economy purposes, but how convenient it is when the memory suddenly fails to deliver on the requirement of something a bit more substantial, or boredom dictates an immediate end to a rapidly growing disenchantment with a subject. But even the shortened version etc still retains a certain air of respectability. Thought I'd just mention that while I tried to remember *whither* I was bound. Neatly avoiding a preposition to end the sentence with. Ah yes! Faraday. Mr Faraday has a lot to answer for, or rather for which to answer.

Alexander Graham Bell: Graham Bell invented the telephone. He was a Scot determined to make himself the biggest posthumous nuisance ever, and – let's face it – whom hasn't he annoyed with his bloody infuriating contraption. Every time you get into the bath it rings (the phone not the bath). Every time you go for a quiet siesta, brrr bloody brrr, off it goes. Alexander Bell left Scotland to go to America but no one could understand what the hell he was on about. He got so lonely that he thought, 'I know, I'll invent a method whereby I can talk once again to people advanced in culture'. Unfortunately, he got through to Scotland instead of England, but fortunately an Englishman answered the phone. A gentleman called Watson who, incidentally, had just got into the bath, heard the brrr brrr, hurried down and picked up the strange looking instrument from where the sound emanated and heard 'Ah wants ta see ya, de ye ken' (note Scottish accent). This is recorded as the first intelligible words spoken on the telephone which I feel may well infringe the Trades Description Act.

An off-shoot to the standard telephone is the mobile. Now it seems that society can't manage without this little beast, it is to be seen and heard throughout the land and has replaced barking dogs, cats pissing in your garden and litter louts urinating up your fence as the biggest and latest nuisance to invade our lives. It is also the most dangerous of contraptions apart from the nuclear bomb, but whereas the bomb announces its arrival to selective areas this little piece of aggravation seems quite indiscriminate in its judgement of whom to upset.

Only the other day I was strolling along at peace with the world blissfully unaware of the intrusion that was about to crash into my life. Caught in a daydream and about to engage in some pleasantries with Liz Hurley I hardly noticed this big fellow approaching. As we were about to pass each other, out of the blue he bellowed, **"HELLO."** It was a foghorn like voice that sent shivers down my back. Startled out of my wits I almost jumped off the pavement and into the path of a speeding juggernaut. Trembling, I gathered myself together, had that lorry have hit me someone else (like the paramedics) would have been doing the necessary gathering. I prepared for the assault that I felt was about to follow when suddenly it came to me he was phoning someone. As I gradually recovered I could hear him shouting as he disappeared into the distance,

"I'll be home in about ten minutes." I'd been nearly deafened, almost run over, virtually scared witless, teetered on the brink of a coronary and all because this insensitive loud-mouthed bastard wished to inform his phone mates on the other end that he would be seeing them in ten minutes. Are we becoming a nation of complete morons? Or is the threatened brain damage by mobile phone beginning to kick in?

I'm still not entirely convinced that he needed to traumatise me into a state of nervousness approaching a call for psychiatric reports, and possibly a long term stay at some sanatorium, to impart that which seemed to me at the time to be just an interim report on his progress towards home and to someone on the other end of the phone to whom he would be delivering an in depth and fully comprehensive account of his electrifying and stimulating venture while they were apart. I bet he wouldn't mention the fact that he had almost devastated a senior citizen's life and nearly encumbered some poor lorry driver with loads of paper work making out some completely unnecessary accident report.

After I'd recovered I thought of ringing my MP and getting this phone-obsessed maniac conscripted into the army. Possibly sent to some foreign spot where they torture people who scare old age pensioners like me. They might even consider an operation where they stuff his nuisance mobile phone up his---. Better stop there before my blood pressure goes on a jaunt to unacceptable heights.

John Logie Baird's invention is probably the one that has changed our lives more than any other in the world. John Logie Baird had a vision and turned it into a television. He also invented the video recorder. We can't blame him too much as he only worked on a project that Michael Faraday had started by his discovery of electricity.

Neither can he be blamed for the rubbish broadcasts, and think of all the enjoyment we get from whingeing about them; why! we probably get more enjoyment from whingeing than from the actual programmes.

For labour-saving devices I suppose the greatest is the washing machine. The dishwasher is another great labour-saving device or, as it is sometimes known, the husband. Women in the early part of the last century never had the luxury, or the luck, to have 'new man' to do the household chores. These were things that changed lives.

Medicine in the 19th and 20th centuries advanced by an enormous amount. First we had Madame Curie, born in Poland in 1867, who along with her husband discovered the radioactive elements radium and polonium. They promoted the use of radium as a treatment against cancer. In 1934 Madame Curie died of leukaemia through the large doses of radioactivity to which she had been exposed. She is the only person to win Nobel Prizes in two different sciences – Physics and Chemistry.

Alexander Fleming: Alexander Fleming, who was a British bacteriologist, discovered penicillin in 1928. This was the first of the antibiotics. He noticed it inhibited the growth of bacteria in a culture dish, but it was two other scientists, Howard Florey and Ernst Chain, who developed it into a medicine. It was used to save countless lives during the 1939/45 war and this in spite of the fact that every one else was determined to *take* as many as possible. They were awarded joint Nobel Prizes for their efforts. Now, in the 21st century the ordinary bugs which were sensitive to penicillin have learned a thing or two, they have attended fitness classes and trained to such an extent that they have become super-bugs.

Louis Pasteur: Louis Pasteur was my kind of guy. Born in France in 1822, died in 1895, he was a scientist whose most important discovery was of micro-organisms (no not orgasms granny, steady down). Louis Pasteur discovered that if wine was heated gently the heat would prevent the wine from turning into something akin to vinegar. This method is called pasteurisation. I personally have drunk a few bottles that were obviously oblivious to the very existence of Louis Pasteur and would have been better served on fish and chips and in much smaller quantities than I ill advisedly swallowed. Louis Pasteur also applied the same criterion to milk, but it was not so much appreciated by the drinking classes as it was when applied to wine.

Medicine has travelled quite some distance when we consider how it was in the nineteenth century and even up until the early twentieth century. Imagine going to sea on a man-o-war in the days of Admiral Nelson and prior to that. There you sat having a pint of beer when in walked eight or so blokes looking like mobile settees. It would only be the smile on their faces which would give you a clue to their particular species, so although no other clue would be present and it is a fact that it is only homo-sapiens who smile, it was a sure give-away that they were humanoid, of a sort. They'd buy you a few pints and then invite you to accompany them on their next cruise. In spite of your protestations on your inability to accept their kind and charitable offer due to other commitments they would insist and so you became their shipmates for the indefinite future.

Great! a free sea voyage, forget the rough seas, the maggots in the food and the every day vomiting all featuring and adding spice to the journey, you could be entering into an experience only those who were in the right place at the right time would be experiencing. And before you can say 'lead balls' there you are surrounded by them. They're coming in like a night at the twelve lane local bowling alley. Unfortunately, they're not that orderly in their rush to inflict pain on you, in fact the only order they have and the only similarity with bowling is to knock over a few pins. The problem is that the only things that come anywhere near to looking like pins are arms and legs, and because of their lack of experience in the matter of what to knock over, they are suddenly aiming at you. But this is where the medicine comes in; there is none. One of these big balls, because of the lead poison factor affecting its brain, has decided that your leg needs some adjustment, but being not of the greedy breed, only take it off half way up to the knee. Two days later the stump you are left with begins to swell, smell and turn a sort of florescent green. Now there's nothing wrong with florescent green it's just that you don't want half of your left leg that colour, looking so bulging and smelling like a dung heap.

You show this to the ship's captain who advises a visit to the surgeon (or as he is better known, old saw bones). Anyone with an inclination towards that which may be termed squeamish should turn away, or close their eyes now. Remember, this is a time before anaesthetics had been discovered, so no ether or nitrous oxide (laughing gas), in fact from this time on the only thing remotely to do with laughter would be as you toppled over every time you tried to kick some cheeky little sod's arse because he insisted on calling you stumpy, on top of which you'd forgotten there was only air where the lower part of your other leg once was.

"Right, let's 'ave a look," says old saw bones our resident surgeon prodding the bulging, reddened, puss filled sac. Our resident surgeon is really the ship's carpenter seconded into the ranks of the medical profession simply by the process of elimination, this process being, that as he *was* the ship's carpenter he was the only one with a saw. Other crew members had sharp knives all very useful for slicing through flesh and soft tissue of the enemy where bone severing would not be required, but slightly under qualified for bone gnawing. However, the carpenter's saw was not only sharp, but jagged and quite familiar with hacking through obstinate wood, so obstinate bone would cause it little problem.

Now we have our victim (sorry patient) and our butcher (I mean surgeon) and a saw perfectly adequate for ripping through the toughest bone. What we need now is a quick acting, pain quelling, nerve soothing agent. What better than a bottle of rum? So our patient is plied with enough good old navy rum to fell the strongest of men, even an elephant should one be found and requiring it. The surgeon, because of his weak stomach for blood, will finish the bottle off. Now we have a re-enactment of a scene from history and of course good imagery of physical suffering and mental grief, and the patient won't be feeling too ecstatic either.

Our brave seaman will now be, hopefully, 'impervious' to pain, but old saw-bones will be impervious to our hero's cries for mercy anyway. With the help of four or five of the fittest, finest and strongest of maties to reassure our gallant champion that it won't hurt, and to hold him down just in case a slight miscalculation of the pain factor has been made, our intrepid carpenter-cum-surgeon will now commence with that which is required in order to prevent the fungus spreading further up our friend's leg. In the interest of humanity and just to explain that there are others less lucky than him, our saw handler offers some comforting words "Well at least you're alive," a rather moot point at this stage of the proceedings.

The look of despair and fear radiating from the drunken stupor which now masks a face that is hardly recognisable as anything human gives the impression of "I'm not too bloody sure if 'alive' holds any advantage." The operation goes quite well, for the surgeon, who is by this time in the middle of the voyage and has become quite adept at this kind of sortie into amputations. The flesh has been severed and some loose skin, hanging like an overlong elastic thigh bandage, is turned up, this is to fold back later on in the proceedings, this will be required assuming the patient has not expired aided by trauma and alcoholic poisoning in the meantime. Using the sharp serrated edged implement the fearless surgeon grinds through the bone causing two of the not so resilient aides to rush to the ship's side and deliver their latest meal into the mouths of waiting voracious fish. The blood and pus are by now flowing quite liberally and the wound must have a cortisone applied to prevent infection.

"Get the tar heated," cries the good carpenter-cum-surgeon. The tar, when sufficiently heated, is applied to the stump and a horrendous hiss, as the blood and pus evaporate into an acrid smelling vapour, can just be heard above the patient's plea for deliverance and the thunderous noise of the intolerant waves dashing against the ship's side. The fluids congeal and the flow is staunched. Now there is no likelihood, or I should say less likelihood of infection, the surplus skin is sewn into place and from what is left of the anaesthetic (rum) a celebratory toast is offered to the King/Queen.

Why you may ask was the King/Queen toasted? Well! it was tradition and was only right and proper that when you had given a part of your leg on behalf of the monarch he/she should be allowed to reap some reward for allowing you that privilege and honour.

These things which I reveal are only taken from stories handed down through the tales of old seamen and the well-informed historians. I myself, and I speak with a heart full of regret, was never privileged to lose a leg in the service of my country, and I feel the telling may suffer because of it. However, I can say that on several occasions I have been legless, but that was mainly through the use (or possibly misuse would be a term more appropriate) of rum as a social stimulus rather than a pain killer and after several visits to the urinals and a few hours in a comatose state the legs returned to some kind of sanity and were, thankfully, still attached to my body. On reflection I don't think that counts too much as bravery, more like inane silliness and an inability to realise that when you're slipping to the floor instead of sitting on a stool it's time to go on to lemonade.

Then there was the art of dentistry which also benefited from the discovery of nitrous oxide. The pain of toothache may not approach the pain or trauma of having your leg hacked off, but it is still quite an ordeal. However, imagine the ordeal before Alexander Fleming came up with penicillin. In those days it would not be some trained specialist sensitive to the needs of the individual, no indeed, it would be the barber in civvy street and the ever-durable carpenter-cum-surgeon-cum-dentist in the navy.

Teeth, given to the rigours of every day munching and crunching on things they are not at times too conversant with, will, in a fit of ill will, go bad. Now that's ok, but then they decide that they aren't going to go without putting up a gallant show, and to do this they need to inflict as much pain as possible in the short time left to them. They know in their heart that they're no match for the leg-gnawing-thing, trauma wise, but in the pain scenario they can offer quite a good fight. They also know another ploy; invite an abscess to stay for a few days. Let him bring along his full bag of tricks; the redness, the swelling, the pus and his own bucket load of throbbing. That's where Alexander Fleming comes in. Penicillin hates Mr Abscess and his buddy Mr Pus, so now Mr Tooth could only have the services of Messrs Abscess and Pus for a limited period.

Prior to this, to remove a tooth which so obviously offended, it was necessary to do it without any pain killing drugs. It is not pleasant to contemplate, but there you were in agony, when you discovered that the cure was going to eclipse the discomfort by a very large amount, but this pain had to be ended. The dentist, ignoring the fact that through your life you had mostly tried to avoid pain, but pain would now be invading your life without the advantage of any meaningful numbing process, would begin his work. With his sturdy knee delicately ensconced in your stomach and his hairy hand (grasping a pair of pliers normally reserved for wrenching obstinate nuts from rusty bolts) stuffed down your throat, the tug of war is on.

After much sweating and swearing, grunting, grinding and gouging finally out comes the offending tooth. Then, the last thing you needed to know, "Oh! dear! it's broken off, never mind I'll soon get that little old stub out." The carpenter-cum-dentist uttered his words with the joviality of a man about to gift his victim with pleasure rather than more pain. Big, sharp, indefinable instrument in hand, off he'd go prodding, poking, digging and delving just searching for the last surviving remnants of ivory, or stub as he called it. At last he'd finally got it cornered and despite desperate resistance the fraction of offending tooth finally succumbed, as, in all probability, would your sanity at this point.

Now, and in no small measure, we must offer our thanks to those dedicated men of medical research, namely the Flemings of the past, who have made the removal of teeth much more tolerable. A hole in our bank account is the greatest pain we now have to endure. Dentists usually make sure we aren't too deprived of pain when they offer their bills and when they utter the phrase "Ahhh! yes there is quite a large cavity there," it's never too clear whether he's referring to your tooth, or making a prediction on the not too distant health of your bank account. With the amount of teeth God supplied we need to be vigilant with our savings as visits to the dentists will be regular and rewarding experiences, that is regular for us and rewarding for the dentist.

Because of a few dedicated men and women who devoted their lives, in the nineteenth and twentieth centuries, to the relief of pain we are now able to lose various parts of our bodies, especially teeth, with as much enjoyment as we can muster, secure in the knowledge that when the dentists says "This won't hurt a bit," and provided you are not too attached to your money, it won't. So all in all we can endure the experience in a much more relaxed attitude than our forefathers, or for that matter our foremothers.

As a person who finds pain unbearable, even in small doses, my gratitude and appreciation goes to all those scientists whose efforts deserve my unreserved thanks and I would like to record my deepest admiration, to those people of the past, who in their own way, through dedication and hard work have made pain a thing to look forward to. My heartfelt THANKS.

Before I leave the subject of pain there is something else I've noticed; over the past few years the teeth that I'm now left with have entered into a pact with my jaw and their common enemy seems to be my tongue. Some mornings as I teeter between sleep and wakefulness, wondering about the crucial points of theology, or whether I am prepared for the walk to the bathroom, my jaw will, without warning, suddenly snap shut and my teeth will attack my tongue. This is an involuntary manoeuvre planned and executed solely by the pact of jaw and teeth and without consultation with my brain. At this point theology takes a back seat to excruciating pain and theology becomes momentarily irrelevant as my body is jerked abruptly towards attentiveness. The reason for this onslaught is not immediately apparent because as far as I'm aware my tongue is quite a good-natured little organ whose sole role (sole role; that's very poetic) is to manoeuvre my food into places where my teeth can access it and chew it without eating half my face away. We can't have maliciously marauding mandibles and molars munching merrily away at their own tongue, that is really very unethical, and bloody painful too. So if there are any scientists out there who can explain the reason why one's teeth, which have acted responsibly for seventy odd years, quite unexpectedly take on this rogue persona and attempt to shred one's own tongue, please do so. Maybe those men of science would like to devote a few hours in order to arrive at a solution before my teeth decide to attack on some other flank and completely devour my whole body.

On the subject of various medicinal aids, which I take to ensure my hard earned cash doesn't fall too quickly into the hands of extravagant little ones with little knowledge of how to treat it, namely my grandchildren, I revere those medical aids with a respect they so richly deserve. Never ignoring the fact that if I don't, some day they will throw a fit of temper and I will be no more. However, one thing which I found very worrying was that on arriving home the other day I discovered a letter pushed through my door which stated that there was a high level of police activity in the neighbourhood due to the concern they had over the drug issue, so not to worry. Worry! I should say not, it had been so long since I'd seen a policeman in the area I doubt I would have recognised him/her anyway, and now we were about to be inundated with a 'high level' of them so I expect they let them out on certain auspicious occasions. Everyone in the neighbourhood had apparently received a leaflet, every house, flat and bordello in the area had one, even those who were using or supplying drugs, except the local pharmacist, I think they forgot about him. This leaflet warned the residents to watch out for 'users'. It read; 'Be on the look out for hard drugs users,' it then gave the criteria to take as evidence of their activity on which to base your suspicions: vacant looks, some staggering when walking and fidgeting about on the doorstep for a long period of time. After reading it I came to the conclusion that, unless I'm very careful, I'm going to be spending rather a lot of time enjoying the company of the local plod on night duty trying to explain away the reasons why I'm vacant, stagger about, arrive home late and have to fidget for an interminable amount of time in order to get the key into the lock. I can envisage some nosey neighbour getting on the phone to the local cop shop and just for the hell of it getting me hauled in for a drug test. Bearing in mind the amount of medication I need to take just to see the sun set and hopefully to see it rise again the next day, I should think It will be a pretty exhaustive test and a very long stay. Should Osama bin Laden get caught at the same time it's a fair bet that he'll be out before me.

In the process of aging, deafness is another one of those irritations which follow you until you slow down, and then ambush you while you aren't concentrating. From hearing a pin drop on the planet Mars your hearing regresses to a point where you're lucky if you can hear when (or rather if) someone offers you a free drink. However, deafness can be an asset at times, it can relieve you from questions you prefer not to answer, give immunity from household tasks and allow you an in-depth insight into people's view of you. It can save you pounds in cash if you can't hear the excessive demands the grandchildren are making on your bank account utterly convinced that you are the sole owner of that establishment called The Bank of England. Deafness also gives the notion of fatuous foolishness which places you in the category of the sub-normal, therefore you can avoid too much scrutiny of your behaviour. It seems to give the impression that you are embracing the imbecilic faith and this will give rise to alarm in your family and much merriment to strangers. In my case and with my past record, fleeting moments of madness could always be observed, especially during periods when the moon was at its fullest. Now it is the sane moments which are fleeting.

Most other ailments that attend us as we wind down on life's activities, such as poor eyesight or forgetfulness, and a weakening constitution (which will be fine providing you don't eat too many Indians or Chinese - takeaways obviously not people) can be endured. But as soon as someone mentions deafness, you always get a childish chorus of, 'WHAT?' and then, because they all think it's original, funny and clever, they will kill themselves laughing, unfortunately 'kill themselves' is metaphorical language; bloody jackasses or WHAT?

Another thing; just before I drop off to sleep I've heard a little unintelligible nasal noise which sounds like the word 'um', and then oblivion until my bladder fills to over-capacity. This is quite acceptable if I still have the ability to arrive at the toilet before the overfill overflows, the worrying thing is if the overflow flows over before I reach the bog. This would be a condition called incontinence; incidentally, with incontinence you should make sure you have a good absorbent mop, plenty of disinfectant and a change of bed linen at all times, and of course a sturdy pair of rubber pants would definitely be an asset. Although I've written incidentally, the condition is a touch more serious than the word *incidental* would imply, so anyone reading this, who may live long enough to luxuriate in the tender warmth of their own urine, should be prepared for the worst and hope for the best. As luck will have it I still wake up before I actually piss the bed and mostly make the sanctuary of the bog and avoid the afore mentioned cleaning paraphernalia.

When people of my age were young, back in the late thirties and on into the forties the language was quite dissimilar to that which is spoken today. Not the entire verbal communication, but certainly a few extra words have come into popularity which were never even heard of then, others have had their meanings changed. Take grass, (not literally please) that was the stuff your father made you cut if you got caught idling around at the wrong time, now it's used to help you idle around at any old time. The butcher would say 'Would you like a joint for the weekend?' and you just knew he was referring to meat. Now if you say 'Oh yes please that would be lovely,' you don't know if you'll be cooking, flying or arrested.

'Flying saucers' only crossed the kitchen until the 1940's and then only when your mother had enough of putting up with what your father had had too much of putting down. Suddenly these flying saucers (again a 40's phrase) were to be seen flying even before dad had had his fill. The 'lager lout' (1980's) could enjoy seeing his 'Tupperware' (another addition to the 40's) fly without 'her indoors' (1980's) propelling it. The greatest asset to man's libido came with the 'Miniskirt' (mid 1960's) this transferred the roving eye into the transfixed eye as the male in his never ending search for art became aware of parts of women seldom hitherto seen. From the restrictions of paying 7s-6d for a marriage licence, a visit to the priest, a fortune on sartorial correctness, providing a banquet and all in order to keep the relatives and in-laws in a state of euphoria (or at least from killing each other) man could now view every aspect of the goods he was pursuing without actually placing himself on the doorstep of the Marshall House.

We had a 'cultural revolution' (in the 60's) when people turned into 'Hippies' (in the 70's) and devoted their time to growing their hair long and making love; both activities vigorously pursued leaving little time for much else. 'Yuppies' (80's) in contrast, became 'workaholics' (70's) and they had *very little* time to make babies (in spite of the miniskirt incentive) as they were too busy making 'bread' (70's), and so they had to rely on the 'test-tube' (late 70's) to replace natural procreation. For the rest of us came the infuriating Rubik's cube, this little device could send you into a world of frustration only rivalled in its complexity by my trying to cut my toe nails, which incidentally seems to be getting much further out of reach with each passing week. I've come to the conclusion that either my arms are getting shorter or my legs are getting longer and if my arms don't stop getting shorter or my legs don't stop getting longer I'll end up with very short arms, very long legs and toe nails resembling stilts. The word 'gay' from gaiety indicated splendour, joy, mirth, brightness a sense of fun, but then became a sexual connotation, so I expect although it is, in all probability, a bit more serious in regards to relationships for some who have that kind of inclination, it still retains its fun for some.

For the sportsman there was the Fosbury flop: this was a method of high jumping created by Dick Fosbury (1968 Olympic Games) this revolutionised the high jump, but don't get this confused with the other high jump dad will be for should he encounter the 'Brewers flop' or as it is mostly known, the Brewers droop. There were no user drugs, a fix was something which applied when putting up a shelf, or something you were in when it fell down as soon as you placed anything on it. There were no pills called uppers or downers only aspirins for dads as they tried to duck the incessant sexual demands of mums. I think 'mothers' is more appropriate, mums seems too cuddly a word to associate with anything as physical as that (you know what) act. The word pot was only applied to a receptacle used for cooking, or to a receptacle placed under the bed, and usually referred to as a gazzunder. Unfortunately, gazzunder is one word we've almost lost due in part to 'en-suite bedrooms' and also, the 'incontinence pad' (dates unknown, but certainly after Aunt Edna's time; trust me) must take a few plaudits. We have retained its near cousin the 'piss pot' but this is only to refer to people we aren't too fond of as in 'yer-a-right p p', although some people prefer toss pot and as I am often referred to by both names I personally have no preference and feel equally at home with either. In 1992 the Queen had her 'Annus Horribilis' and when Margaret Thatcher came to power, not wishing to have the Queen's subjects feel deprived, she made sure we were all allowed to indulge in a few annus horriblises or maybe it's horribilii.

Xerox; we never knew anything with spelling such as that and to be honest even now I'm distrustful of it, it sounds more like some sexually *transmitted* disease and not a mechanically *transmitted* message. Coke (Coca-Cola) was a new concept in soft drinks, it had a texture of a smoothness and a taste of sweetness never before experienced. It contained an effervescent sensation with the bubbles twinkling around the tongue and a tang which had the taste buds tingling with delight. That was when I was young and was able to extract every small and delicate detail of flavour that my taste and olfactory desires explored. Now it is a sad fact that not only do the delicate tastes avoid my senses, the ones which I would have thought, in my prime to be overpowering, I'm now able to handle with only a fraction of the enjoyment I once did. Prior to this coke was not to be sniffed at, it was just a fuel, now we can sniff it, drink it and burn it; that's progress for you. People of my generation were born into a world where the temptations were not so great as they are in today's world, there were no such things as 'user drugs' only drugs for medicinal purposes. There were no paedophiles or at least none that we knew of, weed was a wild unloved plant which spread from your neighbour's garden to your dad's and never from your dad's into your neighbour's. The pill had not as yet come, so dad had to be very careful when *he* did. Actually I'm pretty grateful that the scientists waited until after my arrival before introducing the pill, or I may well have finished up as a nasty discoloured blob on the sheet of passion, or flushed down the bog with obscene haste on some cold frosty morning.

On August the 6th 1945 we learned of two names; Enola Gay and Little Boy. These were names that the world would never forget. Little Boy was the first atomic bomb to be dropped. It was dropped on Hiroshima a city in Japan and Enola Gay was the plane that delivered it. Then on August the 9th, Bock's Car dropped 'Fat Man' the second atomic bomb, on the city of Nagasaki in Japan obliterating it with this cataclysmic great wind of evil. The shock and horror reverberated around the world as

Hiroshima and Nagasaki were blown apart; completely wiped out. Everyone thought this was the ultimate in delivering death and destruction, but we had all forgotten about the nuclear scientists, they had other ideas. They came up with the H Bomb, which could kill even more people. The problem is that if these weapons get any more destructive there will be no one left to kill. Of course the up side is that neither will there be anyone left to advance destruction further.

The devil's wind of destruction on such a massive scale is too horrific for the mind to take in. Paradoxically, maybe the threat of such devastation has become the umbrella of safety from complete obliteration. Although man, in his infinite wisdom, had at last found a way to kill tens of thousands of people at one fell stroke, in all probability he had also come to appreciate the result of using it is too ghastly even for him to contemplate. But it is more likely that those people who started wars in the name of religion, greed, or for power, suddenly realised that they too would benefit nothing. They could not hide from the horrors of these immensely powerful weapons of destruction. Delivering total annihilation these new weapons would not grant them freedom from destruction and they would now be in the front line where hitherto only soldiers and innocents were.

Children of the 1940's and 50's played on streets that were safer than today's streets, there was very little traffic and the main danger came from getting too near the horse's rear should he be inclined toward a serious attack of morning ablutions, or practising his kicking. This was the way we were in my childhood and then on through to the 21st century. My generation saw a world war which devastated major cities and major countries culminating in the annihilation of two cities and the killing of tens of thousands of people. Those of us who survived the terrible events of 1939/45 and the generations which followed owe a great debt to the men who were forced into a war that was not of their making, nor of their wishing. It was a war that made sure that democracy would carry on throughout the world, or at least for those who wanted democracy. It preserved the rights of men to speak in freedom, to worship in freedom and to walk in freedom without fear from racists, bigots or bullies; at least that was the perceived world. True democracy does not begin at any specific point in time, neither does it end on some nominated day, it needs constant nurturing and can only be preserved by good people who are aware of injustice and then act to maintain democracy.

We, played our games, fought pretend Indians and killed imaginary Germans, so even in our games war was a prominent feature, but like cartoon characters, we always recovered sufficiently to fight another day. Although there were not the electronic games of today's generation we did have vast areas in which to roam and friends with whom we shared our time. These friends were total and committed, that is to say, some were total and some should have been committed.

The city's boundaries were not so far spread in the 40's and 50's but now urban eats rural at an alarming rate and the countryside gets further and further away. In the 40's and 50's we had one mile to walk or cycle and we were among the trees and meadows, the rivers and flowing streams. There were no cars to transport us, so we biked, bussed, or walked. We whiled away our days in idyllic surroundings, free from the cloistered restrictions and the dangers, whether imaginary or real, that our children and our children's children face.

After childhood, and especially in the forces, we meet people who would lay down their lives for their friends and at times do, but we lose touch with these people and find very few people we can honestly call our friends. When I started to write this book two people whom I'm proud to call my friends are Kenny and Marian Thaxton. Unfortunately, it was mentioned in conversation that it was my intention to try to write down observations and memories of life as seen through my eyes. Here I will demonstrate just one of the reasons, and there are many, why I believe their friendship goes above and beyond the normal of that which would be expected even of the most devoted friends. Were I to casually mention to anyone else that I intended to put into print any of my life's experiences, a great rush towards the emigration office would ensue with a backlog of people applying for passports. Embarrassment would compel friends of a lesser inclination, or indeed of a nervous disposition, to hot-foot it for the hills.

Not so with Kenny and Marian, no sir, why, they even want to take part in it. And that is the quality of their friendship, there are no limits to which they will not go to support me.

It only required the tentative remark "I'm thinking of writing a book," and straight away, ignoring the fact that this could be the end of their civilised world, they implored

"Are we in your book?" grasping my ankles as I hurriedly tried to make my escape.

"No you bloody aren't," I emphatically replied, dragging myself free of their iron grasp.

"To recount tales from our murky pasts would lead us all into prison, deportation, or even on to the gallows."

"Don't worry about it," they shouted "we want to be those prisoners deported to the galley."

"No, no," I replied, as I scurried off down the path "the gallows, the bloody gallows, this will be no picnic."

I could still hear their plaintive cries as they reverberated around their close, entreating me to "Stop . . . stop."

"Please . . . please," they beseeched, "stop." Had I have realised that they were requesting me to stop allowing them to free themselves from the car door which had entrapped them I would have stopped two miles before I did (in spite of what they think).

However, I will say that if I wanted people to be in my corner in any given situation, Kenny and Marian you are the people I would choose; there are no greater friends than you two, you are the tops.

After much consideration I could only think of five other people who I would mention as true friends; Maurice Curchin and John Rogers have been my life-long friends. They have always been there any time a favour was needed and never have they refused or made excuses. Two others are Terry and John Whall. Although we see little of each other these days I know they would not mind if I included them among my friends. To all of them I say, thanks for your support whenever it was called for. Anne England is the last I will mention, but this is a round robin and not a list. You, Anne, have been my navigator through the chill waters of spelling and grammar, steering me clear of the icebergs which await the unwary voyager, or in my case the reckless and incautious voyager. Also, you have given your time freely to proof read my material. It is thanks to your pedantic attitude, and in spite of my ability to delve into an inexhaustible well of foolishness, this piece of work is intelligible albeit with the loss of half the rain forests of South America when you disallowed certain small details to my otherwise impeccable work. So a million thanks to you and to the others I have mentioned, I'd not sacrifice your friendships for money. At this point I would also like to mention, Mrs Lesley Barrett (from the Three C's). Ms Val Thomas (from Thorpe High) and Mr Ken Voyce (from Wensum Lodge). All inspirational in this work, so stand and take a bow, or conversely flee in haste.

In life, time is the greatest thing to preserve, closely followed by friendship. Use your time wisely and your friendship reverently. Time is God's gift to us for life's duration and is but a one-off present, it is not renewable, recyclable, or extendable. However, it is fleeting, and return fares are not an option (as far as we know). True friendship is freely donated by decent people, it seeks no favours, it asks for no reward, and it should be cherished.

And so as we journey with fortitude through life's traumas but enjoying its advantages. From spring's promises on toward summer's glorious fruits, advancing into autumn's ripened harvest, mellowed wines and bountiful stores, we finally arrive at winter sufficiently prepared to see it out and living in hope that next year, because of the prospect of more of life's rewards, in spite of life's disappointments, we will still be ploughing on and enjoying our memories . . . hopefully creating and cultivating a few new ones.